I0567738

FALCON BAY PUBLISHING

Written by Neil Le Amendec

Published 2020

Cover Design produced from Canva.com with Kindle Direct Publishing assistance

E-Book ISBN 978-1-8381029-0-6

Print Book ISBN 978-1-8381029-1-3

"A fool takes no pleasure in understanding, but only in expressing his own opinion" Proverbs 18:2 English Standard Version
"Brexit was a fantastic example of a nation shooting itself full in the face." Hugh Grant

Chapter 1

The sky was a murky battleship-grey, wisped and wavy like a chaotic battlefield filled with Confederate soldiers. Dr Nigel Johnson's office in the Baptist University of Texas hospital was filled with the screams of a hysterically upset woman, like the cries of a woman who had lost her children. Shrills and wails pierced through the corridor. Dr Nigel Johnson was rather bemused and bewildered at such cries. Dr Johnson was removed from the suffering of others. Floating as a ghost on the screams of others, he was detached from the suffering of others on an emotional level. He couldn't care less about the suffering people went through so long as they coughed up the cash and didn't die. Death meant libel cases and lawsuits for misconduct.

'I understand what I told you is difficult to accept...'

'You are saying I that you want to amputate my arms and legs to save my life. Do you not understand how awful that is?' the woman bawled uncontrollably, blubbering like a bleeding baby.

'Mrs Donaldson, I fully understand that it is a very difficult thing to talk about,' Dr Nigel Johnson grinned, empathetically, 'I fully get your upset.' His voice was that of a reassuring counsellor. 'We use our limbs for everything. It is very hard to comprehend life with no limbs. As an orthopaedic surgeon with 30 years of medical experience and 24 years of surgical experience, I fully get why you would be upset.'

Dr Nigel Johnson was a tall and amazingly handsome surgeon, with piercing brown eyes and olive skin. His physic was of an Italian sportsman and he had charm too, perfect qualities of a salesman and a surgeon. Dr Nigel Johnson's voice became that of a school principal. The sound echoed throughout the room at his booming voice, which was threatening, the bark of an attack-dog.

'However, Angelica, to put it bluntly, the pain in your leg is getting worse. I have seen the biopsy results we have done and it is a highly malignant cancer. It started in your ankle but I can assure you it will

spread and fast. You have serious chondrosarcoma of your ankle. It will spread to your other limbs and will ultimately consume your body.'
Angelica continued to sob. Her husband Michael put his arm around her in a comforting way. Dr Nigel Johnson was startled by her response.
'How can I put it to you in a way you can understand the seriousness of the situation. I don't know if you are political or anything. I try not to talk politics in my job for you know, obvious reasons. I am a professional after all,' Dr Nigel Johnson laughed, with cheeky glare into Angelica's eyes.
'What do you mean to talk about politics? I am an Evangelical Christian and a Trump-supporting Republican. What has this got to do with my cancer?' Angelica spluttered. Angelica was too upset to really
'Oh really? Wow, you say that you are a Republican. Well, as a matter of fact, I am also a Trump-voting Republican. I can happily tell you I am likewise a Republican. Surgeons are good Republican voters,' Dr Nigel Johnson grinned.

Angelica was completely confused by this. She was a Republican, having voted for the Republican party all her adult in every election. It was a religious duty of every good white Evangelical to do so. The Democrats were after all the Demoncrat party or as she once heard in her church, the party of Demoncratic rule, giving power to Satan and the power of darkness over the country. She was not some kind of person who talked politics at every waking time of the day or some kind of political pundit. There was however certainly a focus on politics that were directly linked to her faith. Abortions, gun rights, Israel, pornography and other issues were all issues that were all Christian issues. Trump was in her mind, appointed and anointed by God himself. This and all his deficiencies were no vice or contradiction. God can choose anyone, one of the pastors at her church once said. It was just, well, why would politics be part of her cancer? Could cancer be a political issue?

'In all due respect sir, I do not see how my cancer has anything to do with my political beliefs. They are personal to me and I do not wish to talk about them whilst I am with you,' Angelica said forcefully. Angelica had tightened up, crossing her arms in disbelief at what Dr Nigel Johnson was saying. Dr Nigel Johnson smiled and paced around his office, looking out of the window onto the world outside.

'Oh, I am sorry. I always get caught up in the political world outside my job. It is really easy to become obsessed with politics. Believe me. Sometimes I want to be a politician. Well. We know that Trump is facing a tough time at the moment from critics. I want you to know that I would never turn on Donald Trump. He is a fantastic president. The best president since Reagan. I remember Ronald Reagan. I voted for him. It was one of the first elections that I ever voted in.'

Angelica looked around the office, looking at the numerous medical certificates on the wall and saw various photos of Dr Nigel Johnson. The office was a consultation office, bland white paint for the walls, wooden furniture all in dark brown finish. Dr Nigel Johnson was not a surgeon that was the first recommendation but Angelica's husband Michael had suggested him. He was a contact of Michael; someone Michael had met various times but Michael never stated why. This was a good enough reason to have him as a surgeon.

'Is politics something that you enjoy?' Michael asked.

'It is something that I get immense interest in. So, I am a surgeon that likes to compare what I do to things outside of surgery. After all, it is hard to understand surgical procedures when you haven't done a medicine degree. So I try to compare the surgery I do to things outside the surgery. Like a novelist I suppose, writing allegorical fiction.'

Angelica appeared to be skeptical. She didn't read much other than the Bible. The Bible was the inspired word of God, whilst all other books were written by mankind who is flawed. 'I don't read allegorical fiction. I only read the Bible.'

'Well, parables are like what I tell. You know parables, don't you? Well, the way I will discuss your cancer is like well, like the Mexican border crisis. We know about the Caravan. Well, that is like the cancer you have. The cells inside of you are replicating uncontrollably and soon, like the Caravan of migrants on the border will invade and infect your body. If we think of cancer as migrants on the US border, I think you will understand the importance of intervention, don't you think? We have to make you great again, like America.'

Intervention in a crisis of immigration and cancer. Of course, the regular talking point of US conservative talk shows. Immigration was cancer. America had to be made great again. And Angelica had to be saved from cancer as the US saved from immigration from Mexico.
'We need to take back control, Angelica. If we lose control over the cancer, the same way we lose control of the border, you die. That is why I am proposing a radical treatment. No other surgeon would advocate this but then again, no Republican would have even thought about saying what Donald Trump was saying,' Dr Nigel Johnson sounded more intimidating and empowered, his voice that of a demagogue.
   'I am still not convinced though,' Angelica cried, 'I mean I don't want to lose all my limbs. How am I supposed to be able to do things by myself?'
   'We need to take back control over the cancer. We need to take back control over your body.'
   'But how on earth do I take back control over my body if I am losing my limbs?' Angelica whined.

Taking back control of one's body via amputation. This was reactionary, to say the least. For Angelica, this was unthinkable. Why was that even a possibility? Amputation was not a way to gain back control of one's body. Amputation did not mean control but a lack of it. Yet, Dr Nigel Johnson was insistent. Gaining control meant the loss of limbs.
   'I think the loss of limbs shouldn't be seen as a negative thing at all. Have you heard from the experience of amputees? It can be seen as a positive thing to have your limbs removed. It is possible to take back control.'
   'Positive? How on earth could it be a positive? And take back control when I lose my limbs?' Angelica rebuked, aggressively.

'Well taking back control is possible if you have life insurance. You can pay-out of $3,500,000 if you have all your limbs amputated.'
'$3,500,000?' Angelica shouted in disbelief.

'Oh yeah. Think of what you could do with that much money. Pay off your mortgage. Buy a new house. Plus, who needs limbs now when bionic technology could well mean that legs and arms are obsolete. Within a decade, there will be bionic technology that could mean that people with bionic limbs will have a significant advantage with those who do not. Think that you could ten years from now have the strength that surpasses your husband. Losing your limbs will benefit you long term. Think of having this amputation as a long-term investment into bionic technology. You will be able to one of the first people to benefit from the new technology that is going to be developed in the next 10 years. Hell, there will be people who will have amputations so they can get this new bionic technology.'

Angelica seemed rather perplexed now. It was a ridiculous proposition; having all your limbs amputated could be beneficial to someone. Yet Angelica pondered it for a while. Perhaps Dr Nigel Johnson was giving a good proposition. Perhaps becoming an amputee was an advantage, an adventure. Who would have thought that losing your limbs was an actual advantage? Who would have thought that losing all your limbs would free a person? Yet, this wasn't a decisive decision, her believing that it was right to have her limbs all amputated.
'Do you have any questions?' Dr Nigel Johnson hissed like a rattlesnake.
'So, is it definite that I would get a substantial pay-out? I mean $3,500,000 would mean having my limbs amputated would be a good thing somewhat. Such money is positive.'
'Do you have a life insurance plan?' Dr Nigel Johnson asked.
'Yes, we do...'
'Then most certainly. Many of them cover health conditions that people may develop. Given its severity, it is very likely you receive a

substantial pay-out. $3,500,000 is most likely but who knows, perhaps you could receive a $10,000,000 pay-out because your disability will have a significant effect on your life but I can't quite such a figure due to it being used against me of course,' Dr Nigel Johnson grinned.

'Any more questions?'

'What are the prosthetics currently like on the market?' Angelica asked.

'Well, they are amazing for those with money. For you, we are talking high-quality prosthetics because assuming you get a high pay-out from your compensation, you would be able to afford the high-quality expensive prosthetics available on the market.'

'Okay, we are done for today. Thank you, doctor.'

'Thank you. Remember to rebook your appointment with my receptionist to see me again. Your life is on the line. If you wait, you will die,' Dr Nigel Johnson said in a harsh, hissing voice.

Michael and Angelica drove home on Highway 30. There was hesitancy among Angelica as they drove down the interstate. Angelica was 52% behind the quadruple amputation and 48% dead-set against it. Of course, in a presidential election, these numbers would have been decisive. Barack Obama won re-election winning the 52% of the popular vote. But presidential elections were once every 4 years. A quadruple amputation was for life. Once it had happened, there was no going back from it. The surgery was permanent. There was no going back once it had been done. Amputation was final, complete and total. A total, clean break of the body.

'How did you think that went?' Angelica asked Michael.

'That is more the question that I should ask you.'

'I am certainly not entirely behind the surgery at all. Losing all my limbs is an extreme policy to take.'

'It is.'

'Do you want me to be permanently crippled?' Angelica asked.

'Didn't you listen to him saying about bionic limbs to replace the limbs you lost?' Michael said.

'Do you believe that?' Angelica asked hesitantly.

'I think that technology is improving. The money seems good though.'

'What the $3,500,000?'

'Yes.'

$3,500,000. That was a lot of money. For a middle-class couple with no children, that could be enough for them to retire on. Put half of it into investments and then live off the income. There was no need to contemplate working or if you did need to work, then reducing the number of hours needed to work. And of course, there was healthcare. The USA, with its ridiculous healthcare system, meant that $3,500,000 could pay for any eventuality regarding healthcare costs. For Angelica, this was an attractive proposition. A $3,500,000 pay-out from her life insurance company would be an amazing event in her life. Even if she had no arms or legs. A stumped millionaire was better than not being a millionaire at all.

'What about your job though?'

'What my oil engineering career? What about it?'

'Well you earn a lot of money, don't you?' Angelica uttered.

'Money is not that important though is it?'

Well, it was. Angelica's choice to have a quadruple amputation at all was in part since she could receive $3,500,000 life insurance pay-out. Money is emperor in America. It had the power over life and death, controlling every aspect of American life and had no equal. Given that money was so alluring, this monetary handout was enough for Angelica to consider having the quadruple amputation. Plus, there was the need to take control of the cancer and stop it from spreading. Why did Michael go from saying that the $3,500,000 pay-out was amazing in saying that money was not important?

'I thought you said that the $3,500,000 pay-out is an amazing opportunity and now you saying the money from your job isn't that important. Which one is it?'

Michael laughed emphatically, 'My job is not of your concern. Your life is considerably more important than the job that I do.'

'So, what does your job involve then?'

That was a good question. Supposedly, Michael was the chief Oil Engineer Consultant by trade, dealing with running oil drilling in Texas. That meant he held one of the most senior posts of an oil company in Texas, a company which he held a 5% stake in. Practical would define Michael's thinking and attitudes. Dealing with problems would be done based on his own experiences and intuitions rather than basing it on theoretical ideas or education. Michael was in his early thirties, slightly older than Angelica who was in her late twenties. Michael was well-built, with strong muscular physique after years of weight-lifting and training at the gym. He had sharp blue eyes and golden blonde hair.

'You know my job, Angelica. I work as an Oil Engineering Consultant at an oil company. I can't tell you much about it, due to the confidential nature of the trade. What I will say is that the money from that is not that much in comparison to the $3,500,000 pay-out,' Michael said cautiously.

'But it is still money that you could not be earning if I were to lose my limbs.'

Michael sighed, 'I suppose. Your life is more important than my job. We have got to take back control, haven't we? We need a clean break from the cancer.'

'Well, that is the reason why I am going to get the surgery. I don't feel 100% behind the surgery. I feel 52-48 behind the surgery. Someone has sawn my entire body in half right now as my intentions are split down the middle.'

'I wonder what your family will think about your decision to have a quadruple amputation,' Michael pondered.

'Don't talk about it. It won't go down well. You know what my family is like. Particularly the Nora and Erica dilemma.'

The tension between Nora and Angelica had been steaming up for years. Nora was a lesbian. Angelica disagreed with her "lifestyle choices". Disagreed was too light a word. Angelica thought of herself as an evangelical Christian alongside her husband Michael. Nora and Erica had been partners for years, although they could not get an official marriage union together as this would break the family and cause a rift. The Brians' Family Compromise was that Nora and Erica could live together but not sleep together when they were visiting the family. The decision for Angelica to have her limbs amputated would cause a rift that would be the gateway for the breakup of the Brians family. Nora and Erica's unofficial union was that she wouldn't be cast out of the Brians family for being a lesbian. This was a stance completely taken by Angelica who thought her Christian beliefs to be incompatible with a sister who was a lesbian.

'The one thing that could bring about the end of my family. I can never support my sister marrying another woman.'
 'Well, that is your own belief...'
 'No Michael it is not my belief. It is from scripture. As it says in Leviticus 18:22, a man lying with another man is an abomination.' Of course, she didn't mention not mixing fabrics or not eating cheese with meat.
 'Well, you can believe what you want to believe. But I warn you, the Brians family will break apart if you carry on the way you are going.'
 'I honestly don't care. Homosexuality is an abomination.' Not like the pride of the rich people was also an abomination. God was after all the God of the television, the source of much Angelica's theology.

 'Don't you want the $3,500,000?' Angelica asked. The allure of the money was tempting her to the operating table.
 'The money is good. I keep saying about my job. But there again my job is nothing, nothing compares with keeping you alive.'
Michael looked deep into Angelica's eyes. Her eyes were a delicate hazel colour, which at times became a vibrant dark green. She smoothed her chocolate-brown hair with her hand. She was curvy, if

overweight, having a medium-creamy complexion, somewhat tanned but not entirely. Angelica was in many ways typically American; her aspirations were entirely material, she rarely read any books except the Bible, which she read either daily or weekly. The desire of $3,500,000 was taking control of her mind, like a powerful opioid, seeping into her mind until she craved the day her arms and legs were gone so she could become a millionaire. $3,500,000 was enough money to live on for the rest of your life; plus, Michael's job was in an exceptionally high paid. She could just have prosthetic limbs or bionic limbs as Dr Nigel Johnson suggested. Even if they cost $400,000, she would still have $3,100,000. She could buy a new car, a new house and have a luxurious vacation every year. Perhaps even expensive jewellery. So much for the 52% decision. Amputation means amputation. Even if a mind was hesitant for such a decision, there was always decisiveness. It was always possible to make a titanic success of the amputation.

'I am glad that you have been won over by the surgery,' Michael said. 'We need to take back control.'

'I am still very hesitant. It would say that I am 53% behind the idea.' 53% is 1% more than 52%. Not really much of a difference, unless you were a political statistician.

'Yes. Being 53% behind something is better than 30% behind something. Politicians would love to have 53% of the voters on their side. So, I am glad you are 53% behind the decision. Home sweet home,' Michael said, as the car arrived back at the home they were living in.

It was a 4-bedroom detached villa in the Dallas suburbs of Texas. It was a ghostly white colour, steel grey roofing and two storeys tall, a small backyard with a single tree. The house was surrounded by a large wall and fenced in as a bastion of middle-class decadence. It was a fortress, fully protected from any form of an intruder. A Stars and Stripes flag stood at the front of the house, which towered over the house like a powerful demi-God to be worshipped, feared and adored. Kneeling to it was a blasphemy. When they had parked the car in the garage, they went into the house. The house was decorated in patriotic bunting that was dangling down from the ceiling; the floor in parts of the house was a varnished wooden floor. The walling was painted in a pale brown and white. Decorating his home was a way of Michael to paint his ideology onto the wall; maintaining the ordinary and the status quo. The lounge was adorned with pictures of Michael and Angelica together; their special relationship kindled a sort of romance that seems to weather any storm. Michael knew that it was a façade. The lounge contained a gigantic television that dominated the front of the room and behind that was another Stars and Stripes. The floor was made of varnished wood, with a rug in the center of the room, blood crimson with patterns. Upstairs were four bedrooms; all were empty except the bedroom that Michael and Angelica shared. The empty bedrooms were used to store things and for recreational purposes; Michael kept some rifles in one of the rooms upstairs, locked in cabinets. These rooms had a piece missing from them; their white walls unstained from the lack of activity in these rooms.

'So, I order the pizzas, then shall I?' Angelica asked.

'Yes, a good idea.'

Angelica phoned up to order the pizzas before sitting in the lounge with Michael. They looked at each other. Michael smiled. 'Perhaps we could do you know what this evening. I do like it you know.'

Angelica smiled in returned. 'Oh really.' Her voice sounded voluptuous.

'Why don't we try something new. I wouldn't mind if you wore latex...'

'Oh my. You have been watching porn, haven't you?' Angelica's tone was ardent and paranoid.

'No of course not, why would I do such a thing?' Michael said, his voice in a sort of disbelief.

'A woman knows things about her husband, Michael. An absolute sign you have been looking at porn is a change in sex habits...'

'I don't know what you are on about Angelica. All I wanted was something different,' Michael sighed.

'Your wife is potentially dying without having all her limbs amputated and you say you are bored of sex? How could you be like this Michael!' she screamed at him.

Michael sighed. 'I just wanted something to spice up the mood, ease the tensions after what the surgeon said today.'

Angelica wept, tears drowning her body into a fit of sobs. Michael just looked at her and sighed.

'I am sorry,' Michael whispered.

'BDSM is the sick depravity of Liberalism in our society. Liberals have fetishes. They fetishize everything. Drugs, homosexuality, abortion, latex or leather catsuits. Only a Liberal would want to have BDSM sex with his wife.'

Of course, Angelica didn't mention Neo-Liberals. They fetishized the free market.

'Take that back now!' Michael boomed, 'I am not a God-damn Liberal. Liberals believe in equality and I certainly don't. Hence a wife shall submit to her husband; that ain't a Liberal idea.'

Angelica didn't respond, looking away from Michael staring out of the window.

'I, sometimes don't know why we married each other, Michael,' she murmured.

'Neither do I.'

'We are different people. Now I have to text my mom. I am taking back control of this. That includes our sex life.'

Michael squirmed. Angelica texted her mom, sister and brother about the consultation and about the potential $3,500,000 settlement that she could get in compensation and about how it was important for herself to have the operation. She knew it was a life-changing operation. Angelica wanted to take back control of her life.

Chapter 2

Wilma, Angelica's mother, lived on a ranch about 75 miles north-west of Dallas, close to the Oklahoman border. The landscape was barren, open sky for miles as if God has stretched out the land to become a carpet under the heavens. The grass was long, coarse and a dry yellow, in parts and green that spread for miles by the road. The ranch that Wilma owned was unique in the fact that it contained sheep as the main animal on the ranch. Wilma was not the most successful farmer in the world but brought up three children including Scott and Nora, who were Angelica's siblings. The road up to it was a dirt track, bumpy with long grainy grass at the sides. Cows were chewing on pieces of grass and sheep, which meant that Wilma's farm was nearby. After passing past the fields and the dirt tracks, the farmhouse where Angelica grew up became visible. It appeared to be decaying, the roof needed repairing. Tiles had fallen off. In Texas, where there was rarely any rain, a few missing tiles would not affect the structural integrity of the house. The dust had blown onto the walls of the outside of the house, weathering the house to a rusty-red and burnt-umber. Wilma didn't have the money to repair the house. Wilma was now struggling and kept herself above the water, now that Angelica's father Norman had died recently. Wilma's maiden name was Orangeman but she married into the Brians family.

Wilma stood out on the step, with a smile on her face, dark glasses and silvering hair, her face was radiant at the sight of her daughter returning home. She had a benign face, friendly smile and seemed as if she could be a friend to anyone. Wilma did own guns, though these were mainly bolt-action rifles and shotguns. She wore a checked t-shirt and jeans, not the clothes that a 63-year-old would wear but this was rural Texas and looking pretty wasn't an objective for those who work on farms.

'My darling Angelica. It is so good to see you again. How are you my sweet diamond?' Wilma said with a gleaming smile.

'I am okay mother.'

'How are you doing Michael? Are you well,' Wilma asked.

'Yes ma'am,' Michael said in a formal greeting.

'Why don't you come in and make yourself at home? I will make us a drink inside.'

After getting out of the car, Michael and Angelica went into the house. The house was decaying. The wallpaper which was from the 80s had faded to a grim yellowy-grey and the floorboards creaked at the first steps on it. The lounge hadn't changed much since the 80s; the room other than the television that could have come from a campaign room Reagan's re-election campaign. The couches were a mouldy-green, faded to a pale color, whilst the curtains were a bleached ochre. In the corner of the room was a Stars and Stripes flag, which had not faded over time. There was a cabinet filled with old plates and cups,

'What drinks would you like?' Wilma asked

'You have Coke, don't you?' Michael said bluntly.

'I have that, just for you,' Wilma replied in a warm response, 'what about you sweetie-pie?'

'I'll have a coffee. You don't do tea, do you?' Angelica said.

'No honey, I don't do tea. Tea is such an English-thing dear. Why would you ever drink that?' Wilma sniggered.

'There is tea in Texas, but you better not drink it. That is the stuff you put in cars,' Michael interjected.

'I have it every so often. I have always wanted to go to England on vacation.'

'Well, maybe you should someday.'

'Well good news, the pound has crashed since 2016 thanks to them voting to leave the European Union. I suppose they are taking back control whilst people like myself take control of their currency,' Michael laughed.

'You trade currencies?' Wilma asked.

'I trade all sorts of things. Trading the pound is a sort of wildcard. Great to do if you are in the know of UK politics. But not advisable if you don't know about politics.'

Wilma left the room for around 5 minutes. Michael and Angelica looked at each other. Michael rarely talked about his trading habits. He mentioned things fleetingly, every so often mentioning that he traded commodities, stocks or currency. But it was never for too long since he didn't want to draw attention to his tendencies that he had.
   'You know Scott, Nora and Erica are coming today.'
'Erica? Really? Isn't your mom super-conservative evangelical? I thought she would not have them together under her house.'
   'No. She says she doesn't condone their actions but says that Jesus would love them none the less. She suggested our informal Brians Family Compromise when they came to stay at Easter once. She and our family allowed them to live together provided they didn't get married or have sex when they were staying with family. Scott is all for it, mind you. He is a bloody Liberal.'
'I can't stand queers,' Michael said. 'Better not bring that up in the conversation mind you. It'll end up like a battle in the civil war, knowing the views of your brother would side with your lesbian sister and her partner.'

Wilma returned with a cup of coffee and a glass of coke.
   'Thank you so much. You are always so kind to us,' Michael said.
Wilma laughed. 'Oh, you are so polite.'
 Wilma brought herself her coffee and sat down with Michael and Angelica.
   'I have some news for you, mom,' Angelica said, breathing in deeply.
   'What news?' Wilma asked.
   'About the cancer diagnosed in my ankle. Well... Dr Nigel Johnson says that he will have to amputate both arms and legs to stop the spread of cancer. Amputation means amputation,' Angelica replied, tearfully.

'I am so sorry to hear that. That is awful news,' Wilma said, wrapping her arms around Angelica.

'I was worried telling you.... I didn't know how to respond,' Angelica cried, bursting into tears.

'Why were you worried about telling me?' Wilma whispered, her voice dismayed and confused.

Angelica sniffed and became calmer. 'I was worried about how you would respond when I said that I was going to go through with the procedure. I might be entitled to a pay-out of $3,500,000 according to Dr Nigel Johnson. '

'$3,500,000? That is a lot of money. More than the money I received from Norman dying.'

'It would mean losing my limbs though...'

'I am sure the family would help out.'

As soon as Wilma had said that, there was a knock at the door. Two young women and a male stood outside. The women were holding hands as girlfriends, a controversial thing to do in Texas. Well, outside the big cities and particularly outside Austin, the Liberal part of Texas. They both had shoulder-length hair, one had red hair and the other was a brunette. The male was a big set, muscular like an American football player with a beard and glasses. He was not what you would imagine as an oil engineer, like Michael. Unlike Michael though, he was an offshore oil engineer and thus earned more money. To Michael, this caused much tension, since Scott was considerably more liberal than himself. Despite working in the oil and petroleum trade, Scott was a Liberal. This always baffled and disgusted Michael, who thought that Liberalism sort to destroy the petrochemical trade. Scott justified it by saying the wealth generated from petrochemicals and natural gas could pay for renewable energy.

'Nora, Scott and Erica. How lovely to see you come today! Come on in,' Wilma exclaimed enthusiastically.

They went and sat on the couch opposite Michael and Angelica. The tension settled in, like that of an international conference. It appeared they were gathering to discuss some kind of treaty with each other. The brown eyes of Scott glared at Michael whilst Angelica scowled at the lesbian couple facing them. This stand-off, this family feud that dated back for many years. Angelica had no intention to recognize the legitimacy of the relationship between Erica and Nora. The Brians Family Compromise was just that, a compromise. It was hopefully a way of keeping the peace in the family but appeared that it would not last.

'Well, can I get you a drink?' Wilma asked.

'Coffees for us will do,' Nora said, looking intently into Erica's eyes, before smoothing the red hair.

'What would you have Scott?'

'Do you have whiskey?'

Wilma laughed, 'You and your whiskey. You know, you need to be careful otherwise you might dehydrate in the Texan heat. We are a few hours away from the nearest hospital.'

'I'll have a soda afterwards anyhow,' he replied.

After Wilma left the room, the tension rose in the room to Defcon 3. The standoff was almost inevitable and shouting was now a foregone conclusion. The two factions would inevitably split into

'So, Nora, how are you and Erica doing?' Angelica asked with a snarling voice.

'We are doing well. We have some big news for you,' Nora replied chirpily.

'What news then?' Angelica's voice becoming rather sharp and aggressive. She knew what Nora was going to say.

Erica showed them her engagement ring. It was an azure sapphire and diamond ring that glistened in the light. Both Michael and Angelica scowled as if they had smelt some dog faeces on their shoe.

'You have ruined our agreement, haven't you?' Angelica shouted.

'What the Brians Family Compromise? Since why does it matter you? I am not able to make the choices myself. Anyhow, I heard you were having some major surgery that you had decided,' Nora replied.

'I am…. I am having my legs and arms amputated,' Angelica said tearfully.

'That is unfortunate,' Nora interjected, with an unsympathetic voice.

'You have to bring up this at such a traumatic time, don't you? Where are your support for me and my surgery?' Angelica demanded.

'Okay, Angelica. I will let you know where I stand,' Scott said, his mind reflecting on the situation. 'I believe you have not thought through the implications and the whole idea of the surgery to any length. You have visited one surgeon who has given the most extreme treatment around. Have you ever thought of the financial implications of such surgery? What if the pay-out is much lower than you have thought? What about other, less extreme procedures or other surgeons? And to think that you are undecided.'

Angelica had discussed to both Nora and Scott over Wattsapp before the conference but told them not to discuss their feelings until the meeting the next day. It was obvious that it was going to become heated.

'Listen, Scott, I am running out of time. The tumor is killing me. The chondrosarcoma that I have is exceptionally aggressive. Dr Nigel Johnson has said that he needs to act quickly to save my life. We need to take back control, okay? A quadruple amputation is better than no amputation at all.'

'Yeah, Scott. My wife is dying don't forget that!' Michael interrupted

'Do you know what life is like as an amputee? A quadruple amputee, Angelica? Have you reflected on how limiting it is?'

'Scott, Dr Nigel Johnson has said that there is not enough time. To take back control of my life, I needed to act now….'

'And what if he is wrong. You see I have asked my doctor about this procedure and thought the procedure was ridiculously absurd. Look you told us that you were only 53% behind the idea of having the amputation. What an absurdity to have a quadruple amputation when you are only 53% behind the idea of having it....'

'Who is this doctor of yours?' Nora interrupted.

'My family doctor...'

'They aren't my family doctor though, are they?'

'Do you even know about medicine and medical procedures or healthcare at all Angelica? Look what qualifications does this surgeon even have? Do you have any understanding of surgery or healthcare at all?' Scott engaged in an irritated voice.

'Umm well... I watch.... Err.... Grey's Anatomy...' Angelica bumbled.

'So, I guess you know nothing about it then.'

'And you know a lot, don't you? Mr Know-it-all? Typical Liberal attitude to have....'

'My politics have nothing to do with the conversation. Why does this family always have a political argument?' Scott replied

'I don't know how you can be a bloody Liberal-Commie when you work in the oil industry like myself,' Michael stated, bluntly.

'Because I feel that we need better public services and want a better life for people...'

'Why don't you move to Scotland and Nora with Erica move to Norway or Sweden hey? They are like Norway and Sweden getting married, Communist Socialist hippies! You aren't pure Americans. Americans don't believe in government helping people. Americans believe that the individual helps themselves. That isn't American.'

Scott sighed deeply, whilst Nora and Erica just looked at each other awkwardly. Wilma re-entered the room with cookies and drinks.

'Anyone want a cookie?'

The cookies and drinks were put on an old table in the center of the room. The Brians family was at peace for a short time. Political scientists have calculated that one of the major factors behind civil wars is the lack of food. And the food that was presented reduced the tensions in the room so that there was less fighting.

'What were you arguing over this time? Why did God give me a family that is in permanent strife?'

'Well, why don't you tell her Nora, why were we arguing? Angelica said coldly.

Nora showed Wilma Erica's finger and Wilma's face dropped. 'Well, I wasn't expecting that. Well... That has blown me away,' Wilma said.

'Is that it? Is that all you are going to say, mom? Aren't you going to say about the Brains Family Compromise we all signed,' Angelica groaned.

'You and that again. It was not a proper contract but just an agreement between us so that our family wouldn't break apart,' Nora said.

'Don't you understand what marriage in Texas and around the Christian world is?'

'Tell me, I want to know,' Nora sarcastically replied.

'Marriage is a sacred bond between man and woman. When people have sex, they become bonded with the person they have sex with. So, God intended to make sex between a man and a woman in marriage...' Nora yawned at Angelica's lecture.

'Do you even care about God and your salvation Nora? The judgement of the Lord is coming, the end is coming, God is sanctifying America and making it great again for his return. You won't be apart of his flock when he does return.'

'Since when have you become the arbiter of God's justice?' Nora scowled.

'I follow the Bible; I go to church...'

'Erica and I go to church...'

'Well it is a church of the devil and false teachers and you know what the Bible says about false teachers! They go to the worst part of the hell! Fire and everlasting pain will be the result of your love for Erica.' Rage had taken over Angelica's thoughts.

'I thought Jesus loves everyone...'

'Queers, liberals, atheists, the adulterous, covetous-Commies, Democrats, feminists, will all be going to hell. I can assure you of damnation for what you do with Erica.'

Nora sniffed, trying to hide her tearful response from her sister who had no acceptance for her and Erica's marriage.

'And you Angelica, let's take advise from you. You who are having your legs and arms amputated for what purpose?' Scott snarled.

'You Scott… You never see anything wrong with Erica and Nora's breaking of a sacred bond created by God?'

'No, because unlike you or any of you in the family, I abandoned religion for a while. I don't go to church.'

'You will likewise go to hell…'

'What have I died yet? Am I dead already? Must have died in a car crash before we got here.'

He looked at Nora and Erica and winked at them. Nora smirked somewhat at his wink but Angelica didn't understand irony. The irony was in short supply among conservative Evangelicals from the Southern US. The irony was a more Liberal-elite coastal thing,

'What do you mean? You are alive Scott, not dead. Hell is fire and darkness where there are weeping and gnashing of teeth.'

'Indeed, it is. A place with other people. As Sartre said, hell is other people.'

Wilma sighed. 'I love Nora whatever she becomes Angelica and accept her because Christ accepts me.'

'But she lives a life which is sinful…'

'Don't we all sin?' Wilma said.

'No, we don't. People who live in willful sin and refuse to change will go to hell. More the point, Nora has violated our agreement that they agreed to.'

'You are a fine one to talk, aren't you? You who having your limbs amputated. Do you not think about that this surgery might be a mistake?' Nora said.

'No… you and Scott…'

'This I don't understand. You lecture me on my life with Erica and yet you are unwilling for us to talk about your decision for surgery. I mean Scott is right. You are only 52% or 53% behind the idea of having your legs and arms amputated. Why on earth are you having the most life-changing surgery on such a whim of a feeling? I could not imagine someone ever deciding they were going to have their legs and arms amputated with 52% of themselves believing that was right.' Nora's voice was irate.

'It hasn't got anything to do with your lifestyle.'

'You decide to have your limbs amputated on the basis that your life is threatened but worse in your text, you said about how you could receive a pay-out of $3,500,000 and have new bionic limbs. You really have bought into what Dr Nigel Johnson is saying,' Nora said, frustratedly.

'You show no support for me. I don't entirely believe in it myself. Just open to the idea...'

'What? Oh, you hypocrite. Talk about hypocrisy. You expect me to support you having your surgery when you are unwilling to support my love for Erica. Now you pretend that you want us to support your pathetic decision to have all your limbs amputated simply because "you want to take back control". Goodness only knows what you want to take back control of.'

'I am family to you! I am your sister. Do you not care about your sister?'

Nora was quiet. She contemplated what she would say. Family meant to love. It meant kindness and looking out for one another. Angelica had done none of that. Ever since Nora had come out as a lesbian, Angelica had been torturous. Angelica had claimed this was to do with the fact that she was merely trying to save her from eternal damnation. Yet there was no such love or kindness to her. Just in spite. Pure coldness. Yet Angelica, despite her Evangelical credentials didn't live a particularly amazing life herself, Nora thought. She went to church, listened to Christian music and could cite Bible verses on everything. Angelica though had no warm heart. Inside was no desire to help people other than to spread the word of God. That was sufficient. 'To be honest, no not since the way you have treated me and Erica.'

'How could you? How could you say that? You awful person!' Angelica cried.

'You expect me to support you having surgery and having your limbs amputated when too be honest you have merely accepted the treatment plan given to you by a surgeon who wants to rip you off, quite literally. You won't support me because of my sexual orientation so don't expect me to support you.'

'I thought family is supposed to stick together...'

'Yeah like knifing me in the back because I am gay.'

The war of words was obliterating the relationships within the family. Wilma was torn by the conflict between her daughters. She did not endorse the relationship between Erica and Nora but loved Nora no matter who she was. Yet Angelica could not accept Nora's status as a lesbian because she believed it was morally wrong. Angelica felt cold at the lack of love Nora had for her, despite her unwillingness to accept Nora. Contradictory though it was, Angelica did not see anything wrong at completely disagreeing with Nora's lifestyle. Scott disliked the fact Angelica was lecturing Nora when she didn't like being lectured herself about decisions that she was making.

'Do you ever consider whether you are wrong Angelica?' Scott asked.

'Whatever do you mean?' Angelica exclaimed.

'In the way, you think, what you believe, in the way you treat others. I mean I am just baffled really. You expect Nora to support you having an extremely intensive medical procedure when you are unwilling to support her or even at least accept her when she is a lesbian...'

'Because she is wrong.'

'What if going to Dr Nigel Johnson was a mistake and his treatment plan completely flawed? There are other doctors you know. Have you thought about seeing one of them?' Scott asked.

'I get a $3,500,000 compensation pay-out. We need to act now.'

'You expect us to sympathize your position, for us to support you and look after you when the reason why you want the surgery is that you want a $3,500,000 pay-out? All that emotion is crocodile tears...'

'You dare say that about my wife, you commie-liberal! Even if she doesn't get the money pay-out, I will love her unconditionally.' Michael shouted.

'The only way you have got to argue against me is to call me a Communist and a Liberal, which I must say is ridiculous because liberals believe in democracy and Communists don't. You really are a pathetic couple.'

Scott got up, gurgling all of his whiskey done before going outside to cool off from arguing. Angelica curled up into a fetal position and cried into herself.

Both Erica and Nora decided to join Scott outside. Angelica and Michael sat inside with Wilma.

'I am sorry it has to be like this,' Wilma said regretfully. 'If only our family could just get along.'

'It is Nora's fault. She wants to be a lesbian. She chose it. She chose to live with Erica and chose to get married to Erica.'

Wilma sighed. 'I love Nora no matter who she is.'

'She sins against God. She brings judgement on herself. I will have no part in her life.'

'Just remember she is your sister. Even if you can't bring yourself to like her, she is your sister and played an important role in your life.'

'But my loyalty is to God first.'

'Love others. Isn't that what the Bible says?'

'But I can't simply accept who she is. I must reject and denounce it. I can never accept her if she wants to live a life of sin.'

Wilma looked serious. 'If you want to be like that, fine. You are your own person. But let me tell you this Angelica.' Angelica looked as if she was about to argue. 'Listen to me. You can't expect your brother and sister to support you if you refuse to support them. Love isn't a one-way ticket. You do not have to agree with someone on everything they do to love them. Only treat them with kindness that you would want to be treated.'

Angelica looked down. 'Sorry. I cannot treat Nora with kindness when she chooses to live a sinful life.'

Chapter 3

It was Monday. Michael was at work for the entire week. He was spending the entire week away from Angelica. Supposedly, Michael was spending the week assessing oil drilling sites across Texas but also in the oil sites in North Dakota. The company was looking to acquire more sites. Angelica was alone by herself. The house was pristinely cleaned by Angelica. She had spent the majority of the morning cleaning the house, hoovering, dusting, washing the floors. The floor gleamed. The light pine-green walls and white panels made the house look friendly, like a forest of nature; despite Michael working in the oil industry. Angelica was going to phone up her life insurance provider, Laurence and Johnson, which provided not only life insurance but pay-outs for health problems.

'Hello, you have reached Laurence and Johnson, I am Lillian. I am going to need your name, your address and your policy number,' the female voice said in a customer service drone

'I am Angelica Donaldson, my policy number is 15188406 and my address is....'

Angelica was hesitant about whether again it was a good idea to carry on with the procedure.

This was a conflict inside of her. Divided she was on the issue. She had made it out when she was with the family that she wanted the procedure, but now she was doubtful if she could get the money. Plus, there was a life without limbs. Imagining a life without limbs is to imagine a fish with no water. It is impossible to imagine the life-changing reality of not having limbs. They are used for practically everything. To live without limbs would mean the end of life as Angelica knew it. That was hard to accept. The phone call was to confirm whether she would get the pay-out or not.

'Hi, Angelica. How can we help you today?'

'I am phoning up because my surgeon Dr Nigel Johnson who I have been referred to regarding bone cancer in my right leg. He recommends a quadruple amputation due to it being a cancer that is spreading...' Angelica stated.

'I am so sorry Mrs Donaldson to hear this,' the customer service advisor droned, her voice instinctive and without a particular emotion.

'I am phoning you up because he says I could get a pay-out of up to $3,500,000 if I had the surgery. Now I think that would be a lot of money and would help be able to get my life back. Do you offer any pay-outs regarding such procedures and what amount are you likely to be able to cover?' Angelica queried.

'Umm well, I can have a look for you now. How long have you got at the moment?'

'I have time today.'

'Okay. If you hold the line, I will be able to respond to you.'

'Thanks.'

The telephone went to the pop music wait, where a song played for hours in the background, driving the people who waited up the wall. Angelica sat and huffed, sighing whilst looking out of the window. She had a vibration in her jeans pocket. Her cell-phone with the phone number of Dr Gina Benjamin-Cruz, her family doctor. Angelica did not want to have two phone calls at once, so she slid the red bar on her cell phone to the left to hang up on Gina. 20 seconds later her cell phone vibrated, with the number of Dr Gina Benjamin-Cruz. Again, Angelica groaned before hanging up on Dr Benjamin-Cruz. Dr Benjamin-Cruz left a voice message on Angelica's answer box on her cell phone. Angelica looked up her answer message.

'Hi Angelica,' Gina's voice sounded alarmed, 'Listen carefully. I am phoning to you because I have some vital information about your cancer biopsy. Please, could you call the clinic back so we can discuss the findings on 972 481 558 620? That is 972 481 558 620. Thank you.'

The phone call ended. Angelica was bemused. What was Gina phoning for? What were these findings? Angelica was contemplating phoning up. She put the number into her cell phone but heard the voice of the customer service assistant phone, so she put down her cell phone on the table.

'Hello, Angelica?'

'Hi.'

'It's Lillian here. I have investigated the computer system for the pay-outs that we cover. Your contract does provide a pay-out for cancer diagnosis and treatment. Given this, we would pay-out for you…'

'How much? How much?' Angelica demanded.

'It varies depending on various factors. Your coverage is platinum coverage which means you get the most money, plus have the most likely for a pay-out. I will need to talk through the terms and conditions of such pay-out. Never the less, you would receive a pay-out.'

'Tell me how much I would receive?' Angelica shouted

'Anywhere on my screen of $35,000 to upwards of $3,700,000.'

'$3,700,000?'

'This is entirely depending on the situation, the seriousness, advise from doctors and covered entirely by terms of conditions…'

Angelica was ecstatic. $3,700,000. $200,000 more than what Nigel Johnson was saying. What could she spend the money on? Her mind was racing and she couldn't concentrate on what the woman on the phone was saying about terms and conditions, the details of such a pay-out. Taking back control of her life never felt so good. Angelica's mind raced through images of her new life. New bionic limbs, a mansion, an amazing car, hot holidays. No worries about having your arms and legs completely removed. The considerations around that could wait. All that mattered was the thought that she could become a millionaire. So what that she was becoming an amputee.

'Did you get all of the terms and conditions. Do you need me to send to you a copy of all the terms and conditions to you?'

'Send me an email and I will read it later,' Angelica responded.

'Is there anything else you would like to talk about?'

'No thanks.'

'Well, Mrs Donaldson thank you for your call and have an amazing day.'

Angelica put down the phone. Her heart was raising. She would be a millionaire. The pay-out would make her wealthy. With Michael's income, they could move to a fancy new mansion. She imagined swimming in an azure-blue swimming pool, with the crisp Texan blue-sky above her and sipping a Long Island Iced Tea at the side of the pool. It was unbelievable. Who thought that Angelica would become a millionaire from having her legs and arms amputated? Then there was the simple necessity of surviving through the cancer. She had to stop the tumor from spreading. Angelica asks thought that being an amputee could also be considered a freeing experience as you had been freed from having limbs.

She flipped through her phone and deleted the phone call from Dr Gina. She did not see the point in listening to Dr Gina. Angelica trusted Dr Nigel Johnson. She believed that Dr Nigel Johnson was competent and that he was ultimately trustworthy.

Angelica turned on the television. Television was to Michael and Angelica a major source of entertainment. Tablet computers, smart-phones, Angelica could afford the best of the new technology available. This is in part because of the job that Michael did. His salary let Angelica and Michael have a living that the rest of the world would envy. They had three cars. They lived in an exclusive gated community. They had everything they could ever need. Angelica wanted more though. How deep she desired more and more wealth; a mansion with a swimming pool that was 2 meters deep. The most opulent jewellery. This operation was going to give it all to her. Never mind being without arms or legs, the helplessness and inability to act on one's will. Angelica did not care. All she wanted was the $3,500,000 pay-out. Losing her arms and legs were all a means to an end.

Who needs limbs anyway, Angelica thought to herself. Such a weird thought, of incomprehensible weirdness, of denying a basic necessity was part of the delusion that Angelica had bought into. She could have new bionic limbs that Dr Nigel Johnson had said. Technology solved all of mankind's problems. Simply invent a device to solve a situation. And the problem goes away.

Her phone bleeped when she received a text.
Are you okay for tomorrow? her friend Elizabeth Londres texted her. Elizabeth was Angelica's only Latino friend. Elizabeth and Kate Sunderland were meeting up for coffee as a girl's morning out with Angelica. They went with Angelica to Dallas Cornerstone of God Evangelical church, a megachurch who had 4 services a day, each with 3,000 participants. In such a crowd, it was impossible to meet new people but Elizabeth, Kate and Angelica all met at a Bible study group. Now, they were friends despite their differences. Kate was the wife of a truck driver whilst Elizabeth was a nurse. Perhaps, Elizabeth was one of the only friends who were honest to Angelica. There were differences between them. But at the end of the day, the Bible could unify them.
Yeah, I am thanks. Angelica
The same place of the Hypo-Caf near Whiterock Lake?
Yeah, Elizabeth seems a good idea.
Alright, see you tomorrow.

White Rock Lake was a lake right in the heart of Dallas, about 8 miles to the north of the city center.
On the southern side of the lake, was a large garden which was beautiful and tranquil to walk through when you were feeling down. Angelica wondered what Kate and Elizabeth would be thinking about what Angelica was going to tell them tomorrow about her surgery. Still, she believed whatever they thought, nothing could distract from having a pay-out of $3,700,000. Her thoughts were encrusted with gold-leaf with the thought of that much money. Still, it was not that she hadn't got money at all. It was just, well, money was the only real consideration when discussing to have all of her limbs amputated. After all, it was extreme to have all of your limbs amputated just because the doctor said so.

She turned the television on a conservative talk-show.

'Yeah, those migrants are a cancer,' one of the panel members said.

'Woow, wooh you can't say that.'

'Why not?'

'We are a nation of immigrants...'

'They are though. I mean those on the caravan, they threaten the foundation of the nation. Too many migrants coming over here undermines the fabric of a nation. Undocumented immigration is cancer.'

'They aren't immigrants though they are refugees...

'Right, they are the same thing. Undocumented migrants, refugees and asylum seekers are all the same. They are a cancer.'

To Angelica, the words cancer and immigrant continued to repeat themselves like a mechanical process. She knew they were a sign from God, of a word from God. What more did she need to decide whether to have her limbs amputated than an actual word from God himself? Perhaps that was the sign she needed, watching a conservative talk-show, was actually a prophetic message. Like Trump taking control of American borders, Angelica was taking back control of her body.

Oh Lord, thank you for the divine word of your prophecy in watching this program. May I submit to your will in having the operation Lord. Thank you, Lord, for our president Donald Trump, who was sent by you to deliver us from the darkness. Please Lord confirm this is your message for me to have the surgery. I am submitting to you, to the knife, to have my legs and arms removed.

She turned over the channel to EPPTV or Evangelical Protestant Pentecostal Television, a large televangelist channel. The show was called *Trump: Prophecies of God and America revealed*. The speaker was preaching on how Trump was sent by God to lead the USA to a great Golden Age.

'Trump is like Solomon. Solomon had many wives. So, has Trump. Yet Solomon wrote three books in the Bible. David was a strong leader and people celebrated that he killed tens of thousands. He led Israel into a

Golden Age. Trump is a strong leader and is leading America into the Golden Age. David was a man after God's own heart, so is Trump.' The church leader's voice boomed like a political orator, shouting with fiery passion at the crowd, with violent hand movements in a brown suit. The crowd were shouting amen, multiple times to the words the preacher was saying, with cheers and claps at his words.

'It is clear, God is making America great again. The right political leadership is restoring us to a greater America. America will be great, with God praised again and our flag respected, not burnt by Liberal-Marxists who want to destroy our constitution. Trump will pack a Supreme Court filled with conservatives who will push forward God's agenda in America. The constitution is based on God's laws...'

Angelica went off to make herself a coffee. The words boomed from the television. A voice from what seemed from the heavens came through the television. Angelica burst into the room.

'To you at home watching, I believe that there is someone out there who has a life-threatening illness. They have seen a surgeon or a doctor, and they have proposed some extreme treatment options. Phone up our number which is 404 1924 722 723. That is 404 1924 722 723, press 6 now and speak to one of our advisors,' the voice from the television exclaimed.

Angelica fell to her knees, feeling overwhelmed with emotion at the words. She was certain at the words, that they were for her and she yet was hysterically upset. Emotionally deluged by her situation, Angelica did not want to pick up the phone to talk to the advisors.

'You are upset. I know you are. Phone our advisors on the number below, that is 404 1924 722 723 and they will be able to help you.' Angelica, trembling with fear picked up the phone, barely being able to contain her emotion.

Hello, you have reached through to the Evangelical Protestant Pentecostal Television helpdesk. May the grace of God be upon you. The voice of the end of the phone was that of a female, robotically calling out responses. *Press 1 if you want to donate money to EPPTV. Press 2 if you want to phone your appreciation and thanks for the show. Press 3 if you want to receive financial blessing from God. Press 4 if you want to receive help in your life regarding your family. Press 5 if you want God to bless your life. Press 6 if you want to receive help regarding health concerns. Press 7...*

Angelica pressed 6 instinctively.

You have selected you to want help regarding your health concerns. Press 1 if you want an advisor to talk and pray with you about having an abortion. Press 2 if you think you are ill but not quite sure what it is. Press 3 if you have been diagnosed with a terminal illness and want to donate money to us. Press 4 if you are sick with a life-limiting condition and want us to heal you. Press 5 for general healing and donation for our healing team to heal others. Press 6 if you are having major surgery or treatment, recommended by a doctor. Press 7...

Angelica pressed 6 again. The phone went through to Christian pop music, the glib song of thanks, a blessing. The repetitive music went into a cycle. Angelica tried to hold back her tears but she sobbed into her tissue. She remembered when Dr Nigel Johnson first said that he would have to amputate her arms and legs. She desired to please God and she wanted the $3,700,000. But it was overwhelming.

'Hello, you have reached the health advisors team at EPPTV. My name is Jazmine. What can I help you with today?' a trite female voice asked. Angelica blubbered, her voice spluttering with whimpers. 'Hello…. Can I help you?'

'Hi… I was watching your show and… I felt God was speaking to me… I have been diagnosed with bone cancer in my ankle and the surgeon has advised a quadruple amputation… I don't know where to turn to… I could get a pay-out of $3,500,000 if I have the surgery…' Angelica wailed.

'Oh, I am so sorry. Well the Lord has a plan for every one of us. In the dark parts of our life, God watches over us.'

'Is it the Lord's plan to have the surgery? I think God is saying that I should the surgery.'

'Of course. Whatever the Lord says, you will obey.'

'Do you think I should?' Angelica was frantic in her voice.

'Whatever the Lord says.' The answer was mechanical and robotic. There was no discussion of theological issues, no consideration or comfort. It was purely up to the response of the caller to make. Perhaps if the caller was phoning up about abortion, then perhaps the response would be less robotic. Angelica was alienated by these responses. She was hoping for someone who was a Christian to talk through her decision to have her arms and legs amputated. This wasn't happening. Instead, she was talking to a call handler that may as well have been a computer.

'So, I want to know what God says in this over my life. Should I have my legs and arms amputated or not? That is the question.'

'The Lord needs to be glorified...'

'Answer my question?'

The advisor went silent for around 20 seconds. 'Did you say you will get $3,500,000 pay-out?'

'That is correct...'

'Well, you know EEPTV sees wealth as a blessing from God. Perhaps this really a sign from God from him that he wants you to have the operation. Perhaps financial blessing really is God's hand.'

Angelica wailed some more. 'Thank you. Thank you. I must submit myself to the will of God and the surgeon's hand!'

'As it says in Proverbs 10:15 "A rich man's wealth is his city and the poverty of the poor is their ruin". God blesses people with wealth. Sure, it may not seem a blessing to have all your limbs amputated but remember God has complete sovereignty and control over everything, from your cancer to the surgeon who will operate on you. Everything is the purpose of God. Perhaps the $3,500,000 is for you because God wants to bless you in mysterious ways.'

'How can losing my limbs be a blessing?'

'Because you are financially better off. Can't you see? God uses this situation to make yourself better off. Besides, God can heal an amputee.'

'He can?'

'Yes. I mean he healed lepers why can't he heal someone who has had their arms and legs removed? God has complete control and can do whatever pleases himself. I mean what about getting prosthetics, surely they are a gift from God? Think of all the new prosthetic limbs that are available.'

'They are?'

'Yes. And the technology is improving all the time. Praise God.'

'Well, I have never heard that prosthetics are a gift from God.'

'Everything in existence that is good is a gift from God. God blesses us every day and most people do not see his blessings and take him for granted.'

'I see. Thank you for helping me today,' Angelic whimpered.

'That is okay. May the Lord bless you,' the woman said emotionlessly. Angelica hung up the phone. She was emotionally shattered after talking about her health problems to the woman on the phone who appeared to be a computerised voice assistant with about as much emotion as a crow. Still, it could be worse. Angelica knew what she had to do now. She must submit to the knife and have her limbs amputated. For God willed it.

Chapter 4

Dallas was a city surrounded by many lakes. About 3 miles from the center of downtown Dallas was the lake known as White Rock lake and a garden known as Dallas Botanical Gardens, a large green area with trees and beautiful flowers that swayed in the wind. Angelica sat in serenity to the wind that lightly blew. Spiderworts waved in the wind, like a winter tide. She was reading her Bible app on her smartphone and read it quietly in the breeze. The sun was risen and shone radiantly, golden beams of light that blessed the world. Angelica knew that her meeting with Elizabeth and Kate was going to be a difficult discussion. Top of her discussion was whether she should have her limbs amputated or not. This was going to dominate her conversations until the surgery itself. Of course, it was the biggest decision of her life; to have her limbs amputated or not. If she didn't have the amputations, the cancer could spread or so she thought. Every day, Angelica tried to convince herself of the surgery. I am taking back control, Angelica thought. I need to save my life, Angelica repeated to herself. The cancer cells are taking over my body, like immigrants taking over America. Of course, her only Latino friend Elizabeth Londres, a nurse didn't fit into a bad immigrant type. She was American born after all and was most of all an Evangelical Christian. An American born foreigner but a Christian, so Angelica found that acceptable. Angelica didn't talk about the problems of immigration to Elizabeth as she thought it wasn't very friendly. Kate Sunderland was another true American; blue collar with a husband who was a trucker and stayed at home to look after the kids.

'Hi Angelica,' a voice said. It was Elizabeth, a curvy 33-year-old with glasses. She worked shifts and so was able to meet up with Kate and Angelica. She was a surgical nurse herself, someone who knew far more about healthcare than Angelica. Perhaps she could persuade Angelica not to have the surgery.

'Hi Elizabeth, I hope you are okay.'

'Did you read the Bible chapter which was set by the Bible study leader?' Elizabeth asked.

'Yes, it was Proverbs 3:5 and 6. "Trust in the Lord with all your heart and leader, not on your understanding. In all ways submit to him and he will make your paths straight".'

The group had been looking at the trials of life and God in their Bible study group. They knew that Angelica had bone cancer. This Bible study was rather important. Angelica, having her limbs amputated was an extreme event. To say it was a trial of life was an understatement. They were yet to find out about the surgical procedure that Dr Nigel Johnson was offering. She was going to tell them today to Elizabeth and Kate today.

'That is right. Shall we walk to Hypo-Caf?' Elizabeth asked.

'That is a good idea. Kate is meeting us there.'

Elizabeth and Angelica walked through the park, the sun shining down on the cool November day. Angelica limped, due to the pain that she had in her ankle. The cancer was there in her ankle. It needed to go. The choice of having a quadruple amputation was an extreme option, but it was completely necessary in Angelica's mind. Amputation means amputation and Angelica was going to make a complete success of it.

'Have you been watching the recent mid-terms. I think it's great news that Beto O' Rouke lost to Ted…'

'My politics is a private matter due to my job,' Elizabeth smiled. 'I do know how much you and Michael are Trump supporters.'

'I believe he is a man sent by God to set America back on the straight and narrow.'

Elizabeth chuckled. 'Really?'

'Yes, I believe it.'

'The same way you believe Obama is the Anti-Christ and Clinton the daughter of the devil?'

'Absolutely.'

'Ahh. I stay away from politics. Give to Caesar what belongs to Caesar and give to God what belongs to God. We should pay our taxes of course…'

'Bloody Liberal-Communists. They want our property and our money.'

'Taxes pay for important things and I think it's our Godly duty...'

'You are a Democrat, now are you?' Angelica asked angrily.

'What? This is why I don't talk politics with you, Angelica. You are so aggressive to other people who think differently to you,' Elizabeth whined. 'Why are so obsessed with politics or more accurately believe so fervently that the Democrats are evil?'

'It's in their name DEMONCRAT. They are the party of Satan worshippers. Beto O' Rouke would have turned Texas into a cesspit of filth, sin and corruption. There would be healthcare for all including abortions on demand, youths smoking Marijuana and burning the flag and there would brothels and strip-clubs on every street corner...'

'Actually, Angelica don't Republicans go to more strip-clubs and brothels then Democrats? it's a well-known fact that strip-clubs do well when the RNC comes to town.'

Angelica grimaced, her clenched-mouth becoming that of rottweiler but she did not say anymore.

'Shall we talk something else other than politics?'

Every conversation that Angelica and Elizabeth about politics ended with Elizabeth stating that she
had not got the time due to her job as a nurse or that she would rather not talk about politics because she said the Bible didn't give enough evidence to support various claims that Elizabeth clung to. This sort of tension between Elizabeth and Angelica in politics didn't strain their relationship too much. After all, they focused on Christianity.

'There is such a handsome surgeon at the hospital that I like,' Elizabeth exclaimed.

'What is his name.'

'Albert Sanchez. He is a Vascular Surgeon. I mean surgeons are always more manly than doctors,' Elizabeth laughed.

'Are you going to date him?' Angelica asked.

'Well... I mean... I don't think he even knows that I like him. We both have of course really busy lives.'

'That is cute. Is he a Christian?'

'I don't know...'

'Well, you know what it says in scripture. Don't be unevenly yoked. You know the rules. Christians shouldn't date or contemplate dating or marrying those who aren't Christian.'

'But I like him. What if he believes in Christianity but doesn't go to church? I mean he could go to church and still be a non-Christianity.'

'You should date people who go to church. That is just how it is.'

'But I want to date who I love. Christians are a fine one to talk. How many of them get divorced or live in loveless marriages?'

'I have been married for many years...'

'Do you love Michael?'

Angelica paused for a minute. She looked up at some birds that flew over their heads. It was a hard thing to contemplate, loving Michael. What was love for Michael? What was their relationship? 'I do.'

'A long time to answer.'

'He has been odd lately.'

'What do you mean?'

'He asked for sex the other day...'

'Oooh. Slightly saucy. Fancy you talking about sex with your friend. I thought you said sex was a private bedroom thing for Christians.'

'He said he wanted me in latex. I was horrified by it. I guess he was watching porn or something?'

'Yes, you know what men are like. Either he watched some porn with it in or some suppressed sexual fetish. Or both.'

'Yeah but come on. Michael comes to church with me...'

'How come you know that Michael is a practicing Christian?'

'He talks about it. He goes to church. He prays with me.'

'Does he practice his faith? You challenged me by asking about Albert.'

'Well... I think he does.'

'We'll just keep an eye on it. He may have reasons for it.'

Kate met them at Hypo-Café. She was sat at a table by the window, looking at her phone. Kate was an overweight woman in her mid-thirties who wore a ruby-red baseball cap with "make America great" etched in white letters, white t-shirt and blue jeans. Her face was lavished with makeup, false-eye lashes. Her husband was away trucking for the week across the United States and so left her alone.

'Hi, Angelica.'

'Hey Kate,' Angelica said, embracing her quickly before letting go. 'How are you doing?'

'Well, I am doing fine. And yourself?'

'Well, could be better. It's what I was meaning to tell you...'

'Shall we order a drink?' Elizabeth asked.

'Yes. We should. You look well Lizzy,' Kate said.

'Thanks. Please don't call me Lizzy. You know I hate that name!' Elizabeth said.

'I know how to push those buttons,' Kate laughed.

'I think I will just have a coffee and some donuts,' Kate said.

'I will stick with a coffee. Perhaps 3 cookies,' Angelica stated. Angelica sat down and was very quiet looking at the table. She was gathering the courage to say to Kate and Elizabeth about her intentions of surgery. Elizabeth went up to order the drinks. Telling your friends that you planned to have your legs and arms amputated was bad enough. Telling them that you were only 53% behind the idea was another thing in itself. It wasn't really enough of decisive support for making such a decision. Really, surgery like that required complete support for the idea. Being only 52% or 53% behind it was not really enough to justify it.

'I love the donuts here. They are so good,' Kate said. Kate lacked the intelligence to really involve herself in the level of discussion that Angelica and Elizabeth usually involved themselves in. Her intelligence was that of gut-feelings rather than thought out beliefs.

'So, do I,' Angelica replied, quickly with little hesitation.

'You seem pretty tense Angelica. Everything okay.'

'I'll wait for Elizabeth to come back.'

Elizabeth after paying sat down with Angelica and Kate. Kate looked at Elizabeth who in turn looked at Angelica.

'You seem upset Angelica. What is wrong? Are you upset by what we were saying on our walk here?'

'What no!' Angelica snapped. Elizabeth was taken aback by the sudden outlet of emotion.

'What is wrong? We are your friends.'

'I met the surgeon, Dr Nigel Johnson, a few days ago. He said I needed a quadruple amputation on all my limbs because of the risk of the cancer spreading. He said that I could receive a massive pay-out of $3,500,000 because of it. I phone my life insurance company and they confirmed that I would receive a pay-out but were vague to how much I would receive. I wanted to know what you were thinking of it.'

'$3,500,000? That is fantastic!' Kate Sunderland said.

'Really?'

'Yes. Think of the money. If someone were to offer me to have my legs amputated for $3,500,000, I would say count me in.'

'No Kate. He said he would need to amputate all my limbs because the cancer is spreading rapidly across my bones, vessels and arteries. The only way to stop it was a below-knee amputation of both legs and below elbow amputation of both arms.'

'Well its what the doctor says. You need to stop the spread of cancer. You do what you have got to do. You know, take back control.'

Taking back control wasn't a thought-out policy-implementation but rather a statement of the stomach, rash and impulsive. Kate had practically no understanding of surgery or medicine. She wouldn't think about what doctors or nurses said, just her gut intuition to tell her what to consider. Elizabeth though looked more concerned but was silent and had not interrupted Angelica when she was talking to Kate. Angelica smiled and hugged Kate. 'Thank you, Kate. My family except for my mom all rejected me having the surgery but you care for me.'

'If I have to take care of you I will. Of course, some of that $3,500,000 would be nice.'

Angelica laughed. Elizabeth frowned and shook her head.

'You don't seem so eager Elizabeth.'

'Honestly please listen to me. Do not listen to Dr Nigel Johnson. You do not need all of your limbs amputated. That is absurd. There isn't a type of bone cancer in which you would need a quadruple amputation. It is a ludicrous treatment plan,' Elizabeth said dismissively.

'What? And you know what is right for my body?'

'I am a nurse. Any bone cancer can be operated and removed by removing the section of bone or the most radical solution amputation of one limb. Do you know which bone cancer it is?

'I can't remember... chondrosarcoma I think Dr Nigel Johnson said?'

'Right do you know the usual treatment for chondrosarcoma rarely includes amputation. The treatment plan would usually involve the removal of the cancerous bone growth in the section of bone. Quadruple amputation is not used ever for that kind of cancer. Please, I would recommend you see another surgeon. That treatment is completely the wrong kind of treatment'

'You aren't a surgeon. You are a nurse. You haven't got a clue about bone cancers,' Angelica snarled. It appeared that Angelica now knew more about bone cancer than Elizabeth. Or so Angelica believed.

'I am a surgical nurse actually.'

'Oh really. Wow,' Angelica said sarcastically. 'You would know a lot about bone cancer treatments.'

'I have worked in operating rooms when they have removed them so yes. I think I know about them,' Elizabeth calmly replied.

'You must be an expert then.'

'I know more about them than the average Joe six-pack. It is my job after all.'

'Too bad. Dr Nigel Johnson said I needed it or I will die.'

'I am surprized the medical board haven't stripped him of his license to operate. That is a clear unnecessary surgery. Why on earth have you not reconsidered it? Angelica, what on earth are you doing to yourself? Why would you amputate your limbs like this or reconsider the treatment?'

Angelica was hesitant to respond. Her mind was all over the place on this issue. She didn't know what to think sometimes. Despite her aggressive opposition towards Elizabeth, she was never wholeheartedly for the quadruple amputation. She believed she needed to take back control and that $3,500,000 was a good pay-out for herself. But there was the niggling doubt that the entire project was completely stupid. After all, who would think that planning to have all of their limbs amputated was a good idea? Would it not have been a good idea for Angelica to get second advise on having her limbs amputated? And yet here was Angelica turning down all of her second advise for no apparent reason other than being right. She didn't want to be proven wrong. 'It is necessary. He said the cancer would spread without it,' Angelica said tearfully.

'Do you even know bone cancer spread? I guess you know about it more than me now.'

'I just think you are jealous of my pay-out. I don't need to listen to advise from nurses like yourself.'

Elizabeth glared at Angelica in the eye. 'Listen Angelica. Please, I do this for a day job. I beg of you to consider what I am saying and what I am saying is that having all your limbs amputated is ridiculous.'

'Why?'

'Because I believe it is wrong. You are being lead to believe that you need a quadruple amputation when the reality is no medical professional in their right mind would do such a treatment package. It goes completely against any necessity and goes completely against best practise. Please don't do this on yourself, especially if you are not 100% for such a procedure.'

'Why would he say it if it wasn't necessary...'

Elizabeth moved her index finger and thumb together in a repetitive fashion. 'He wants money. He'll get more money for the surgery. I don't know how he has managed to convince you or why you are so strongly believing that it is the right action.'

'That is ridiculous. You are just envious of surgeons...'

'I am a healthcare professional! I know this,' Elizabeth shouted, slamming the table

'You don't know my body. You don't know everything there is to my body or the cancers that infect me. You don't know. You don't know what will happen. But Dr Nigel Johnson does.'

'I do. I can tell you are buying into a surgeon who wants lots of money.'

'I don't care what you have got to say,' Angelica said. 'I will get the surgery and the pay-out again. This sounds like project-fear to me.'

A vibration and ringtone came from Angelica's handbag. The same number 972 481 558 620 from Gina Benjamin-Cruz, her family doctor. Angelica hung up on the number. She did not want another opinion on her Chondrosarcoma. How would these people know any better than her when making the decision? It was her body and she made the decisions. Even though she was divided on the issue, this division wasn't changing into going against the idea. After all, she could have listened to Elizabeth. Why wasn't she reconsidering her choices?

'Who is that calling you?' Elizabeth asked.

'No one.'

'Tell me. Who is that person.'

'My family doctor.'

'You hang up on your family doctor? Why?' Elizabeth asked in a bemused voice.

'They keep phoning because they want to talk to me urgently about my bone cancer.'

'You are hanging up on your family doctor when you have a life or death condition? Are you insane?' Elizabeth yelled.

'What can I say? I am fed up with listening to experts. People as a whole are fed up with listening to experts. That is why we vote for Trump.'

'It's your health! Your body. Your life...'

'I am taking back control of my body over this cancer...'

'By having all your limbs removed?'

'Yes. I am.'

'I don't know what else to say.'

'Your support.'

'No, I will never support someone having surgery for something they don't need.'

'Fine. Elizabeth. I don't want to talk to you anymore. I don't need you. Kate and I will continue without you. Pathetic Mexican middle-aged singleton.'

Elizabeth's face dropped; her eyes saddened. Her friendship to Angelica was strong despite of the differences in opinions and for the fact that Angelica was at times racist. 'Is that what you think of me? The woman who bought you your snack, a Mexican middle-aged singleton. ...'

'No not really. I wanted your support and because you didn't give it to me, I am removing myself from your friendship.'

Elizabeth was quiet for a minute; her arms crossed her eyes avoiding looking at Angelica. 'I was born in America,' she whispered.

'Shut up Mexican. We aren't talking again. Okay? For now on I will not sit with you in church. I won't go to the same service as you, okay?'

'So much for love and friendship,' Elizabeth whimpered exhaustively.

Friendship and community collapse over the rash decisions that people make. As Angelica drove away from her meeting with Elizabeth, she felt relieved that she had ended the friendship. There was no reason to believe her. It was her body and it was she who was going to make the final decision of whether she was going to have the amputation or not. Expert opinion was not going to make her reconsider her choices. And if experts were not able to persuade her, then no one could. That Sunday, Angelica avoided going to the 10:30 am church-service. She knew that Elizabeth always went to that service when she was not working. It was possible to completely avoid her, since the church was so large that it was possible to not see the same people twice. Instead, Angelica was going to the 2:00 pm service, the afternoon service. It was identical to the content of the 10:00 am service. It was possible to hover in church services, absorbing worship and then disappear for the week without it having any impact on your life. Angelica thought it would be nice to spend some time with Michael before church in the afternoon. They curled up on the sofa together watching television. Angelica looked intently into Michael's eye.

'Michael? You will love me without arms and legs won't you?'
Michael smoothed Angelica's hands affectionately. 'Darling, I will love you no matter what comes of the surgery. I know it will be different without any arms or legs. But I will love you no matter what.'

'Michael, you understand that the reason why I have the surgery is well to take back control of my body, to save my life and not simply to get a large pay-out? I do it because I am in complete control of my body and will not allow other people to tell me what to do. Amputation means amputation and we are going to make a success of it.'

'Cupcake of course I do. We don't need the money. Even if you receive nothing, I will love you with all of my heart.'
Angelica kissed him on the cheek. 'You are such a wonderful husband.'

'Hmm. At least I try. You were saying that your meeting with Elizabeth wasn't that good.'

'She was saying that I didn't need to have all my limbs amputated and that Dr Nigel Johnson just wants the money.'
Michael laughed, cackling to what Angelica was saying. 'She is a nurse. Of course, she would say that. Nurses and doctors don't get along. Doctors know best. Nurses are best submitting to the will of doctors.'

'Like wives to husbands?' Angelica smiled.

'Absolutely. The only good nurses are women. Men should be doctors. Or surgeons in this case. Female surgeons? Well, that would be kinky I suppose.'
Angelica chuckled. 'That is naughty,' she whispered. 'Very naughty.'
Michael grabbed hold of Angelica and pinioned her to the sofa, pushing her arms down to the sofa. 'I am very naughty. All that work in the oil field, all I wanted was to come back here and just and have a naughty time with you.'

They kissed and embraced, becoming physically aroused, groaning before being interrupted by Angelica's cell phone.

'That damn cell phone interrupting us!' Michael shouted. 'Who is it? What do they want?'

The number 972 481 558 620 flashed up on her screen, with the name family doctor popping up on her screen.

'Who is it?'

'Dr Gina Benjamin-Cruz.'

'Well answer it then!' Michael said frustratedly that he was unable to continue with the act of domination.

'Hello, Gina. Look this isn't a good time...'

'I don't phone patients usually on a Sunday. You must understand how important this is.'

'What?'

'I need you to come to my office tomorrow,' Dr Gina Benjamin-Cruz appeared urgent, 'I think there has been a mix up in diagnosis.' Gina's voice was professionally unsettled as if she was looking through papers. 'I need you to come tomorrow ASAP so that I can arrange another biopsy.'

'What do you mean?' Angelica said passive-aggressively

'There is some belief that you.... I will tell you tomorrow. What time can you take tomorrow?'

'Umm say 10:30 am.'

'Okay. Please come, won't you?'

'Yes. I will.'

Angelica hung up the phone. 'Where were we?'

'I am not interested now,' Michael grunted, 'I don't feel like it.'

'Come on. I am really turned on.'

'I have lost it. Sorry,' he said, almost feeling ashamed. 'What else is on television?'

'We could watch EEPTV,' Angelica said.

'Good idea. It is the Sunday service on.'

They changed channels to the preacher on the television, standing at the front of a mega-church, preaching emphatically in his brown suit and red tie. These television preachers were hypnotic, shouting at the front of the stage in front of thousands in a handpicked audience and shouting to thousands of people who tuned in every time the program was on. They listened to Donald Trump and they would listen to televangelists. And the televangelists would say that Donald Trump was set by none other than God himself to save the USA. Not that Obama or Franklin Delano Roosevelt had been sent by God; just Donald Trump. Only Republicans are ever sent by Trump. Angelica was enthralled by watching these televangelists. Christianity was a religion of the television, God's voice would speak directly through it.

'The blessing of wealth and health is not something you hear today from certain Christians. Let me tell you what The Bible says. The Bible clearly says that wealth is a blessing of God and health a sign of his mercy or judgement. Let me tell you the story of Job. Job was a righteous man, a man who followed God without hesitation. The Lord let the devil come down and test Job. Life tests Christians faith. He does. Your health, your job situation, your money in your life, your social life are all signs of God in your life. Let me say this if you have a health condition, it may be a sign of God's judgement over your life. However, don't let me scare you. There may be someone watching me today and wondering whether the Lord is judging you because of their health condition. Let me say this if God blesses you out of this trial by saying an improved bank balance, think of it as God's blessing. Did not after the trial that Job go through see Job be blessed by God?'

Angelica was speechless. This was no coincidence. Why would EEPTV have it on twice in one week about health issues being linked to herself if it wasn't a sign from God? The amputations were going to lead to her to prosperity and were a blessing from God. God was blessing her by having her limbs removed. Having cancer was now a positive thing, a sign of God's blessing on her life.

'I can't believe it,' she said as hypnotically, infatuated by the television. 'What?'

'This must be a sign of God. God clearly wants me to have surgery. It must be a sign that I am to have surgery that I would have my limbs amputated for God to ultimately bless me at the end of the treatment with wealth.'

Of course, Angelica ignored the many people who were not blessed with wealth or health. And why would God give her millions of dollars as a sign of good fortune after her limbs being amputated? Was a test like this to show the love of God or was cancer something that happened to people as part of a corrupted world? It was easy to ignore the millions of people who were not blessed financially by God or by health. For it didn't have the awe and wonder of the miracles of God, it wasn't worth watching.

'What do you mean?'

'Don't you understand? I saw another program on the television about refugees being a cancer. Don't you see? Then another saying Trump was sent from God and now this program saying that financial benefits from illness is, in fact, a blessing from God. God wants me to have my limbs amputated. Elizabeth was of the devil when she said that Dr Nigel Johnson wanted to simply make money from my surgery.'

Angelica's eyes were filled with tears of joy. At last, she had confirmation from her own beliefs and thoughts that God was genuinely confirming that he wanted her to have surgery. The dots had been connected from comparing immigrants to cancer, to Donald Trump being appointed by God to now this clear message from the church service at EEPTV and it all was from God. God wanted her to be an amputee. It was divine will. Never mind the criticism from her family members. They were apostates. Never mind Elizabeth. She may have been a nurse. But she did not confirm the words of the Lord. So, she was a heretic, manipulated by the devil to oppose God's rightful actions. Angelica was right to oppose her. This 52% belief had become a landslide of faith. All that mattered now was becoming an amputee. For a quadruple amputation was better than no amputation at all. It was divinely ordained. She needed to take back control but she needed to obey the will of God himself. Who cared what other people thought? 'I don't see the link myself,' Michael said, bemused. 'Tell me, how are immigrants being cancer, connected to Donald Trump being appointed connected with this church service.'

'Don't you see? I have cancer and immigrants are a cancer to society. Trump is appointed by God and just after saying that, the man said about having medical treatment to phone up. And now this. How else could it be anything other than God.'

Michael grinned to himself. 'Appears someone needs some surgery,' he said, kissing his wife on the cheek.

His wife frowned. 'It is weird is, isn't it. Such a weird thing that I could enjoy losing my arms and legs. Perverse, like some fetish. Because it is the will of God himself.'

'Quite. You will look beautiful with no arms or legs.'

She looked at him and the eyes and kissed him passionately on the lips. This time her phone was not there to disturb them, picking her up and taking her to the bedroom. They were at it for over an hour. The shouts, grunts and noises of intoxicated passion filled the house with an aura of irrationalism. Control and domination, the desire to take back control and lose all of your limbs was a big turn-on for Angelica.

After the hour of passion and lunchtime, Angelica and Michael went to church in the afternoon service. The megachurch was packed, filled with thousands of people as if the entirety of heaven was filling the rows and rows of seats. Musically, the lighting was intense, a rock-concert of a famous Christian band as worship. People sang with an intense purpose, their music echoing with the loudspeakers. People lifted their hands and waved to the intensive emotional music. Various songs played, the tempo and theme, emotionally stirring these worshipers to lift their hands. Angelica was bawling her eyes out to the music as she lifted her arms to her shoulders and spread her hands out as if to receive a gift. Not too long after the singing, the pastor spoke at the front of the church, on the stage in front of everyone there. He spoke on the passage in Jeremiah 29:11, "for I know the plans I have for you, plans for you to prosper". It was emotionally warming. At the end of the sermon, the pastor spoke to the congregation, just before the music played.

'If any of you are going through medical problems or health problems, please come down to the front for prayer. I feel there is someone in the audience who is going to have major surgery soon. Whoever that is please, come down the front.'

Angelica looked tearfully into Michael's eyes and after hugging him, she limped down to the front of the service, past the many rows of chairs to the front of the church, past many people standing singing to the songs being played.   Down at the front were the prayer-team, wearing their ruby-red badges. A young white female, perhaps in her mid-twenties approached Angelica.

'What is your name, how can I pray for you?' she asked softly.

'I am Angelica...' Angelica said, huffing to stop herself from crying. 'I have chondrosarcoma in my ankle, which is a form of bone cancer and my surgeon recommends a quadruple amputation of my limbs to spare my life from death.'

'Oh, that is awful,' the woman said empathetically, putting an arm around Angelica, 'I am so sorry to hear that. I can see why you are upset.'

'I have been told I may get a $3,500,000 pay-out from my insurance company...'

'Money shouldn't be your goal. I hope that you do not strive for money. Remember what it says in Matthew 6:19 "Do not store for yourself treasures on earth". Love, life, faith and kindness are more important than money,' the woman said with compassionate wisdom.

'My husband said the same thing that I may not get the pay-out.'

'Your life is the most important thing. It is a gift from God. Tell me what have your friends and family said about this.'

'They think I am crazy to have this surgery. I have sadly fallen out with them,' Angelica cried.

'That is most sad. I am not going to say I know anything about surgery or whether it is the right thing for you. All I will say is that God loves and cares for you. Even if you make a mistake, he loves you. Shall I pray?'

'Yes please.'

'Oh Lord, thank you for allowing Angelica to come down to the front. Please, may you comfort her at this time and make the right decision. Lord give her strength for this surgery and may the surgical and medical team make the right decisions. Do these things in your name; amen.'

Chapter 5

The doctor's waiting room had classical music playing in the background. The walls were a calm, azure, a light-sapphire color. There were various magazines left around on tables, eclectic and diverse for all kinds of people. People waited with apprehension to see their doctor. Angelica waited on her seat, her legs forming a cross looking towards the ground. The wait was excruciating. To be told that there may have been a mix-up was distressing. She had to wait for the doctor to say what was wrong. Of course, how could there have been a mix-up if it was the will of God? For if God willed the surgery to happen, then it must mean that this what a sort of test. What if this was the test to see that she had faith in God? It had appeared to her that God revealed what she already believed. No need to challenge conventional beliefs. That was not what Evangelical Christianity was about. No need to challenge the way a person lived a life or how they voted or how they treated others. Faith and most of all money and Republicanism were what it meant to be a *White* Evangelical. In any case, many White Evangelicals never even went to church at all, or read the Bible. Yet they had the same faith and most of all voted for The Republican Party. She had prayed about it daily whether it was right to have the quadruple amputation. The objections from her family and friends were confirmation that it was God who wanted her to have surgery. Many people who followed the will of God but were rejected by others.

'Angelica Donaldson,' Dr Gina Benjamin-Cruz said.

Angelica got up slowly and limped towards the door that Dr Benjamin-Cruz was coming from. She followed her down the chalk-white corridor, towards the opened door. Gina looked at her smiling briefly before sitting down at her desk. Angelica sat down in the chair opposite her desk. Her room had a brown bed, besides her desk, with charts on the wall of anatomy and of graphs showing various health conditions. Gina wore a lab coat and blue scrubs event though she worked in a local clinic, not a hospital. She had dark-brown eyes and black hair; her skin was of a permanent dark tan. Serious but friendly was her demeanor.

'Angelica, thank you for coming in today. I am sorry I called you on a Sunday. I phoned you up because I have received some information from the hospital that there may have been a mix-up of diagnosis of your condition. The initial diagnosis of chondrosarcoma may have been confused with a far less serious tumor called GCTOB or Giant Cell Tumor of Bone, clinically known Osteoclastoma. We don't know how this happened, we believe there might have been a patient mix-up in notes. We need you to undergo some more biopsies to confirm this.'

Angelica sighed. 'My surgeon Dr Nigel Johnson seems to disagree with your position.'

'Dr Nigel Johnson? Why what is he saying?'

'He is saying I have chondrosarcoma which he says is exceptionally aggressive I will need a quadruple amputation.'

Dr Gina Benjamin-Cruz looked as if a lightning strike had happened in front of her; completely stunned beyond reason. 'He said you would need a quadruple amputation?'

'Yes.'

'That defies all medical reason. I do not know or understand the medical diagnosis here. No, no. I will find you a different surgeon.'

'Why? Why don't you trust him?' Angelica groaned.

'I have never in all my professional life heard of a case of chondrosarcoma requiring a quadruple amputation. That is absurd. Chondrosarcomas are not treated with quadruple amputations. It is done under the most extreme emergency cases of extreme trauma, crush injuries, infection the most common of these being meningitis or sepsis.'

'You don't trust him?' Angelica growled.

'Are you serious enough to believe this? It is against clinical guidelines. I mean do you know the clinical necessities for a quadruple amputation? I wouldn't recommend this surgery at all. Not for any form of bone tumor, including chondrosarcoma or GCTOB.'

'I don't believe you. How could there have been a mix up in my diagnoses?' Angelica said in disbelief.

'I am sorry that we do not have the details. I would recommend another biopsy and have a second look at these results. We need to rule out all potential misdiagnoses.'

'I will need a consultation with Dr Nigel Johnson before I go through with any new biopsy. Why should a second biopsy be done just because we did not get the right results in the first?' Angelica replied.

'Do you even know what it is like to be a quadruple amputee? In America? It is a horrendous disability to have.'

'I can get prosthetics and new bionic limbs can replace any limbs lost...'

'A lot of insurance companies are wary of paying out for prosthetics. They may pay for some of the cost but are reluctant to pay out for the entire cost. Advanced prosthetics are around $50,000. To pay for you to have each limb would cost $250,000. Bionic limbs are at least a decade away. Just imagine this now. Picture life with no arms or legs. How do you go to the bathroom? How would you eat, wash? Have you prepared yourself for the consequences of being a quadruple amputee?'

'I have watched things on Youtube.'

'Have you met any quadruple amputees without prosthetics?' Dr Gina Benjamin-Cruz asked.

'No... I haven't'

'I have met patients who have become quadruple amputees and let me tell you this, many have racked up enormous medical debts. If you are poor and become a quadruple amputee, there is very little support for you. Good luck paying for bills.'

'My husband will take care of me...'

'What about his work situation? If he became a full-time carer to you, your financial situation would deteriorate rapidly.'

'I think we would cope. We have a large amount of savings. He earns a six-figure salary.'

'That money won't last for years though. I don't know whether you were thinking of having a family.'

Angelica paused for a moment. It was one thing Michael and Angelica rarely talked about. They owned a villa with multiple spare rooms, with plenty of space and yet why didn't they think about children? Michael rarely said anything to her about it. He always wore a condom, but Angelica never challenged him. Lubrication was his argument, enjoyment. Angelica knew that asking the subject and he would change the subject almost immediately. Angelica never understood why he was like this. He didn't say he wanted to be childless but never talked to Angelica about his positions on children.

'I that is a very personal question,' Angelica replied, 'I have asked my husband about it and he has never said either way.'

'I would be very hard to do without limbs. We use our limbs on a day to day basis and without having any plan for how you would survive without limbs means that you haven't thought about the implications of being an amputee.'

Angelica was dazed by what Dr Gina Benjamin-Cruz was saying.

'I have thought about it. You are wrong in what you are saying.'

'My suggestion is that you would at least consider other treatment alternatives. I hope you would at least consider taking up my suggestion of having another biopsy so we could get a second set of results so we could determine if you would really need the surgery or not. Why don't you have a final say; a second chance to make an informed decision. It appears you really haven't thought about it. Why are you unable to reconsider the decision of treatment?'

'I will have to go back to my surgeon though. I am not simply having more biopsies to confirm what cancer this is. What if we get the same results as before? What if there a has been no mix-up of results and you were just lying?'

'I am not lying here!' Gina exclaimed, 'I'm doing what the hospital has told me and most of all what my clinical judgement based on evidence is. I mean a quadruple amputation for any kind of bone cancer is quite frankly the worst treatment plan I have ever heard.'

'But my health insurance company may not pay for a second biopsy. I have already had one biopsy and that should have been enough. In the end how many biopsies should I need? One is enough, amputation means amputation.'

Gina sighed. Gina was not talking to a rational patient who was interested in her health. She was talking to a cultist, a deranged patient who had drunk Kool-aid. She now believed the most absurd treatment plan that Gina had ever come across. To say it was unnecessary surgery was an understatement. It was a surgery that was pointless. For Angelica not to even consider a second 'Go back to Dr Nigel Johnson talk through what I have said and meet me next week. I will forward him the results.'

'I will do that then.'

'Thank you, Angelica, have a good day.'

Angelica left the doctor's clinic and got into her SUV. She was driving out of the parking lot and was heading towards the freeway. The road was busy despite it being mid-day. A phone call with the number of 0010174107420 phoned Angelica. Angelica answered it with her hands-free kit.

'Hi, who is this?'

'Is this Angelica Donaldson?' the female voice asked mechanically, like an AI assistant.

'Yes. Who is speaking?'

'Hi, Angelica. This is Dr Nigel Johnson's PA, how are you doing today,' the PA's voice droned.

'I am well thanks I have just been to my family doctor about the chondrosarcoma that I have. She seems to think there has been a mix-up with my diagnosis and is going to email Dr Nigel Johnson the findings.'

'Okay, Angelica. We have to be clear with you. We need a new consultation to discuss the treatment and to finalize the date of the surgery,' the female voice became more demanding.

'Yes, but my doctor says we need another biopsy...'

'You can come to the consultation and discuss it then,' the voice said almost angrily, 'What day can you do this week. Is Thursday okay at 11:00 am?'

'I'll have to discuss it with my husband....'

'Great we'll see you there at 11:00. Thank you, Mrs Angelica Donaldson and good day.'

The PA hung up on Angelica. Angelica was surprized at the phone call. Why were they phoning her back and so demanding of the consultation? What about going with Michael? She was shocked by the abruptness and rudeness of the PA. Would she not have considered Angelica's situation at the moment before booking an appointment? Angelica decided to ring Michael's number, thinking that he would be busy.

'Hi cupcake,' Michael said.

'You aren't busy...'

'No. Not really. I am just doing paperwork. Why are you phoning me?'

'I went to the doctor's today and they said there may have been a mix-up in the diagnosis that I may not have chondrosarcoma and that I may need a second biopsy to confirm this...'

Michael sighed like a steam engine, 'We can't keep going through new biopsies, Angelica. They made a mistake, did they?'

'Well she thinks there may have been a misdiagnosis and we need a second biopsy to confirm this,' Angelica replied.

'Then what? Have a third or a fourth because we didn't like the results of the second. We need your treatment now, don't we?'

Angelica was surprized with Michael's response. At first, he had been rather opposed to the idea of a quadruple amputation. Suddenly he was all for it. Angelica was hesitant to reply.

'Answer me, Angelica!' Michael shouted.

'Yes. I agree with you. My will can't be subverted by doctors or professionals. Most of all it would be subverting the will of God.'

Michael sounded upset. 'The thought of losing you my precious diamond. How would I cope? I can look after you without limbs. We can get through it. It won't be too bad. After all didn't people survive World War 2?'

Tears welled up in Angelica's eyes. 'You are such a good husband,' she cried, 'thank you for being so supportive of me.'

'That is why you have got to see Dr Nigel Johnson again.'

'Well, his PA just phoned me about having another consultation with Dr Nigel Johnson.'

'What day this week?'

'Thursday at 11:00 am. '

'Yes, I can make that and support you,' Michael said immediately.

'What about your work commitments? How can you just say you can make it?'

'Do not worry about those,' his voice hissed. 'I have no problem juggling my work around my precious diamond.'

'Okay then. I will see you tonight.'

'Bye my lovely cupcake,' Michael said voluptuously.

After turning off the interstate and entering the suburb that Angelica lived in, Angelica went down the street that she lived in. Outside her house drive was a white van that had parked outside the house. The windows were blackout and it appeared to be conspicuous but was randomly parked outside the house, even though the majority of the people were out at work. Angelica decided to get out of her vehicle and take a look at the people who were parked outside her house. Who were these people who were parked outside her house?

'Hello, who are you?' she shouted, limping towards the van.

Just before she reached the van, it sped off like a startled horse up the road.

That was odd, Angelica thought. A random van parked outside her house. Who was spying on them?

Angelica contemplated this when she drove up to her short drive to the villa before closing the gate and locking herself up inside her suburban citadel, protecting her from the outside world. It was an island in an archipelago, Angelica's and Michael's villa was. Worth around $700,000, Michael said he did not want to buy another more luxurious villa because he said he only earned $250,000 a year. In reality, he earned more, much more but never disclosed this to Angelica. She sat inside watching more of EEPTV. Today, she believed there was no divine message. Instead, she relaxed to the television, not having to worry about the problems today. At least Michael was returning from work this afternoon as he sometimes was away on business visits.

Michael came back from work at 6:00 pm. He appeared rather tired and sat down on the sofa next to Angelica.

'Hi Michael,' Angelica said.

'Hello,' Michael groaned.

'How was work today? Angelica asked.

'Alright. Doing various business documents. Nothing I can discuss due to corporate confidentiality,' Michael said.

'Well it's good you haven't had a bad day,' Angelica said.

'How has your day been Angelica?' Michael asked.

'I went to see Dr Gina Benjamin-Cruz as you are aware.'

'Oh yes, you were telling me. That was bad that they had a mix-up in the biopsy report. I still think we should go back to see Dr Nigel Johnson again this Thursday.'

'Definitely. I wouldn't just have more biopsies. If they wanted the result from before they should have got the first result correct anyway.'

'Well at least we are on the same page,' Michael smiled. Michael put his arm around Angelica, 'What is for dinner,' he said.

'Tacos.'

'Nice although I thought tacos were for Tuesday.'

'I thought I would make them for today.'

'Okay. Well, I am looking forward to them.'

The abrupt talk with Dr Nigel Bank's PA did not undermine Angelica's faith in Dr Nigel Johnson, although she was somewhat divided on the issue of whether to have a second biopsy. The waiting room for seeing

Dr Nigel Bank was far smarter and sleek than the one for the clinic of Angelica's doctor. There was a flat-screen television which played various programs. It was currently on a certain Right-wing news-channel, spewing out lies of the migrant caravan heading towards the Texan-border with Mexico. This had been dominating the news recently. The Midterms in Texas had been eventful alongside this news. Beto O' Rouke, a young Democrat narrowly lost to Ted Cruz. This was an act of divine intervention. God had personally intervened to stop a Democrat from winning in Texas. Forget about the political policies of what Republicans in Texas were doing. God was on the side of the GOP; God's Own Party.

'Those bloody refugees flooding our border and bringing crime to our streets in the US,' Michael said.

'It's cancerous the vast amounts of refugees. It makes me think of my cancer,' Angelica said.

'Yes. I think the influx of refugees is rather cancerous. They grow exponentially and then kill a country. I am looking forward to tonight and watching some programs again. I don't want to watch to more of that EEPTV. Or maybe I will go on Youtube,' Michael said.

'But I like EEPTV,' Angelica whined.

'I can just go on the computer or my cell phone.'

An olive skin male came out to greet them. 'Angelica Donaldson,' Dr Nigel Johnson remarked.   'Would you like to follow me?'
They went down a gleaming white corridor and blue-tiled floor towards the office with Dr Nigel Johnson, Orthopedic surgeon MSc, PhD. Angelica limped as her ankle was very painful to walk on. They went through the door into the room in which the fateful day that Angelica was told that she required a quadruple amputation. Both Angelica and Michael sat in front of the desk, with Dr Nigel Johnson.

'So how are you felling Angelica?' Dr Nigel Johnson purred.

'I am okay I suppose. Did you receive the email from my doctor?' Angelica queried.

'Email? What email?' Dr Nigel Johnson appeared confused.

'She said she was sending you an email regarding my treatment package. She contacted me the other day and requested to see me urgently in consultation because the hospital may have mixed up my diagnosis with someone else and that I may not have chondrosarcoma but GCTOB, which is rarer than chondrosarcoma,' Angelica said.

Dr Nigel Johnson raised his eyebrows, 'I see. Well no I have not received any email from her or more importantly from the test department about this mistake.'

'I don't understand. Why haven't you received it? Where has it gone?'

'It is quite possible that no email was dispatched and that it was a mistake on their part.'

Angelica shook her head and looked bewildered. 'I thought she would have sent something or the other hospital giving you the need to do a biopsy.'

'No, I have not received that information.'

'So are you going to offer a biopsy?'

Dr Nigel Johnson looked at Michael who said or did nothing, 'Well we could do. But I do think that Dr Gina Benjamin-Cruz is incorrect in her diagnosis. I have looked over your results and I do believe that you have chondrosarcoma is that having GCTOB or Giant Cell Tumorous of Bone is very rare. It is unlikely to happen in the ankle also.'

'She said that a quadruple amputation was an unnecessary procedure.'

'Now that is lying,' Dr Nigel Johnson stated coldly, 'this procedure, the one I am going to perform is not done without regard from the reality that cancer cells are going to break off and spread. Given their type, it is most likely they will go to other parts of your body including other limbs.'

'Are you saying that she is wrong?'

Dr Nigel Johnson looked at Michael again, who was holding Angelica's hand and smoothing it. Michael subtly nodded.

'Yes. I believe so.'

'So how do I trust you over her then...'

'Because I am more qualified than she is and she does not know the difference between cancers! That is why!' Dr Nigel Johnson shouted. Angelica fell back into her seat.

'Are you dismissing her findings?'

'I am not dismissing them. But come on here, how many biopsies do we need to take? Two, five, eight just to get the right result that they want. They are only saying this because they got it wrong the first time and so they want to change the results. It is their incompetence, not mine.' Angelica gulped and Dr Nigel Johnson looked at her, grinning at her uneasy face.

'Besides I wouldn't trust Gina. Now today, I have the 175-page document that you will be signing before I operate on you. It is called *Article 50- Healthcare Liabilities and Treatment Clauses*. I will not carry out any treatment on you before you sign this contract.'

Out of Dr Nigel Bank's briefcase, Dr Nigel Bank picked up a large bound copy of a paper contract; *Article 50: Healthcare Liabilities and Treatment Clauses*. Angelica looked at it in a perplexed way. 'I have never heard of this liabilities and treatment clauses before,' Angelica said.

'The purpose of this document is to make sure that you are aware of the treatment I am offering you. It is a contract that I and I alone give you and is done so that I am not liable for anything that goes wrong in the treatment or anything that you think about in that you change your mind...'

'I can't change my mind on the treatment you are offering me?' Angelica asked.

'You can but I wouldn't advise it. When you sign *Article 50: Healthcare Liabilities and Treatment Clauses*, you will have signed to say that you understand the consequences of surgery and that will be enough for me to start the ball rolling for you to have surgery. We need it to be final rather than just talk. We need to turn words into action. Amputation means amputation and we will make a success of it.'

Dr Nigel Bank pushed the document over the desk towards Angelica. Angelica opened the document onto the desk and realized the enormity of the task of reading the document. She opened the first page, past the contents and read the words.

Clause 1 e): The patient of said treatment has not the right to appeal against the surgeon or surgical team or the medical establishment on any basis regarding whether the treatment is considered unnecessary or deemed inappropriate by other medical professionals….

Clause 2 c): The patient forfeits the right of any compensation if medical treatment does not have the desired effect or leaves permanent problems for said patient…

Clause 4 f): The surgeon is not liable for any pay-outs or insurance claims that are null or invalidated or reduced by life insurance or medical insurance companies.

Angelica closed the document and pushed the document towards Dr Nigel Johnson.

'I can't sign this document. It undermines my position and I trust you have my intentions at heart but you appear to be only interested in protecting yourself. Perhaps Dr Gina Benjamin-Cruz was right. Maybe I should receive a second biopsy?' Angelica said.

Dr Nigel Johnson looked speechless and turned to Michael who looked concerned.

'Dr Nigel Johnson is only trying to protect himself from litigation charges and being sued. You would I hope never want to sue the man, would you now?' Michael said in a voice of sarcastic reassurance.

'No,' Angelica sighed, 'but I am worrying now, do you know? Why would Dr Nigel Johnson have such an in-depth document if he didn't need to protect himself?'

'I do it on the basis that I am trying to protect myself legally from any form of ramifications. You wouldn't sue me I know but I need to protect myself. In any case that you decided that this surgery was a bad idea and that it wasn't a good idea to sign Article 50, it cannot be revoked and the outcome is surgery.'

She contemplated in silence the document and was about to leave. 'I think I am done. I am ready to go, Michael.'

'Listen, Angelica. Listen very carefully. What are we going to do once we leave here? Are we just going to go back and have more biopsies? What are we going to do about it because leaving this place without any plan of surgery means the cancer will spread unabated? At least signing this article gives us a chance for you to prepare for surgery,' Michael said demandingly.

'I can't just sign a massive legal document without any legal protection. I need to have legal protection.'

'What about your cancer Angelica? Do you not care about the fact that every day you dither about, your cancer is killing you? This is important Angelica. Your life is on the line. You have been dithering about yes, I am going to have the surgery and then no I am not going to have the surgery. The decision is now. Once you have signed the document you won't need to dither about,' Michael said forcefully.

'I just can't sign this document without reading it through...'

'You have already read it through. I am fed up with you just dithering around. You won't be getting your $3,500,000 if you dither about it. Just think this lack of decisiveness means you will lose all control to the cancer. Death is assured for those that procrastinate over important health decisions. We need to take back control. We control all of the cards,' Michael said, his voice becoming angrier.

Angelica sighed. Michael turned the document to the end where the pages were. 'All you have to do is sign here and it will be done. Remember the fact that you will get prosthetic limbs that can replace the ones you have lost.'

'Why are you being so forceful in this? It is my body okay...'

'Angelica, your body is dying. Cancer cells are multiplying without control. You must take back control and accept the treatment,' Dr Nigel Johnson said remorsefully. 'Now or never. Now is the time to take back control. Prosthetic limbs will replace the ones you have lost.'

Angelica picked up the pen, signing the document where the line was next to the cross.

'Thank you,' Dr Nigel Johnson murmured with a conniving grin.

Angelica looked lost, feeling sick at the document she had just signed was the document that gave the authorization for Dr Nigel Johnson to remove her limbs. There was no going back. Article 50 had been signed.

'after all, you have signed this document. Maybe you will change your mind. We will have various more consultations before the surgery. You will need to meet the anaesthesiologists who will measure you so they perform drug calculations. Then we will meet for the final time before the surgery. If you do regret signing the document, there is a fee to cancelling the surgery. That will set you back $5,000 cancellation plus a potential $50,000 fee also.'

'$55,000! That is insane.'

'You should read the document, shouldn't you?' Dr Nigel Johnson grinned.

Angelica felt powerless against Dr Nigel Johnson. 'So now that you have signed the document, I can set a preliminary date for the surgery. There is a date that I was thinking,' Dr Nigel Johnson said.

'Which date is that?' Angelica asked.

'03/29/19.'

'I am free that day.'

'Great, I'll just pencil that in. Remember, if you can't face having the operation, do phone up and I will just take the cancellation fee. I know you won't do cancel now, but I always have to make sure that you won't,' Dr Nigel Johnson said with a scheming voice.

On the way home, Angelica looked out of the window of the SUV, her jaw muzzled into her right hand, feeling full of despair.

'Cheer up Angelica. Just think this whole treatment will be over soon.'

'Maybe I was wrong not listening to my friends and family.'

'You have done the right thing. Yes, they may not agree with your treatment plan but I doubt they understand the position you are in. What is it in particular that you are upset with?'

'I think I was put off by the contract. It seemed that he was aggressive and overbearing.'

'Surgeons are of course aggressive. Who would have thought? The orthopedic surgeons are known for being aggressive.'

'Why was he being so dominating though? I am concerned that I have done the wrong decision.'

'The Lord is sitting and smiling on the decision you have made. Have you ever doubted that President Trump that we passionately support? Think of all the things he has said and done. Have you ever doubted him or has what he has said made you question voting for him?'

'No, it has not.'

'So why now do you question Dr Nigel Johnson? You would never question which way of voting in an election so why question having your legs and arms amputated...'

'Because it is life-changing...'

'And voting in elections isn't?'

'I don't know.'

'Needless to say, I will love you regardless of the surgery. You will be mine and I will treasure you,' he said, voluptuously, kissing her on the check when the SUV had stopped at a set of traffic lights.

'What will you think of me when I have no arms and legs?'

'I will think about what a beautiful woman I have as a wife.'

'You are wonderful to me. '

'Even though you said a few nights ago you didn't want me to be your husband? You have no consistency...'

'I am sorry for what I said.'

'You are forgiven,' he grinned. 'I can't let my babe get upset before her major surgery. That would be unfortunate.'

Chapter 6

Angelica and Michael snuggled up on the sofa together. Angelica was mindlessly watching television like most evenings whilst Michael was on his tablet computer. Michael flipped between trading charts and looked at his earnings on his financial trading. Angelica tried to forget what had happened today, burying her thoughts about the surgery and the date, 03/29/18. The date was drilled into her brain. It was happening. Life without limbs. Her cancer needed to be cured. The treatment was necessary, she kept telling herself. She needed to take back control. If that meant amputation, that meant amputation. There was, of course, a large amount of uneasiness though. She had been jumping between extremes. One hour, she felt good about having the surgery and then she felt terrified. She was glad that Michael was fully behind her. Michael was looking up pictures on various websites like he usually did.

'Look, Angelica,' Michael said, pointing to his tablet. It was a picture of an operating room, with surgeons dressed in blue around a patient. Jesus was guiding the surgeon's hand in the operating room. 'Don't you think that is where Jesus is right now? Don't you believe that this surgery is divinely ordained that the fate of this surgery is in the hands of God?'

Angelica looked at Michael in the eyes. She had a reflective gaze in her eyes. 'I do believe God has control of my destiny.'

'Just look at the picture. Jesus is in control of you. He has you and won't let go,' Michael said.

'I believe you,' Angelica whispered.

Michael received a phone call on his cell phone.

'I have to go outside to take this phone call.'

'Okay.'

Michael went outside the room and closed the door to answer the phone call from an unknown number.

'Hello?'

'It's me.'

'Hi.'

'Are you okay to meet tomorrow evening? I need to discuss things with you. Our meeting today, it didn't go that well.'

'I thought it was reasonably productive.'

'I am worried that the agreement doesn't go through. If they…'

'I am seeing this through.'

'How do I know that I can trust you to follow through?'

'I am an asset manager.'

'So?'

'It is my job to the manager to manage agreements, contracts and assets…'

'You haven't given me much faith. I want the money…'

'The agreement is simple. You will get the money once the procedure is done.'

'The procedure? The procedure can't be done unless all parties are willing to it.'

'The article was signed was it not?'

'Yes.'

'Then why do you worry.'

The voice paused for a short time. 'Article 50…'

'The document cannot be revoked. What are you on about?'

'The article signed is not entirely binding. I mean imagine I say in court I have an agreement to…'

'The document cannot be revoked since it has been signed and the parties involved have agreed to it.'

'The stipulation fee…'

'They won't back out of it.'

'How do you know?'

'Once the article has been signed….'

'That article, that contract is no more of a legally binding document then a plan written on a receipt.'

Michael sighed, 'You can meet me tomorrow and then we can discuss it then.'

'Same place…'

'7 pm.'

'Agreed. I have no business in the evening to go to.'
'Okay. Speak to you tomorrow.'
'Goodbye.'

Michael went back inside of the lounge to sit back down next to Angelica. He put his arm around her but she moved away from his embrace. Angelica always had suspicions about the backdoor agreements that Michael was signing.

'Who was that Michael?' she asked suspiciously.

'A business client.'

'I thought you worked as an Oil Engineering Consultant Analyst for a company?'

'We have clients in the oil industry. Who buys oil, Angelica?' Michael sniggered.

'I was only asking.'

'You are so paranoid. You should listen to yourself.'

'Your wife is going through some very difficult medical treatment to deal with life-threatening cancer,' Angelica cried, 'I just want your support. I hope you aren't cheating on me.'

'Cheat on you? How could you say such a thing?' Michael grunted.

'You only a few weeks ago said I would be good in latex...'

'Why are you hanging on to that for so long?'

'A wife knows when a husband cheats...'

'Careful what you say. Be very careful,' Michael whispered impetuously. 'Who is going to look after you when you have had your surgery?'

Angelica spluttered, 'Well... well...'

'Your friends. Where have they gone? Elizabeth? Where is she? And your family, do they support you? I love you. How many other people do?'

Angelica burst into tears, wailing on the sofa. 'I am sorry for doubting you! I am sorry. I am sorry. I am a fool to think you would cheat on me.'

'Look at your family. None of them supports you having surgery. Elizabeth, the nurse, out of hand dismissed your surgery. How could she? When everyone is turning their backs on you, I am not. I will never disown you,' Michael hissed, 'You will always be mine.'

Michael smoothed Angelica's hand, which she would soon be losing, in a calm, affectionate way glaring into Angelica's eyes.

'I have a meeting with someone tomorrow so I won't be here to see you.'

'Who is it?'

'Confidential.'

'I guess it is the person who phoned you.'

'Who it is or what association with this person I will not go into. I must not say who'

'Why?' Angelica said cautiously.

'The government is always hunting you down. Us conservatives have to be wary of the government.'

Angelica was perplexed. Angelica thought that Michael worked in the oil business she thought. Why did he talk about the government hunting him down? Michael had always been a conservative. He always said about the evils of big government, so it was easy to just because he hated paying his taxes. Perhaps there was something more.

'I assume what you are doing is completely legal?'

'Why would I break the law?' Michael smiled, 'breaking the law is how do I put it, not something I would consider if it is immoral.'

What does he mean breaking the law is not something he would consider unless it was immoral? Angelica thought to herself. It could mean that he would never commit a crime because all crimes are immoral or it could mean he would be a lawbreaker if he felt it was moral. Yet Angelica thought it could be something for more sinister. The white van outside her house? No, it was probably just someone lost in suburban Dallas, Angelica thought to herself. She did not want to contemplate anything else.

'How about going to bed? I am tired and want to sleep,' Angelica yawned.

'I will stay up for a bit longer,' Michael uttered, 'I like the night. It is a great shroud of intentions.'

'Okay, you are getting weird. What time will you be home tomorrow?' Angelica chuckled.

'Whatever time I return. I wish you a good day.'

Angelica got ready for bed, washing, brushing her teeth and putting on her nightgown without much thought of what she was doing. Of course, after her amputation, she would not be able to do any of those things. She did not even contemplate this. Why contemplate something bad happening when only good could come from the procedure, Angelica questioned herself.

In a dream-like state, she felt unable to move, trapped inside her body. The room was a bright white, a circular lamp was above her and she heard a bleep of some kind of cardiographic heart monitor, the rustling of paper, talking of people. Angelica lied there in her bed, in a nightmarish visitation. She looked up to see surgeons, their faces masked looking down on her, their arms pointing upwards with skull-white latex gloves, their eyes glaring at one another and then at Angelica.

'Our patient today is Angelica Mary Donaldson, a 32-year-old. She has opted to have her arms and legs removed due to chondrosarcoma in her right ankle.'

'Are we sure this surgery is a good idea? I mean it is rather unnecessary...' a female surgeon asked.

'She signed the paperwork. She is sedated,' the surgeon said. 'You are nothing more than a surgical intern resident after all. No more biopsies. Nurse, scalpel.' The surgeon was aggressive and demanding. He cut into Angelica's arms and she yelped in the discordant electrifying throb of dire agony. It was not pain but electrifying torture in her arms.

'Bone saw.' The screaming of the saw was that of a carpenter's workshop. Angelica watched as the surgeon picked up her arm and then her other arm, and then both legs after severing them from the body. A mask covered her face and she looked down her stumped limbs.

Angelica moved her arms and legs, screaming at the horror that she had just experienced. The experience felt real; a nightmare in which she believed she was real. Of course, it was. The clock was ticking. On March the 29th, there would be no setbacks. Amputation was happening

Chapter 7

The dark night hides the intentions of people; the dark curtains wrapping the purposes of man as they slept. Stars hide your fires, let no one see dark and deep desires. Russell Portin drove his SUV down the dimly lit interstate highway. The sky was black, and its stars had fallen from the sky like a faded American flag. Russell Portin was heading for the center of downtown Dallas. He was trying to save a major deal that looked like it was going to crash. One of the people in the deal was not playing ball.

Russell Portin was an asset manager or more accurately ran a successful trading organisation in buying and selling stock, commodities and currencies. The entire web of Russell Portin was that of deceit and lies; a buying and selling stocks, hedging on the value of currencies. He had multiple offshore bank accounts in exotic places like Bermuda and Barbados, whilst holding them in less exotic places like Lichtenstein and the Falklands. He owned a Bermuda passport. Technically he was a multi-millionaire, worth around in excess of $10,000,000. His wife never knew that. He kept his life as a closely guarded secret. A secret that he had to fight for. He knew the FBI was out to get him. This business meeting was in part designed to create a scheme of funnelling a lucrative business trade that was possible to generate $5,000,000 or $10,000,000 for him away from a tax investigation. A complex tax avoidance scheme that had never been dreamt up before, so outlandish it would be in the pages of fiction.

The moon was hidden. In the blurry world of night driving, Russell thought of his night ahead. He needed this business deal to go through. Simply moving money out of the US was not an option. The FBI could have easily kept an eye on what he was doing. Funnelling money was hard to stay out of the radar of the FBI, who had their nose into everyone's finances. What if the deal collapses, he thought. What is the surgery didn't go ahead?

To predicate a business and tax policy on completely unnecessary and unethical surgery was a gamble, to say the least. It would require the total cooperation of a hospital, of medical staff to do the surgery. Great, he had this. The entire deal was resting on the surgeon, who had been acquiescent in the whole deal and an unwilling patient, who was hesitant to have the surgery. It rested on that. If the surgery did not go ahead, Russell would have a considerably larger tax bill or much worse.

The downtown of Dallas was lit up like church candles at midnight mass. The skyscrapers flickered in the dark, their green, red and white lights were harsh on the eyes. Red lights rippled off the water; foaming blood after surgery or murder. Towards the center of the city, the lighting was brighter but still, the night was draped in darkness, a thick black. He parked up his SUV in a parking lot. In a dark black suit and brown polished shoes, he stepped out of the SUV. He carried two holstered firearms on him, a wise idea when heading out into the darkness of Texas. Russell never knew who would shoot at him first; a gang member or an FBI agent. That did not matter to Russell. It was a Second Amendment right after all.

Russell walked down the street to a restaurant. Business deals in a fast-food restaurant was never a good plan. He sat at the table and after ordering a coke, he looked around at the kind of people in the restaurant. There were all kinds of people, businessmen meeting their clients, men out on dates with women. Children weren't in sight. Most men wore suits, smart casual attire. It was Texas after all. Still, Russell knew this was the place to do business. His business partner arrived after 15 minutes of waiting. He looked Italian, perhaps some kind of Mediterranean ancestry.

'I am sorry I am late, Russell. I had been called in for emergency surgery at 4 pm. I had to do some surgery on a trauma victim in a road traffic accident,' the surgeon huffed.
'Oh dear,' Russell said, somewhat empathetically.

'A young female. 19 at one of the universities in Texas. I amputated an arm and a leg due to crush injuries, repairing a fractured pelvis as well. Still could have been worse,' the surgeon smiled.

'Indeed, much worse,' Russell smiled. 'Does she have health insurance?'

'I can't tell you confidential information,' the surgeon said suspiciously, looking around the restaurant.

'I feel so sorry for that girl,' Russell grinned, 'waking up and seeing that you have lost a set of limbs. I was thinking of funnelling money to her, you know as an anonymous gift.'

'Don't bother. Charities and churches will look after her,' the surgeon spluttered.

Russell laughed. 'I wish they would. To business.'

'I am afraid of our business plan. Our strategy is not working. Does the entire business flow through based on this one surgery?' the surgeon asked.

'It is imperative. The plan is simple. The money will flow through per limb you amputate. $250,000 a limb. That goes into the business holding account. You understand the business don't you?'

'I do.'

'You are a company and the surgeries perform are the services of that incorporated company. You subcontract your surgery to the hospitals in the form of a business contract. Now, normally surgeons they pay taxes on employment or self-employment. Instead, you do not pay any taxes because you charge $0 for your salary. Instead, you derive all of your income from profit, which means you are paying a lower tax rate based on capital-gains.'

'Genius,' the surgeon smiled.

'I know. Now this, this surgery is a way of me to dump $1,000,000 of business costs, which of course means tax deductibles due to healthcare expenditure. I move that money through to the business holding account, meaning I take a 75% cut on this surgery, which means I would only have to pay a reduced rate of tax. I can of course ship it to another bank account without any the wiser.'

'I do surgery all day and waste my life because people like you make millions and keep all the proceeds.'

'It is a hard life. I have to spend as little money as possible in the US because the Fed will keep an eye on what spending you do. Still, I have a reasonable life.' Russell took a sip of coke. 'Aren't you having anything? Wine, beer, coke?'

'I'll have a coke. Did you know coke can dissolve bones and clean up blood from a roadside crash?'

'Really? How enlightening.'

A young curvy waitress came over and took some drinks orders before going back into the kitchen. Russell eyed up the alluring woman. Breasts and steak were always good on a woman for Russell. Never mind what his wife thought. She wasn't here to tell him what to do.

'A nice young woman,' Russell whispered.

'You would be too distracted as a surgeon. There are a lot of them around in the OR.'

'Kinky,' Russell said voluptuously.

'I won't ask about your private life.'

'Business is a rough world. You wouldn't believe the kind of world it is. Partying, sex, drugs, drink. Trading is a world of living to excess, being part of the Mile-High Club on seven-figure salary. All of the desires you could ever want.'

'Tell me then, why did you marry your wife under such circumstances?' the surgeon inquired. 'You want a world of fun and she is what, a Bible-thumping, Trump-voting, TV watching Neanderthal with a good figure that you want to destroy?'

'She is easy to control. Easy to manipulate. I can have power over her that you could never have over other women. A lot of women would be more curious about what I do. But she doesn't seem to care.'

'That is good.'

'The fact the patient even elected to have this surgery is in my mind the absurdly ridiculous part of her stupidity. She genuinely believes this is either some act of divine intervention, that somehow God wants her to have surgery. $3,500,000. I earn that every so often.'

'Ludicrous.'

'The patient may change her mind. What if she changes her mind on the day?'

'The surgery will still go ahead.'

'Have you explained to the anaesthesiologist or any of the medical staff of what you are going to do?'

'No...'

'What happens when they find out?'

'I will be able to use my contacts in the hospital to keep me out of trouble.'

'Be sure that you do.'

'I can be sure. What are you going to do with her after the surgery? She will be dependent on others.'

'She'll have an electric wheelchair,' Russell said, 'that she can operate with a stumped arm.'

'What about everything else? Restroom, washing, eating. Literally everything, how have you thought it out, given that you will be tied down?' the surgeon asked philosophically.

'I can do a lot of it myself. I will leave her 5 hours a day or do more work from home.'

'Can you do that?'

'A lot of my trading I can do from home. Besides, I won't need as much money as before,' Russell smiled. 'The trading I have done recently gives me an outstanding amount of around $5,000,000.'

The surgeon nodded. The restaurant appeared to be rather busier than when they first arrived, the noise picked up so that no one surrounding them could hear the conversation.

'Do you require to go to the office to trade?'

'No, not really. I could do a considerable amount of it at home,' Russell said.

'And why don't you do that?'

'My wife would find out what I did as a living.'

'And what is the problem of that?'

'It would make her doubt me as a person.'

'Is that a problem?'

Russell sighed. 'I can't let her know how much money we have right now, can we. If I showed her how much money I made, she certainly would not have had the surgery from you.'

'That is true,' the surgeon said.

'She went to our family doctor and she advised against you being the surgeon,' Russell said.

'Who is that?'

'Dr Gina Benjamin...'

'Oh her.'

'I didn't say her name.'

'Don't need to.'

'Really?' Russell asked, 'there could be multiple doctors with that name.'

'I don't think there are. Besides, I know the doctor by their name. Benjamin-Cruz is a pathetic doctor.'

'What if she believes the doctor?'

'She won't.'

A few days after Russell had done his business discussion, Angelica went with Michael to a Bible study group. This had been the first one they had been able to go to after her treatment plan by Dr Nigel Johnson. Some of them had contacted her about their concern, only for Angelica replying that she would only discuss to them in person about the treatment. The Bible study group met around Jeremy Schmidt's house, who was married to Frances, who happened to be a non-Christian. This upset Angelica and Michael, who thought that Christians should only marry other Christians and that marrying non-Christians was against the Bible. Jeremy seemed to not agree with this teaching, they thought.

Jeremy and Frances lived in a reasonably large villa on the outskirts of Dallas also. Jeremy was a manufacturing engineer and Frances owned a small business. Elizabeth Londres, Kate Sunderland both went to the group. Other people in the group of importance included Bernard, a lawyer, Tina, a Japanese car salesperson and Callum who was a rocket scientist for a start-up company. It was a random group of people, given the nature of America Evangelical Christianity but it worked. The house had a large entrance, with a spiralling staircase. The dining room and kitchen were conjoined to create a large space. The walls were painted downstairs in red, white and blue, which was Frances choice. There were pictures of nature on the walls downstairs and pictures of Jeremy's and Frances' family, pictures of all the children. The Bible study group were having tacos, a wrap of having individual fillings like a pick n mix. The open and friendly atmosphere hid the discordance that hung over the meeting.

'I hope you guys have had a good week. We were studying last week about Proverbs 3 verse 5, which is a very important verse in the Bible, don't we all agree?' Jeremy said.
Elizabeth had a smirk on her face. 'Perhaps we could discuss about this in a group about trusting God with all our hearts and not leaning on our understanding. I think Angelica can start us off in this subject.'
All eyes were pointed towards Angelica and she scowled at Elizabeth, 'Thank you Elizabeth for your kind volunteering,' Angelica said sarcastically, 'I wasn't here last time when you were going over this Bible verse but I can say this that I have had a very turbulent couple of weeks.'

'Tell us what has happened,' Jeremy said. Jeremy was already aware of roughly what was going on between Elizabeth and Angelica. Elizabeth was a friend of Frances, who told Jeremy what was going on with Angelica.
Angelica took a large gulp of air. 'I have visited my surgeon Dr Nigel Johnson twice in two weeks to talk about the bone cancer I have in my ankle. He has recommended a quadruple amputation on my limbs to

save my life. I would appreciate you praying for me that the $3,500,000 pay-out that I can receive will come through quickly and that I will relish this new life that has been given to me from God,' Angelica said, tearfully.

'Wow,' Callum interjected, 'I have never heard of a quadruple amputee for bone cancer. That is quite extraordinary.'

'That is because she wants to ignore all medical advise about the surgery from her doctor and press on with having the surgery done by Dr Nigel Johnson regardless of its effects on her life,' Elizabeth said with a cruel, bitter voice.

'You Elizabeth are a cow. You did not want to support me in my surgery unlike Kate who has been right behind me from the start,' Angelica groaned.

'A cow?'

'Well, you may as well be an ass for all I care. We know what asses are...'

Elizabeth gave Angelica a dirty look. Asses or donkeys, what a kind thing to call your ex-friend, 'It ain't all about politics honey-bun. I am unwilling to talk about politics. It is *you* who wants to make it a big deal. I really cannot understand why you are obsessed with politics....'

'We are living in the end times! Do you not care about the rates of abortion, the promotion of gay rights and the depravity our country is going down? The election of Trump is part of God's plan to make America great again.'

'Amen sister!' Kate said. Michael nodded in agreement with his wife. The rest of the group sighed and shook their heads in disbelief.

'Look we all have disagreements with our friends, family and spouses. My wife and I do not vote the same way as many married couples do in this day and age. I have had such serious rows with my wife over the years, it is questionable how we even got together at, isn't that right Frances?' Jeremy said.

Frances was in the corner of the room, reading a novel by herself. She nodded. 'We have had a serious conflict between us,' she replied, 'to the point I do not know how we married at all.'

'Thank you, Frances, for interacting with us.'

'Yes, thank you pagan for interacting with us,' Angelica said snidely. Frances rolled her eyes. 'I am not a pagan. Atheism is not paganism.'

'You are right. You are a child of the devil!' Angelica said brashly.

'Angelica Donaldson. Apologize for saying such a thing to my wife!' Jeremy exclaimed.

This kind of hostility had never really been seen previously. Angelica may have been utterly blunt but she tempered it. This time, she was going all out in her aggression. It was a complete transformation to someone unhinged from reality. Why on earth did Angelica begin to act like a crazed fanatic?

Angelica sighed, rotating her head to look like she cared about Frances. 'I am so sorry,' she said sarcastically. 'Please forgive me.'

'You are forgiven. Atheists don't need religions to forgive. We are kind and loving to people without religion.'

'All of our morals have come from religion. We would think that rape and murder were acceptable without Christianity. Christianity gave morals to us in Western...'

'This is why I don't get involved in your Bible study because of you of Angelica. I thought Christianity is based on love, kindness, mercy and self-control and Angelica displays none of these things,' Frances said, walking off.

Elizabeth was aghast at what Angelica was saying. She did not understand how she was even friends with her, to begin with. Elizabeth always knew that when confronted on a decision or idea that Angelica had, Angelica would defend it like a savage hyena guarding a carcass. What was weird was that she was defending herself *choosing* to amputate all her limbs. Who would choose to have her limbs amputated? Perhaps there was a reason for her to become exceptionally aggressive? There was none. Her decision to get all her limbs amputated was all she needed to become overly aggressive.

'Thank you very much for getting rid of my wife Frances from this decision. I have prayed a lot for her to come to the Lord and you rarely help Angelica.'

'Oh yes, but you should have never married a pagan as a wife. It says it in the Bible, do not be unevenly yoked.'

'It also says in Proverbs 19:20 to listen to counsel Angelica...'

'You Jeremy are a silly little rattlesnake! You rattle off scripture and you act in a way that acts completely contradicts Scripture.'

'Don't point at the speck of dust in your own eye when you have a great plank of wood in your own eye, Angelica. Judge not lest ye shall be judged. For in the same way you judge others, you will be judged, and with the measure you use, it will be measured to you. ,' Jeremy said cuttingly.

Angelica hissed. She wanted to respond to the remark of Jeremy but could not respond to the remark since Jeremy was right.

'Back to the subject at hand, having Angelica's limbs amputated. From where I stand, I fully support her. You know we should always love our wives, even if they have no limbs. I will love and care for Angelica, no matter what matters to her,' Michael said, looking into Angelica's eyes, smoothing her hand.

'Aww thank you, Michael. Do you see? He is such a wonderful husband, my Michael.'

Michael smiled. Elizabeth shook her head. 'Do you guys even understand what it means to have your legs and arms amputated? It is a terrible disability. What can you do without your limbs?'

'Look Elizabeth. I am getting a pay-out of $3,500,000. I don't need to worry about your project of fear. Everyone who opposes me just spouts project fear,' Angelica said forcefully.

Callum tried not to smirk. Getting a $3,500,000 pay-out was the reason? That couldn't be the only reason why someone would choose to get their limbs amputated. 'You think that all who oppose the decision to have all your limbs amputated as being a bad idea as having project fear when it is cancer in one part of your body?'

'Yes, but like Mexicans and the migrant train that rushes over the border, they will take over my body and kill me.'

Callum and Elizabeth broke into hysterical laughter. 'You honestly are comparing your cancer cells to Mexicans taking over your body?'

'Yes,' Angelica said with a straight-face. 'It is serious. Our country is dying out because of...'

'You watch too much right-wing television and listen to too much fake news. How about read a book or watch some factual documentaries by experts before coming out with stuff like that?'

'I have had enough of listening to experts, Callum. Scientists, doctors, engineers, liberal-communist professors the whole lot.'

'So how are you expecting for us to develop as a country without scientists. I work as a rocket engineer so know a thing or two about science. Without scientists, we wouldn't have anything fancy in the US. We would be like an African country. We certainly wouldn't be number one in the world in anything.'

'Why are you even in this Bible study, Callum? Science is a communist, atheist profession full of liberals. I believe in God and the Bible, not science. Science and education are the enemies of scripture. We only need to believe in God for ourselves for the devil tempts us away with education.'

Elizabeth tried not to laugh at what had penetrated Angelica's mind. Angelica watched hours of television, mainly in the form of televangelist channels like EPPTV, which fed her a diet of unquestioning beliefs about scripture, a denial of any outside information and an intake that was so warped it was comical. Plus, not to mention the supply of endless websites she looked at that supported her perspective and news outlets that churned out everything that she wanted to hear. This kind of pervasive ignorance was sadly common inside the Evangelical church, which was filled with the sort of uneducated types who would crowd Trump's rallies.

'Science has built our modern civilization. Everything from your cell phone, to cars, to computers and even the surgery that you are getting, have all been developed from science.'

'We don't need science for us. We need the Bible and God.'

'Ask for no anaesthesia when you go into the operating room. I am sure that having your legs and arms removed with no anaesthesia would be an enjoyable experience for you.'

'Yes, but wasn't it God who allowed us to have anaesthesia? God gave it to us,' Angelica said.

'Who developed the first anaesthesia drug?' Callum asked Angelica.

'It was God. God did. Didn't God do surgery on Adam to remove a rib to create Eve?'

Jeremy grimaced. Angelica's lack of knowledge of the world was jarring. He did not seem to think this was down to her religiosity alone but her unquestioning belief in certain programs, namely the televangelism that was pumped out blind loyalty. The Bible study group was sort of intelligent expression of what Christianity could produce; rationally minded people who were professionals and had gone to university. Now, one of the people who attended the Bible study had become filled with ridiculous nonsense, who believed that she wanted all her limbs amputated as part of her genuine belief that God had called her to do it.

'I mean humans,' Callum said, exasperatedly.

'It doesn't matter. God did the first surgery.'

'So, what about computers, who developed the first computer? Or bacteria or rockets, do you know anything about science and its effects?'

'All I need is God. Science is not what I need.'

'So, if you don't need science, then how are you going to get your limbs amputated then?' Callum asked.

'God works through the surgeon and the surgical team.' Angelica went on to her cell phone and show an image of Jesus standing next to a surgeon in an operating room, disregarding aseptic surgical techniques.

'Do you not see it? Jesus works through the surgical team and operates on the patient.'

'So, can't God work in science and scientists than the same way he operates on people?' Callum asked, philosophically.

'No because they are atheists,' Angelica said thoughtlessly.

'And if they are Christians?'

'There are no Christians in science today.'

Callum shook his head in utter astonishment. 'I am a Christian who studied astrophysics at university. You are acting irrationally by having your limbs amputated. Totally irrational. I cannot understand.'

'God has told me to have it done,' Angelica said.

Elizabeth sighed exasperatedly. 'Why would God tell you to remove your arms and legs and become someone completely disabled?' she said.

'So, I can completely depend on him. To save my life.'

'That isn't what you said to me. You said you wanted the $3,500,000 pay-out. Which one is it, to rely upon God or to receive a large life insurance check?' Elizabeth demanded.

Angelica sighed. 'Both.'

'The love of money is the root of all kinds of evil. Do you not see that, Angelica?' Jeremy said.

'How dare you say that I love money!' Angelica screamed. 'All I want is $3,500,000 so I can have a nice life, okay?'

'But what next after that? $10,000,000. $20,000,000. Money over a certain amount does not correlate to increased happiness. Not only that but what price can you put on your limbs?' Callum asked.

$250,000 a limb, Michael thought to himself, smiling as he looked at Angelica.

'Well as long as they can be replaced. I can replace them. That has been the whole plan all along. Once I have my old limbs removed, they will be replaced with some new prosthetic limbs.'

'Prosthetic limbs can never fully replace the limbs that you have lost. They are okay but not quite the same as certain fine manipulations are hard to do with prosthetics. Besides, health insurance companies are reluctant to pay for them,' Elizabeth explained.

'Look at you all, you are just pessimistic moaners who cannot see the benefits of having my limbs amputated,' Angelica said.

'What benefits do you have, having your limbs amputated?' Jeremy exhausted, with an aggressive, exhausted tone like shouting to a disobedient child. 'You will be crimpled, unable to complete basic daily tasks.'

'I just don't think you see the benefits of newly gained freedom and sovereignty over one's body,' Angelica said.

'You don't get freedom once your limbs are amputated. Once they are gone, you will lose your freedom,' Jeremy replied shaking his head.

'You are just all doom and gloom merchants; you are project fear.'

'We are not project fear,' Jeremy said, 'we are trying to project reality into the situation.'

'We can argue all night about whether Angelica is right to have the surgery but are we going to study the Bible or what?' Kate asked.

Everyone became quiet for a second. They had argued for quite some time about whether Angelica should have a quadruple amputation or not. No one even stopped to question whether they should just bury the hatchet and focus on Bible study. Instead, theology was thrown out of the window and instead it was focused on a distraction. The argument was trying to convince Angelica of how ridiculous it was to have a quadruple amputation for chondrosarcoma that she had no understanding of. There was no consideration about whether Angelica would go through with it or why even Angelica had believed this ridiculous idea. Why on earth was it a good plan? It made no sense. Not even for the $3,500,000 pay-out. Was it a good trade to have all your limbs cut off to receive a $3,500,000 check? Perhaps this would be on a reality-television channel or something.

'We are having a serious discussion, Kate. We need Angelica to understand how important her decision is and how bad it is,' Jeremy said.

'I have already signed a deal with the surgeon.'

'Even if you signed a deal, there are exit clauses within a deal.' Jeremy said.

'Michael and I would have to pay a $5,000 exit cost to the surgeon. He said it could be as great as $55,000. That is not worth it.'

'You don't think to pay $5,000 is worth paying so you could at least think of the consequences of keeping your limbs?' Jeremy asked.

'The deal has been signed. Amputation means amputation.'

'What losing your limbs is a process that you will undertake simply because you have signed a document to say that you will pay $5,000? Are you really that kind of person?' Elizabeth asked, mystified by Angelica's intentions

'I am doing what is right. I need to stop cancer from spreading. The surgeon said I can have prosthetic limbs which he has said will be the same as previous limbs.'

'But they are not, Angelica. They are worse than your current limbs. It would be the worst deal ever. Having your legs and arms amputated when you don't need them to, whilst you would be crimpled for the rest of your life. Without any chance to change your mind. Why are you going for this?'

There was some hesitation with Angelica. Perhaps, it had finally dawned on her what a ridiculous proposition that she had come to believe in. Why would someone go to amputating all of their limbs to stop cancer from spreading when their family doctor had said otherwise? Angelica became aggressive and started to shout. 'I think this is all just project fear!' Angelica bellowed. 'You guys aren't my surgeon and therefore know nothing about my situation. You are just out to go against me. In that case, fine. I am cutting off my connection with you people! We are exiting this Bible study group, aren't we Michael.'

Michael was distracted by his thoughts. 'Eh, what? Oh yes whatever you say,' He said reassuring Angelica.

'You are cutting off your limbs and now you are cutting off your friends? Why would you leave this agreement we have? Why would you leave this community? I mean leave doesn't have to mean leave? You could remain with us and...'

'I want to be free from your control, do you understand? Leave means leave. Come on Michael, we are leaving. Do you want to join us, Kate?' Angelica asked.

'Damn right I am behind you. They were on at you for hours wasting everyone's time.'

Kate, Angelica and Michael all got up to leave. Angelica hobbled out of the room, as cancer inside her ankle was growing more painful by the day. The other people just stopped and just looked bewildered at to what just happened.

'What is going on with Angelica?' Jeremy asked.

'I guess she has become an extremist,' Elizabeth said. 'She has become deluded.'

'What has become of people in the US today?' Callum said exasperatedly.

Chapter 8

After seeing her anesthesiologist for the surgery, Angelica went back to Dr Gina Benjamin-Cruz for one last time. Michael was joining her this time, sat down in the waiting room sat next to Angelica, smoothing her hand for reassurance. Such reassurance would not be given when Angelica was going to become an amputee since she would not have any hands to hold at all. Prosthetic hands would not have nerves in them. Michael knew that Angelica would most likely come out from the meeting with Dr Gina Benjamin-Cruz as the same person she went in; someone who had already chosen to have the surgery. Dr Gina Benjamin-Cruz was going to attempt one last time to make her change Angelica's mind on her treatment plan.

'Are you looking forward to the surgery?' Michael said, smiling softly at Angelica, smoothing her silky brown hair. He looked intently into her brown eyes.

'I am nervous,' she admitted. 'It will be very different without arms or legs of my own. Getting used to prosthetics will be difficult.'

'Aww. Poor Angelica,' Michael snarled. 'You will always be loved by myself though. No matter what happens.'

'I appreciate that you will always be at my side. No one else gets my decision.'

'You never know, it might just boost our marriage,' Michael grinned. Angelica smiled intently at Michael. She was glad that ultimately Michael had her in his arms even if she had no arms or legs herself. He would always have her.

'Angelica.' Dr Gina Benjamin-Cruz said when coming into the reception.

Angelica hobbled out of her chair towards the door that Dr Gina Benjamin-Cruz was coming from. She limped painfully down the corridor towards the door with Dr Gina Benjamin-Cruz's office. They entered and sat down facing Dr Gina Benjamin-Cruz.

'Has the surgery date been ratified?' Dr Gina Benjamin-Cruz asked.

'March the 29th, 2019,' Angelica stated.

Dr Gina Benjamin-Cruz shook her head and looked uncomfortable. 'Are you really sure that you want the surgery? Because it is an extreme treatment package that I would not recommend.'

'Absolutely.'

'What about seeing other surgeons, Angelica? Have you not reconsidered the grave decision of having your arms and legs amputated?'

'Angelica has already made up her mind, Gina. She does not need a second opinion on whether she should get surgery or not,' Michael said, forcefully.

'You are not in charge of Angelica...'

'I said she has made up her mind Gina! You always want a second choice, a second vote on whether to decide a different treatment option. And Angelica has always made it clear, she wants the amputation of her limbs to take back control of her body from cancer.'

'But how is it taking back control of your body Angelica if you have no control over what you can do anyway?' Dr Gina said bewildered.

'I get to decide my own destiny and my own treatment plan.'

'But this treatment plan is ludicrous,' Dr Gina Benjamin-Cruz said bluntly, 'having your limbs amputated does not gain your independence or your own destiny. It just makes you crimpled.'

'I think we have had enough listening to elitist liberal experts like yourself,' Michael said.

'What?' Gina asked, deeply puzzled by what Michael said.

'You hear me. We have had enough of listening to liberal expert elites. All with your fancy liberal arts degrees,' Michael sneered

'I am a certified doctor, with degrees in...'

'Oh, cool story. Do you know something, we too have seen a surgeon with a degree? His name is Dr Nigel Johnson. But unlike you, he isn't a fancy liberal,' Michael snarled

'My political opinion has nothing to do with my professional advise. We will leave politics by the back door thank you. I have had enough of you and your wife talking about my politics.'

'You cannot separate your political views has everything to do with your professional life. Everything is political. Even which surgery options you have.'

Dr Gina Benjamin-Cruz looked bewildered and was lost for words. To believe that surgery could be influenced by your political views was to her absurd. She did not understand that politics and surgical procedures were one of the same, that a surgeon or doctor's political views mattered in offering medical advise. After all, why would someone have their limbs amputated by a surgeon simply because they had conservative political views? Weren't all surgeons judged not for their political views but by their competence? It was ridiculous to do such a thing.

'Come on. Listen. Why would you want all your limbs amputated simply because Dr Nigel Johnson is somehow a Republican? Is that what it comes down to?' Dr Gina Benjamin-Cruz frowned.

'No it is because he has said that I need to take back control of my body,' Angelica said.

'But they are perfectly healthy limbs!' Dr Gina Benjamin-Cruz exclaimed.

'Fake news,' Angelica replied coldly.

'How can you say that?'

'You are spreading lies about my health. Dr Nigel Johnson says I am going to die without the surgery.'

Dr Gina Benjamin-Cruz shook her head in astonishment. 'I am a doctor. Why would I spread fake information about your health? I would lose my job and my license.'

'Because you don't like Dr Nigel Johnson and don't like my decision,' Angelica said

'I think your decision is completely absurd.'

'And I disagree with you.'

'Disagree with me if you want to. But within healthcare, we only look at what is best for the patient.'

'That is false. You only are interested to perpetuate your own career and your own income. You and Dr Nigel Johnson are rivals when it comes down to treatment options and you want the most money. So naturally, you will talk down Dr Nigel Johnson,' Michael said.

'I am losing my patience here. I am only trying to help you make the best decision for your healthcare,' Dr Gina Benjamin-Cruz said.

'I have made my mind up. I will be having my legs and arms amputated. I need to take back ownership of my body and my future.' Michael walked out with Angelica under his arm. Dr Gina Benjamin-Cruz merely shook her head in utter disbelief.

'We won't be seeing you again,' Michael said down the corridor.

'Good,' Dr Gina Benjamin-Cruz uttered under her breath.

That day was long. The two men smiled and laughed together like two leaders plotting world domination. The sipped wine together in a luxury restaurant, far grander than the one before, with marbled floor and golden décor, not the average restaurant in Dallas. A restaurant for the global elite. Russell Portin slurped at his spaghetti carbonara on his plate, lapping it down like a dog.

'It's good news what you are telling me about the patient,' the surgeon said.

'Quite. The patient argued against anyone who was persuading her not to have the surgery,' Russell slurped.

'That is what we were hoping for. What changed?' the surgeon asked.

'When you are told you have made the wrong choice in a discussion, you tend to defend your position even more, despite how absurd it is. It is called cognitive dissonance. We learn it in trading as making sure that you have trades which are rationally based, not ones based on emotion. Cognitive dissonance is dangerous when you are a trader as you can routinely making the same mistakes if you are unwilling to adapt and change your instincts or positions,' Russell Portin stated.

'Quite. Well, it has seemed to work. The patient's stupidity means that she will succumb to our plans rather.'

'Our tax-dodging plan is working.'

'It is good to see your plan. I mean now, thanks to you I can save thousands on my tax bill to the government.'

'What do you plan to spend the money on?' Russell Portin inquired.

'Well, I haven't really thought about it. I mean doorbell I am doing well as it is. Being an orthopaedic surgeon pays very well indeed.'

A waiter came over and poured some more wine into the glasses. There was a deep sense of pleasure in the ability to convince someone to completely and utterly destroy themselves, all to make themselves

'What do you plan to do with your tax savings?' the surgeon asked.

'I don't know actually. I mean I just like to save money for its own sake.'

'But you don't know what to do with it?'

'The problem with all these loop-holes and particularly this one is that they are illiquid. What I mean by that is you can't just draw the money out of them. You understand to pay yourself a dividend instead of a salary as it saves on your tax bill, right?' Russell said.

'Of course. You told me this. I trust that you will be able to make a lot of money for me.'

'Yes. I will save thousands of dollars.'

Russell Portin remembered his first meeting with the surgeon. It was 7 pm, the world had darkened to a black as the pall had blotted the daylight out of the sky. The faint phosphorescence of the twilight vermillion and copper-orange had faded to dim candlelight. He was ready to go home when he received a phone call to answer from his mobile number. It said an unknown caller. The surgeon looked rather puzzled.

'Hi? Who is this? Who has my number?' the surgeon asked suspiciously.

'Greetings Dr Nigel Johnson.'

'Who are you? How did you get my number?' Dr Nigel Johnson was infuriated.

'I am just inquiring about your taxation that is all. I am a trader and financier and could help you with your tax return...'

'I do not care. I do not take calls from people I don't know,' Dr Nigel Johnson said with an agitated voice

'My wife needs surgery on her leg.'

'Really. Too fucking bad.'

'You don't want to help?' the voice asked

'Well, phone up my receptionist and we can do it by referral okay? Now I need to...'

'Listen, Dr Johnson. My wife has a chondrosarcoma. She has been diagnosed a week or so ago. She is waiting to see another surgeon. All I am going to ask is to meet me so we can go through your business and talk about my business proposal.'

'What has that got to do with surgery?'

'A lot.'

'I am not interested....'

'How much tax do you pay at the moment?'

'Too much. Now excuse me...'

'What if I told you that I could save you thousands of dollars in tax...'

'Interesting stuff. Now you must understand that I have....'

'Well, I can offer you $250,000 a limb.'

Dr Nigel Johnson stopped and wanted to hear it again. 'Run that past me again.'

'Meet me in Parking Lot 41 just off the freeway 406, near the aquarium and Akard Station.   Tomorrow at 9:00 pm'

'Tell me...'

'I'll be in a black SUV. I will text you when I am parked up.'

Dr Nigel Johnson was surprised. $250,000 a limb was a very high price to pay. Who and why would someone pay $250,000 to have limbs amputated? It appeared to be an extreme proposition. Absurd, the idea that someone would pay that much money for an amputation, given the going rate was between $20,000 to $60,000. Why would someone pay

$250,000 to amputate one limb? It appeared to be utterly ridiculous. And yet it intrigued him. He decided that he would pursue it since it seemed such a good proposition.

The night had rolled in and Dallas skyline was lit up with light from the buildings beneath. The street was quieter as the evening set in. The parking lot was near a tall pencil-shaped skyscraper, with large skyscrapers dotted around the parking lot. The trees swayed in the light evening breeze. Dr Nigel Johnson drove near to the parking lot and went into after buying a ticket, going up each level of the parking lot. There was no black SUV parked up anywhere in the parking lot. He parked his car on the middle level and waited. There were hardly any cars parked in the parking lot, it was mainly empty. Everyone had gone home for the night. Other than the odd person who was staying late at the office, there was no one around. Dr Nigel Johnson waited. He checked his cell-phone. No response. After 10 minutes of waiting, there was still no response. Dr Nigel Johnson was become tired and frustrated, about to give in before his cell-phone started to ring with *Unknown Number* flashing up on the screen.

'Sorry for the lateness,' the voice said.

'You were almost wasting my time. Where are you?' Dr Nigel Johnson shouted impatiently.

'I am parked in the corner bottom left on the ground level.'

'Okay meet you there,' Dr Nigel Johnson said exasperatedly.

He drove down each level quickly with no consideration of people that may have been in the parking lot. In the corner of the ground floor was a parked up black SUV. Dr Nigel Johnson drove aggressively towards it before parking up next to the vehicle. The windows on the sides were tinted, so it was difficult for people to see into the SUV. The door of the SUV opened and a tall blonde-haired man in a suit got out of the vehicle and walked around the vehicle. The man stood outside the car looking in at Dr Nigel Johnson, who was somewhat scared of this man's movements.

Dr Nigel Johnson wound down his window and looked at the man in the suit.

'Who are you and what do you want?' Dr Nigel Johnson asked.

'I am Russell Portin. I am a financial trader. I own a multi-million-dollar enterprise and I am worth myself in the region of $4,000,000. One of my trade worth $200,000,000 and I am entitled 5% of the earnings. That means I could have $10,000,000. The problem is tax. Such a large amount of money would After all at a colossal amount.'

Dr Nigel Johnson got out of his car and stood facing Russell Portin. 'Why do you want me? Why are you paying me $250,000 to amputate a single limb? This makes no sense?'

'Because healthcare treatment is tax-deductible, I can make sure that I pay you $250,000 to carry out the surgery. If you help me set up yourself a business, I can help you save hundreds of thousands each you.'

'So, you are paying me $250,000 to amputate a single limb with cancer....'

'No, I am paying you $250,000 per limb. That means $1,000,000.'

Dr Nigel Johnson squinted and looked bemused, '$1,000,000? You are trying to trick me, aren't you?'

'I seriously plan to pay you that much money to you, if I keep 75% of the returns for that surgery as profit and the rest, you and your staff keep, whilst future returns will be 20% each.'

'Oh. So, I am only going to get $250,000 for the entire procedure. That is less than what you are advertizing for.'

'The reason for this is simple. I am trying to cut my tax bill and if I pay you $250,000 to amputate four limbs, I think you would accept.'

'I think that there is a lot wrong with your entire plan. First off, why are you doing unnecessary surgery on someone to avoid tax? It seems ridiculous to begin with.'

'I do it because the patient needs surgery to remove bone cancer.'

'Can't you just pay to have this bone cancer removed?'

'No. I want her to have the surgery.'

Dr Nigel Johnson looked perplexed. 'Why? What is the point?'

The man smiled macabrely. 'The point is to have absolute control of her life. Absolute power.'

'That is rather how can I put it... disturbing. I don't think that is a good idea.'

'Why are you asking for my intentions anyway?'

'Because we must be able to understand what is the best course of treatment.'

'Well all I want her to be is completely dependent on me and my existence, to have absolute power over her and who she is, to benefit from her being dependent on me and my existence. When a woman in a relationship has power, they can shape it into many things that they would like.'

Dr Nigel Johnson looked puzzled by his response. 'I don't understand why you would want to completely control her.'

'Perhaps I am not so happy about our marriage. Sometimes we need to save things.'

'What has this got to do with an amputation?' Dr Nigel Johnson asked curiously.

'Sometimes amputation is needed to take back control. That is all.'

'What about prosthetics and about her being able to function? She would be completely incapacitated without any limbs at all.'

'I don't honestly care.'

'I still think it is questionable with the ethical side, unnecessarily amputating all her limbs.'

Russell looked rather removed from the conversation. 'I guess I will find another surgeon then.'

'I am though rather intrigued though.'

$250,000 for one limb was about half of what Dr Nigel Johnson made in an entire year.

'How are we supposed to convince her that she needs the surgery?' Dr Nigel Johnson asked.

'Exaggerate her symptoms. She isn't clever and can easily fall for it if you emphasized that this was taking back control of her body from cancer.'

The first meeting formed a business relationship that allowed on the one side saving Dr Nigel Johnson tax payments and on the other side, a means for Russell Portin to avoid tax.

'So, Russell, how is this tax scheme going to work?' Dr Nigel Johnson asked.

'You subcontract via a company now don't you?'

'Yes, on your request.'

'This company I invest in and then I can claim tax deductibles on my capital gains tax. You do not pay yourself a wage instead you tax a dividend based on the income we receive and based on the calculations of how much money I funnel into the business every year.'

'How much do you plan to put in as investments?'

'$1,000,000. This, of course, I can take off a tax-deductible, which means I save tax revenue. The first surgery under your new company is critical though because it creates a trail that I can hide my business dealings under.'

'What have you done?' Dr Nigel Johnson asked.

Russell smiled and chuckled. 'Put it this way. I have millions of dollars in assets all over the world. The FBI and the IRS would be interested in my taxable assets.'

'I see.'

'When I put money into the company, this I will put with my friend's account. The one whose wife is having her limbs amputated.'

'Indeed.'

'Except this surgery, it is reversed because I am paying you under Russell Portin and taking out under my friend's account.'

'How haven't the FBI not caught you if they associate you and your friend together?'

'By having a carefully planned life,' Russell smiled. He sipped his drink. 'For me to hide from the FBI is to have my friend and I look almost identical but to have two separate passports and citizenship of two different countries.'

'Clever.'

'They have some suspicions. They are after me I believe.'

'What do you plan to do?'

'Carry on as normal. They could never bring me down. They need firm evidence.

'ID fraud could be easy to detect.'

'They haven't done it thus far,' Russell said, 'Russell Portin is a Panama citizen or so I say. I own a small apartment out there under the name Russell Portin. But I would never live there. My friend lives in Dallas.'

'What if they detect you? Will I be brought down as well?' Dr Nigel Johnson asked with a concerned voice

'Well not directly relating to the scheme. All you have to say is you do not know the scheme...'

'Which is a lie.'

'The main problem is, of course, the surgery. The Article you made her sign protects you from liability?

'I think so. She is totally aware of what I am doing.'

'Then I think it will be okay then.'

Dr Nigel Johnson nodded. Russell took a sip of his drink.

'That covers me then.'

'What does the Texas Medical Board do about unnecessary surgery cases?' Russell inquired.

'The patient signed The Article 50 agreement. She is liable herself since it gives her that she was fully aware and is responsible for the choices she made regarding her treatment.'

'I am concerned that our business venture could be brought down by that case.'

'You were the one who suggested removing all her limbs.'

'You agreed with this,' Russell said aggressively.

'I know.'

'Do you think we should turn back?'

'Of course not. We won't get caught. And even if we do, what are they going to do to us, lock us up in jail? I don't think so,' Dr Nigel Johnson laughed.

'Indeed. Well, give me a notification when you want to speak to me again,' Russell said.

'Michael's wife is seeing me 2 weeks before the surgery just to go over a few final touches. On 03/29/19, its arms and legs away,' Dr Nigel Johnson joked.

]

Chapter 9

Angelica stared outside at the tree in the garden. It was a dead tree; the leaves on the tree had fallen off months ago. Angelica contemplated her life and the surgery she was going to have. It was weeks away before the surgery. A frightening realization that she was going to become completely incapacitated haunted Angelica. Yet she still believed it was the best decision. Nothing could change her mind. Not even her family. Her mom was coming down from Northern Texas. Wilma had managed to convince both Nora and Scott to visit Angelica at her home in Dallas. Ever since the visit to Wilma's farm, Nora and Scott had refused to talk to Angelica, given the fact that Angelica was exceptionally hostile to Nora over her relationship with Erika. The tension in the relationship had been simmering for years and it finally erupted into a conflict at Wilma's house. Now, Erika had gone off to work allowing Nora to visit without any condemnation from Angelica.

'That tree has been dead for a while, has it?' Wilma asked.

'Yes, it has,' Angelica said tearfully.

'A shame. Tell me what is wrong Angelica?' Wilma said with a voice of unease.

'I am scared of... the surgery... am I wrong in doing it?'

'No, not at all. Why, do you regret it?'

'No. I don't regret signing the document required before the surgery. It is just, I have faced so much opposition about it. I have been mixed feelings for weeks over it. Sometimes I think it is great and now I am frightened of the outcomes.'

'Michael will always care for you,' Wilma replied. 'He is always going to be there for you.'

Angelica frowned. 'I do hope so.'

The doorbell rang. Angelica hobbled to the front of the house and the door. It was Scott and Nora.

'Hello, do come in,' Angelica said, aloofly.

Both Nora and Scott entered the house and sat down next to Wilma.

'Can I get you guys a drink?' Angelica asked.

'Coffee will be fine. Scott what will you have?' Nora asked.

'Make that two coffees.'

Angelica went and made the drinks, leaving Nora, Wilma and Scott by themselves.

'One of Angelica's friends, Elizabeth contacted me recently saying she is very worried about Angelica,' Nora said.

'Yes, she has fallen out with her, hasn't she?' Wilma asked.

'Elizabeth tried to persuade Angelica away from the surgery and Angelica became aggressive towards Elizabeth.'

'Really?' Wilma asked. 'I am torn about Angelica.'

'She asked if she could join our meeting....'

'What? Does Angelica know?' Wilma said agitatedly.

'No, of course, I haven't told Angelica.'

'This is going to turn out nasty.'

Angelica hobbled back into the room with the cups of coffee and some cookies.

'Thank you, Angelica,' Nora said.

'That is okay Nora. How is Erika?'

Nora looked at Angelica with a bemused expression. 'Erika? Yeah, she is okay. Why do you ask?'

'Just wanted to see how she was that is all. I wanted to apologize for what I said up at mom's house.'

Nora sighed. 'It hurt us what you said.'

'I can see that. Hence, why you refused to talk to me for a while'

'Absolutely.'

The doorbell rang again. Angelica hobbled to the door and was surprized to see Elizabeth at the door.

'Hello, Elizabeth. I thought we weren't speaking...'

'Yes, we weren't. But Christians don't just let their friends do silly things,' Elizabeth said, 'Are you going to invite me in?'

'Um, of course,' Angelica said.

Elizabeth went and sat down with Angelica's family inside the living room.

'Well I thank you for coming to see me,' Angelica smiled.

'It is okay,' Wilma said, 'You are important to us.'

'It is good to see that I am loved by people.'

'We are here to discuss about your surgery. I don't know anyone in this room who really feels that the surgery you are having is a good idea but we have decided to at least discuss with you one final time about whether you would at least consider changing your mind,' Nora said

Angelica picked up a cup of coffee and sipped it. 'What was I going to say? I don't think I can change my mind. I have made my decision and that is the end of it,' Angelica moaned.

'Yes, but really Angelica, we think this is a really bad position to be in given that you are only weeks away from having your arms and legs taken away from you and you are unwilling to change about this position,' Nora said.

'I have signed an Article that cannot be revoked. Once it has been signed, the surgery is now inevitable.'

'But that is complete nonsense. You can change the outcome if you wanted to,' Nora said

'I have thought it through and made my decision. That is final.'

'What for such a life-changing surgical procedure?' Elizabeth said.

'I have made the decision and I am sticking by it.'

'But it is a ridiculous decision. Sorry but you have been conned by Dr Nigel Johnson. He had made you believe that the surgery is going to be some easy thing that he can do but the reality is how disabled you will be after the surgery.'

'I will cope in the end. I will get prosthetics.'

'Even life with prosthetics is going to be very challenging. There is no easy way of having a quadruple amputation. Besides prosthetics have to be replaced when they wear out,' Elizabeth said.

'It is happening now. The decision has been made and that is that. We need to get the amputation done,' Angelica said sadly.

'Can't you reverse that decision? Can't you have another surgeon assess your Chondrosarcoma? It just seems that you have rushed to decisions without any thought,' Elizabeth said.

'I can't. The decision has been made and that is it.'

'You just keep saying that the decision has been made. No final decisions have been made,' Scott interjected.

'I have made those final decisions.'

'But the decisions you have made can be changed.'

'They can't be changed. I have made my mind up and that is that.'

'Why don't you want to have the choice to change your decision on the most important decision of your life?'

Angelica sighed deeply, breathing from her nose out to her mouth. 'Because I have made a decision and cannot change my mind. That is the reason.'

'So, you will have your legs and arms amputated because you don't want to change your mind?' Elizabeth asked.

'Correct.'

'I am sorry but this makes no sense,' Nora said.

'I have made my decision. It is the decision that has been made and that is the one I am going with.'

Elizabeth and Nora shook their heads in disbelief whilst Wilma welled up with tears. The discussion was circular. Angelica was not changing her mind on the surgery because she hadn't changed her mind. There was no reason. No actual articulation of thought. Just that it was her decision and she wanted to go with it.

'Please Angelica, would you not consider to at least listening to your friends and family on such an important choice?' Wilma cried.

'I am listening. The fact I have allowed people to come round and talk to me shows I am willing to listen.'

'But you are not listening because you aren't changing your mind,' Elizabeth said exhaustedly.

'No. I have made my mind. Even if I don't get the $3,500,000, it will still be a good choice.'

'But why?' Elizabeth and Nora exclaimed.

'Because I have taken back control of myself. I am making decisions about myself as a free person.'

Elizabeth and Nora burst out into uncontrollable laughter. 'You are taking back control of control of yourself by having your legs and arms amputated? Are you trying to pull my leg, Angelica? That is hilarious,' Nora cackled, 'I have never heard something as stupid in all my life as you trying to take back control by cutting off your limbs.'

Angelica grimaced and had a face of thunder, her eyes appearing owl-like in rage. Yet she did not comment.

'Why can't any of you just accept my decision?' Angelica sulked.

'Because it is an absurd decision. It makes as much sense as having oral sex with a dog with rabies...'

'How dare you, Nora, for saying such a disgusting thing! Vile, filthy language.'

'Whilst I wouldn't compare your surgery to having sex with a dog with rabies, what I would say is that your treatment option is completely ill-advised, to say the least,' Elizabeth interjected. 'I would never advise a patient with a Chondrosarcoma to have a quadruple amputation. Not a single medical expert would recommend that course of action; no doctor nor surgeon nor nurse. It is a very dangerous decision you have made. All I would say is now that the deadline to surgery is very near, that you would contemplate, pray and reflect on your decision. Once you are on the operating table and the anesthesiologist applies the mask, it will be too late.'

Angelica put her head into her hands. There was a hope that she was able to change her mind, to recognize the utter absurdity of her actions. After a sniff of tears, Angelica rubbed her eyes. She frowned before restating her position.

'I am not changing my mind because my surgery is my decision. We need to get the amputation done. I have made the decision and that is that. I am doing this because I am. I am doing this because the Lord has told me to because I need to take back control over my body, because cancer is killing my body and because I will receive a $3,500,000. It will start bad but it will get better. I will have prosthetics and bionic limbs fitted.'

There was disbelief. No changes in her mind. Nothing. The utter impending disaster was not changing. The negotiation to change her mind had not worked. Not one piece of argument had appeared to work. Angelica was insistent. She would not change her position on amputating her limbs. Why was she being so unreasonable? How could she not see how absurd it was?

'Why do you think God wants you to have your limbs amputated?' Elizabeth asked.

Angelica sighed, 'I was watching television and the voice of God spoke through the television.'

Angelica couldn't decide the difference between televangelism and the voice of God. To her, the television was the voice of God. But God didn't only speak through the television. God spoke through other media including on the internet, on social media, on her laptop. The Bible was only one way that God chose to speak to people. God could talk to people in many ways, but for Angelica, the way Angelica thought God spoke to her was through the television.

'So you think that God wants your limbs amputated because he was talking to you through the television?' Elizabeth said who looked completely bemused by what Angelica was saying/

'Absolutely. God has told me that my limbs have to be amputated. If it is Godly ordained, then you cannot stop me from doing it that. For the will of man is not the same as the will of God.'

'But God would never tell someone to have their limbs to be amputated. Why would he?' Elizabeth asked.

'Because his will and control of life means he demands obedience,' Angelica said sternly.

'Yes, but why would he ask someone to have their arms and legs amputated? It makes no sense.'

'We must never question the will of God. We must simply obey his command,' Angelica replied.

There was no questioning of whether this was mistaken, of whether Angelica was wrong. She believed that she was hearing the voice of God through the television. And when people were telling her that it was wrong, the more she believed that it was God's will. The fact people were opposing her made her feel that it had to be God. After all, Jesus' kingdom was not of this world. The $3,500,000 pay-out must have been a gift from God; a sign of God's blessing.

'But what purpose does God have with you having all of your arms and legs amputated?' Elizabeth asked.

'I don't know. Perhaps the $3,500,000. I don't know.'

This lack of awareness and blindness was shocking to Elizabeth, who shock her head in disbelief, 'I can't believe you are doing this. We do not approve of this and think you are wrong doing this. If this is what you want, we completely oppose this.'

Chapter 10

Angelica turned on her television to EEPTV, the television channel she always watched. She was hoping for some divine inspiration, perhaps God would talk through her television to tell her whether she should have the surgery or not. Alas, nothing happened. God decided not to speak to Angelica through her television that day. There was not even any guidance from a voice of wisdom, a pastor, a minister or some kind of preacher. The preacher today talked on about the dangers of sexual sin, including masturbation. Angelica hadn't masturbated for a while. Michael was the one who had a good time sexually with her. So was it necessary for Angelica to hear about masturbation?

Angelica sighed. She switched the television off and decided to read her Bible. She opened the Bible to a random verse in Proverbs. *Better is open rebuke than hidden love. Wounds from a friend can be trusted, but an enemy multiplies kisses.* She closed the Bible. Angelica was openly deriding of these words. Her entire family and friends had rebuked her for having the surgery, but now the Bible was saying that this was a good thing. She ignored the words and looked on her tablet computer at pictures of amputee women, imaging herself in a couple of weeks ending up exactly like them. What was it like being a quadruple amputee? She never really contemplated how much she used her arms and legs, never considered what her life would be like without any limbs. Angelica thought that she could simply get prosthetic limbs and that would solve the situation. And yet this did not seem likely to change her situation.

The front door opened and Michael burst into the sitting room.

'Hi Angelica,' he said energetically.

'Hiya,' Angelica replied glumly.

'What is wrong?' Michael asked.

Angelica huffed. 'Is my surgery a good idea or a bad idea? Friends and family came round to say that my surgery was a bad idea, that it was a mistake to get my arms and legs amputated,' she cried.

Michael sat next to her, caressing her, stroking her hair. 'My darling, you have made the right choice. Let no one else tell you otherwise.'

'Why? It makes no sense why you would be saying it...'

'That is because everyone else is wrong. Everyone. You know it is a bit like being a Republican in New York City or godless Austin closer to home. Just because everyone around you votes Democrat, doesn't mean that they are right. The same here, just because they all say that the surgery you are having is wrong, doesn't mean it is.'

'But they are saying it is a really bad choice...'

'Everyone said it was a bad choice to vote for Donald Trump. And look at what he is doing? He is making America great again. The same with you. Dr Nigel Johnson is making Angelica great again. Oh look it even that is MAGA.'

Angelica chuckled, smiling and intently looking into Michael's azure blue eyes. He was hypnotic, caressing Angelica like a doll or a puppet.

'What have you been up to today then,' Michael asked voluptuously.

'Oh, I have been rather bored,' Angelica blushed. 'There was nothing on television. They talked about sex and masturbation on EEPTV. I haven't masturbated well sine...'

'I do it all the time.'

Angelica giggled. 'You shouldn't do that. It is a sin.'

'Not when I am doing when I am thinking of you,' he smiled.

'Oooh,' she said, turned on by his gaze.

'You will always look beautiful to me,' Michael grinned. 'Always.'

'You are too loving towards me.'

All a means to an end, Michael thought. 'No, you just are so adorable and lovable. The best wife a man could have.'

Angelica shed a tear at those words. At least Michael loved her. She could trust Michael to go to the ends of the world for her.

'Oh Michael. Come, let us go to the bedroom. You have deserved it after a hard day of work and by being such a nice husband.'

Michael picked up Angelica and took her to the bedroom. The groans and moans of Republicans mating were that of the faint, strangulated person in an animatronic suit. Passionate conservatism in the bedroom, nothing out of the ordinary, missionary like the Evangelicals that flooded to go out and vote for the GOP. Angelica never deviated from being a good-girl conservative in the bedroom. Michael however always had a libertarian streak that he just could not get out of Angelica. A low-tax state was Michael's dream but was it too hard to ask for a state that didn't regulate the bedroom as well?

'Oh, Angelica. Couldn't we spice it up? We just do the same thing again and again,' Michael grunted.

'What do you mean?' Angelica groaned.

'The same thing every single time.'

'You don't like that?'

'I find it nauseatingly boring,' Michael complained, 'the same procedure again and again.'

'I thought you loved me.'

'That doesn't mean I don't. When you become an amputee, things are going to change in our love life.'

Angelica, looking up to the man who was on top of her, became repelled by him. She was scared that he would say things like this. The time when she was most vulnerable, the time when she was most disabled, she would become a pawn in her husband's sexual fantasies upset her soul bitterly.

'What do you mean?' she uttered with a hint of disgust.

'You will find out soon enough. For now, just relax,' he said thrusting her and kissing her on the forehead.

Angelica tried to push Michael off but Michael pinioned her down like a patient strapped to an operating table.

'I love you,' he groaned, smiling at the sweet release before collapsing to the bed, panting out of breath.

Angelica stared to the end of the room at what Michael was saying. What did Michael want from her? She knew what he said about latex. Michael was changing, becoming more provocative in sexual fantasies. Knowing her place, Angelica was not in a position to actively stand up to him. The strong do what the will and the weak do what they must. Angelica was not in a strong position of bargaining in the marriage.

After putting some clothes on, Angelica left Michael to have a nap, turning on her television to EEPTV again. She was still waiting for that sign, that prophecy of her decision being divinely ordained. And yet as before, there was nothing. No feelings, no suggestions from the Holy Spirit, no Biblical words to help her. God was not speaking through the television at Angelica as she felt before. The subject on television was prayer and faith. She had faith. Plenty of it. In President Donald Trump, she had much faith and, in her husband, and her surgeon Dr Nigel Johnson. Do I have faith in God, she wondered to herself. Of course, otherwise, he wouldn't have asked her to have the operation. Tomorrow she was seeing Dr Nigel Johnson for one last time before the surgery. She was becoming nervous about the surgery or at least apprehensive. She knew it had to be done. Cancer was growing and it was time to take back control of her life. There was no going back now. No more dithering on the decision. Her friends and family tried to persuade her to change her mind but that was no good now. The surgery was inevitable. The process would soon be completed and she could get back to her life as normal, or so Angelica thought. No real contemplation was given to what would happen if it was awful.

'Have you given the Lord sovereignty of your life?' the preacher on the television exclaimed.

Yes of course I have, Angelica thought to herself. God had complete control of her life. Her surgery was part of God's plan, God's plan for her to take back control of her life. Perhaps she would get $3,500,000. That would be nice. And yet, something was missing. She knew something was missing from her prayers to God about having all her limbs removed. Angelica couldn't think of what she had to remember when praying to God about having her limbs removed. Still, she had already chosen her destiny. There was no final renegotiation, no considering other choices or having a second choice on the matter. Angelica was getting the surgery, there was no other plan. The decision had been already made. Democracy means democracy as amputation means amputation.

Except, Angelica had been thinking to herself about the surgery. She contemplated the advise that her friends and family gave her. She hadn't said this to any of her friends and family but she regretted going with Dr Nigel Johnson as her surgeon. However, despite this regret, there was no consideration for changing her mind. It had to be done. It had to be gotten on with. If she didn't have a quadruple amputation the choice had been avoided. What if elections could be just ignored? That would be the consequence of not going through with actions. Realistically, there was no reason to consider that amputating all of Angelica's limbs. It was plainly absurd. But in changing her mind, Angelica saw that it would mean that she could not commit to anything. When committing to something so absurd, it was important to show Angelica was 100% for it, even when she was only 53% for it. Otherwise, Angelica looked weak.

Chapter 11

The atmosphere in Dr Nigel Johnson's room was tense. Dr Nigel Johnson and Michael looked at each other and then looking at Angelica nervously. Angelica appeared to be having second thoughts about the surgery. She had been thinking about it since the meeting with her friends and family but she did not entirely come out with changing her stance on it until now. She wanted to negotiate a more palatable surgery option where she would only have an amputation in the limb which was cancerous, that was her right ankle, below her knee. This action, Angelica thought was a reasonable decision and one that she thought was the best option. Dr Nigel Johnson, however, was not in the mood for negotiation.

'I have already said to you today, there is no alternative Angelica. We have to remove all four limbs to complete separate you from cancer that is engulfing you,' Dr Nigel Johnson said frustratedly.

'Won't I be a complete disabled person though?' Angelica whined.

'Angelica, what has changed in you? You were so certain of the procedure being right that you have cut yourself off from your family and your friends and now this that you only want the limb in which the cancer is in removed?' Michael said.

'That is the correct medical procedure. My doctor said...'

'Listen. Listen very carefully. They are all wrong. It is all project fear. A medical expert who supports the president you love is an expert that you should listen to. After all, liberals hate Trump. And many doctors hate Trump. But I don't I think he is a great president, like yourself. Opposing the quadruple amputation is pure project fear. The procedure that I am proposing is exceptionally radical, nothing more life-changing than becoming a quadruple amputee. I understand that. But the cancer is going to spread. I am only doing what I need to do. I need all your limbs removed, Angelica. You have to put your faith in me because only I know what is best,' Dr Nigel Johnson boomed.

Angelica was confused and felt shaken, like a dog beaten into the corner of a room. This indecisiveness was in part because she was indecisive about doing the surgery. She portrayed being 100% for the surgery, but she was only 53% for it. Someone would have to saw her body in half to show how Angelica felt about being a quadruple amputee. Why was it project fear to have doubts about having a quadruple amputation? After all, most sane minded people would have thought it to be a bad thing to happen to them, to have all their limbs amputated. But to say to people to actively *choose* a quadruple amputation was madness. No government would actively seek to impoverish their citizens or a company would actively seek to bankrupt themselves. To call this "project fear" was odd, given that there was no benefit in having a quadruple amputation. It was one of the most disabling procedures a person could do to themselves.

'I trust you. It is just everyone else… my family and friends… they think I am wrong in my decision.'

'Well know this. I am a surgeon. They are not surgeons. They haven't got a clue about healthcare. You need to take back control of your body. After the surgery, you will be able to have prosthetics relatively soon.'

'What if they are not as good as my limbs now…'

'Don't you understand? Have you not even listened to Dr Nigel Johnson? You need the surgery and you need it now! You need to take back control of your body! Amputation means amputation!' Michael exclaimed.

Angelica had been contemplating in her mind whether it was the right choice having a quadruple amputation to cure chondrosarcoma. It was inevitable that she was going to have surgery but didn't want the treatment plan that Dr Nigel Johnson was offering so was trying to renegotiate it. The problem was Dr Nigel Johnson did not want to renegotiate. For him, quadruple amputation was the only procedure on offer. There was no other procedure.

'Why can't we renegotiate the fact that I may only need one limb amputated? Isn't that my right?' Angelica asked.

'You don't know how this cancer is spreading. Look your entire body will be consumed. We need to take back control over cancer and the only way of doing this is complete expulsion from the body by the removal of all four limbs. There is no other way of doing it...' Dr Nigel Johnson groaned

'But other people said that I would only need the limb in which the chondrosarcoma is in to be removed.'

'Fake news,' Dr Nigel Johnson said aggressively, 'they do not have any understanding of orthopedic surgery. I am an orthopedic surgeon. None of your friends is an orthopedic surgeon. I need your full cooperation if you seek to live.'

Angelica sighed. 'All I want is a deal in which the limb in which my one limb is removed which has cancer...'

'You are having your cake and eating it, Angelica. You can't expect to just remove cancer by just removing where the cancer is. You have to remove every part of the body where cancer will spread. Just as a wall must be built across Mexico to stop immigrants from getting in, all your limbs need to be amputated. They need to be removed.'

'Look, I have talked to my family doctor and she had persuaded me against...'

'She is not an orthopedic surgeon. I am and you are having your legs and arms removed,' Dr Nigel Johnson said possessively.

Angelica was hyperventilating. 'There must be another way than this.'

'What is wrong with you Angelica? Only a couple of days ago, you were for the surgery. You were on our side. What has changed?' Michael asked

Angelica put her head into her hands, curling up into a fetal position and cried. 'I don't know. I am all over the place with this surgery. My heart breaks over having to go through with this position and I feel torn inside.'

'You need the surgery, Angelica. Dr Nigel Johnson is a good surgeon. That is why we picked him.'

'But I don't know if I want the surgery now! All my friends have persuaded me against it.'

'You have signed an *Article 50* document which means you owe me money now if you decide to pull out of surgery.'

Angelica sobbed into her hands, broken by the choice she was making feeling torn as if her body was sawn in half on an operating table. 'I can't make this decision. I need time...'

'Oh no, you don't. We are having the operation on 03/29/19. You are dying. We need to remove your arms and legs to keep you alive. There are no reasons to change your mind,' Dr Nigel Johnson hissed.

'But everyone has advised me against it,' Angelica wailed a reply. Dr Nigel Johnson sighed. 'Very well. I do not recommend you discontinuing the treatment. You are going to die without it. But I respect patient wishes...'

'No. Listen, Angelica, at least keep 03/29/19 as a surgery date. If you don't want the surgery on the day, perhaps Dr Nigel Johnson can let you decide on the day. Is that a compromise?' Michael smiled, glaring at Dr Nigel Johnson who then nodded slowly in agreement.
Angelica sat up, teary-eyed and red-faced at Dr Nigel Johnson and Michael. 'Um yes. I think that is doable.'

'Excellent. Well given it is only a few weeks away, if you do change your mind, do come in anyway and then we can sort it out then, okay?' Dr Nigel Johnson grinned.
Michael and Dr Nigel Johnson shook hands as if they were business partners before leaving. Angelica was still teary-eyed through much of the ride home in the car. Michael had a wave of cooled anger. He was annoyed at his wife's change of mind given the $5,000 payment to Dr Nigel Johnson.

'Why are you hesitant about the surgery?' Michael grunted.
Angelica sighed. 'I have already told you. All of our friends have criticized my decision. I cannot simply just go ahead with it and besides, I have strong doubts.'

'I have doubts about my job at times. But Dr Nigel Johnson is a skilled capable surgeon. You shouldn't have any doubts about the surgery. If you doubt it, then you will die. The cancer cells are taking control of your body. You are dying. We need to take back control and that means amputation.'

'There are other surgeons though...'

'It is too late for other surgeons. We would have months of appointments and consultations only for you to die. This surgeon whilst advocating a radical surgery plan is the best surgeon around.'

'How do you know? It is not like we have tried any others.' Michael became aggressive. 'We haven't got the time to try other surgeons just because you are unsure of the surgery. We have to stick with what we have got. If you are getting upset about the surgery, then think of something else to pass the time!' Michael exclaimed.

Angelica was becoming emotionally uncertain with all this talk of quadruple amputation. She wished that she never agreed with it. It was too late now, given that it was only a few weeks away from the surgery. She was overwhelmed with the burden of having her arms and legs amputated. What a bad idea it was to even think it was a good idea. But now, the clock was ticking and there was no way of rescinding the Article 50 contract she signed with Dr Nigel Johnson. If she did, she would have to pay a $5,000. Of course, she could pay the $5,000 but it wouldn't simply end there because she would still have her bone cancer, in which Dr Nigel Johnson's language Angelica was dying of. Angelica would have to find another surgeon. That would add time. Still, was that better than having her legs amputated.

'I think I should find another surgeon or take up Gina's advise of having another biopsy,' Angelica whispered.

'No Angelica, no. I will make this clear. Our agreement stands that you are having this surgery. I am not paying $5,000 for you to get out of the surgery with no new agreement in place.'

'Is not my limbs more important than the $5,000?' Angelica asked. There was a moment of silence when Michael hesitated. 'Well, then Michael which is more important $5,000 or my limbs?'

'Don't put me on the spot with those questions Angelica! You can't put a price on your life,' Michael replied furiously.

'I asked you a simple question...'

'It isn't simple. Besides, you wanted the $3,500,000 pay-out, didn't you?'

'Yes, I did. I still do. But I know my limbs are more important than the money.'

There was a general realization that Angelica may decide not to have the surgery, which filled Michael with dread. Michael had been planning for the surgery, making sure that his work in the oil industry was okay and set for him being able to balance life as a carer and as an Oil Engineer Consultant Analysis. Really though, Michael could trade from home. Nothing was stopping him from that. Angelica appeared capricious, completely undecided and wanted more time. It was too late for that. Amputation means amputation.

'So, let me get this straight. You are going to crash out of this agreement with no new plan in place for you to have surgery and just hope that you will find a surgeon?' Michael asked.

'Yes. I mean it can't be too hard to find. We have the money for one...'

'Oh no, I wouldn't go too far with that, Angelica. You don't know how much money we have,' Michal replied.

'What do you mean? Don't tell me we have no money left. How much money do we, Michael?' Angelica asked with a tone of horror in her voice.

'To pay outright for surgery would cost $60,000. We have $45,000 in the bank...'

Angelica glared at him. 'You earn $250,000 a year and we have $45,000 in our bank account. Are you sure?'

'I am 100% sure of that,' Michael lied. He never told her about his other bank accounts. Michael had various bank accounts in the millions stored in tax havens that Angelica never knew about.

'Where has all our money gone?' Angelica cried.

'Never you mind about that. Concentrate on getting better.'

'That was our savings. Our life savings.'

Angelica left Michael to sort out the bank accounts as he was far more competent with finance than her, given his job. It would not cross

Angelica's mind of all of the cunning tax avoidance and even evasion schemes that Michael would use to avoid paying taxes to the government or the Fed as Michael called it.

'Did you know how much money we had in our savings...'

'We had over $120,000, Michael, where has it gone?' Angelica said frustratedly.

'$120,000? What $120,000? I don't know what you are on about.'

'We had $120,000 saved in our bank account and didn't we have some investment funds that we invested into?

Michael frowned. He did not like Angelica talking about investment funds because it touched on secrets that he wasn't confident in sharing. All couples have secrets, Michael knew this but took this to another extreme of hiding networks of business activity away from even his wife. After all, why should she know about clients that Michael had? Michael held secrets that he would keep from his wife. There was no consideration telling her about these secrets.

'Don't even talk about our investment funds! They are my concern, do you understand? Your surgery is a more pressing concern...'

'Why are you trying to shift the subject. You are hiding something from me,' Angelica said.

'I am very worried that you are going to die. You are dithering about whether you are going to have surgery or not but all you worry about is my investments, isn't it?' Michael shouted in a paranoid screech of rage.

'You don't care about me...'

'I love you damn it! I don't want you to die. You just can't accept my love because I am willing to have all your limbs removed for you to live. Even with just stumps, I will love you.'

Angelica was repulsed by Michael's words. And yet she couldn't come back with a response to this as he loved her was impregnable from attack. Michael could not be attacked for saying he was loving her. However, she knew that Michael did not mean that he loved her.

Angelica found it difficult to read the intentions of Michael. She found him opaque in his intentions and goals.

'When we get home Angelica, we are not going to discuss my investments or anything else relating to my money. We are going to talk about you and your operation, do you understand?' Michael said like a school principal.

'Yes,' Angelica whimpered.

Chapter 12

Angelica was alone. It was only a week before the surgery. She had been crying a lot, becoming complete destabilized by the internal torment of having her limbs amputated. Of course, she wanted it gone. There was a desire for Angelica to keep her limbs. Before the other consultations, Angelica was optimistic about the surgery. But now it dawned on her that she was going to lose her ability to do anything. No more control. No more being ability in acting independently. Everything would have to be done for her by someone else. Michael would have a cast-iron grip on her life. No more freedom external to Michael. She wasn't in the mood to watch EEPTV on the television. Instead, she decided to browse the internet on different websites. Angelica felt a vibration from her phone.

Elizabeth Londres, the friend that she had thrown under a bus, had seemingly enough kindness to text Angelica.
Are you okay? Are you able to speak with me? The text went.
Angelica was hesitant in texting back. What was she going to say to Elizabeth? Was she going to say that she regretted making that decision now after talking to her friends and family about the procedure or not? Angelica knew that she did not want the surgery anymore, but was powerless to stop it now. The surgery was completely out of her control. Her surgeon and husband even were more control of her destiny than herself. Taking back control? More like handing it all away to those with considerably more power.
I want to speak to you. Please ring me, Angelica texted back.

There was no response from Elizabeth for quite some time. Why was Elizabeth texting Angelica but not responding with a phone-call? To Angelica, it was if Elizabeth was trying to bait herself into responding to her but then ignoring all later communication from Angelica. Angelica browsed through the internet, looking at websites where people uploaded various pictures of various things. She looked at pictures of amputees and watched videos of amputees trying to live out their lives. A double amputee could carry on relatively as normal. Angelica struggled to imagine what life was for a quadruple amputee. Of course, prosthetics were an option. But Michael never even suggested it to Angelica. There was little preparation for Angelica to become a quadruple amputee. It was just going to happen and it appeared that neither Angelica nor Michael were in any interest in trying to adapt to the situation. The lack of preparation was evident. There had been no consideration of getting a wheelchair, no consideration of prosthetic limbs. There was no consideration of food, toilet, washing or day to day activities. Preparations were not made.

Angelica's phone began to ring.
  'Hey, Elizabeth,' Angelica murmured.
  'Hi,' Elizabeth replied abruptly.
  'Thanks for phoning me,' Angelica said
  'Not a problem.'
  'Any reason for the phone call?'
Elizabeth laughed. 'I was just wondering how you are feeling before your surgery that is all.'
  'I am not wanting to dwell on what is going to happen to me. It is horrible,' Angelica cried, 'Why was I even stupid enough to go with Dr Nigel Johnson? Why didn't I go with someone else as my orthopedic surgeon?'
  'Listen Angelica. Listen very carefully. Get out whilst you still can. Go. End the contract, end the agreement you have with Dr Nigel Johnson. I pray for you. Please think of yourself. Think of the effects of living without limbs across your body...'
  'It is too late for that. I have to go through with it,' Angelica replied remorsefully.
  'What? No. You can have a second chance. You can change your mind on the surgery. Just go back to the drawing board. This is an elective

procedure. Who an earth would have a quadruple amputation in an elective procedure? It makes no sense. You can change your mind on whether you have an elective procedure. Many Americans cancel theirs when they realize they have no money to pay for it.'

'But I would have to pay a cancellation clause of $5,000.'

'Is you being able to have functional limbs more important than having $5,000?' Elizabeth asked.

'I can't change now. It is too late.'

'It will be too late when you wake up on March the 29th with no arms or legs because you chose to carry on with such a ridiculous procedure.'

'But I can't back out now.'

'Why not?'

'Because… I can't. I made the decision and now the decision has been confirmed by the surgeon and my husband.'

'They don't control your body though do they, Angelica?' Elizabeth said frustratedly.

'No. But my husband controls our bank balance. He is in control of what I can spend the money on. He controls this situation far more than I would like.'

'But you can get out of there. You could move out….'

'Where can I go? I have nowhere to turn. Now that I have cancer, I have nowhere to go. I have no money independent of him for health insurance. I would be bankrupt trying to pay for treatment.'

Elizabeth sighed. 'I never thought that Michael was pulling the strings of the surgery. I thought you were in control.'

'I didn't. Until recently. The last meeting, I had with Dr Nigel Johnson, he was completely turned against me. It is as if he and Dr Nigel Johnson were conspiring against me. I have no evidence that they are. But then why would Michael seem to completely defend everything that Dr Nigel Johnson was saying?'

'It is your body after all. You control it. It isn't your husband's decision about what happens to you. You could leave him and move out of your house. It would be hard. I am sure there would be people to support you…'

'No. There would be none. No one would support me. Wives, submit to your husband as people would say.'

Elizabeth sighed. 'But what of husbands loving their wives?'

'I don't think they would think of that.'

'Do what you think is best. If that means leaving, that means leaving. Packing your bag and going.'

'Thanks for your advise Elizabeth,'

'All the best in your future and God is always with you.'

Elizabeth hung up the call on Angelica. Angelica sat, distraught on her sofa. She did not know what to do. Should she leave now? She didn't have the money for health insurance or treatment for her cancer. Michael could just simply cut her off from the bank account. Worse was the fact that any purchases she made she would be tracked by Michael. Angelica had been manipulated into having the surgery but she felt foolish but it was too late to back-track. She had signed the Article-50 paper. The surgery was happening and there was nothing that could be done to change it.

Michael came through the door. There was a large smile on his face as he looked at the crying wife that sobbed continuously on the sofa.

'What is the matter by honey-bun?' he said in a soothing voice, calmly and coolly.

'Why did I sign the contract to have the surgery? Why can't we just cancel it?'

'Aww. You poor thing,' Michael said, with a no hint of genuine sympathy, running his fingers through her hair as if she was a doll, before kissing her scalp.

'Can't you cancel the surgery...'

'That is not possible now. The deal has been negotiated. We will be paying for the surgery soon.'

'But you have taken my control away from me. The control of my life!' Angelica exclaimed.

'Well, amputation means amputation,' Michael hissed like a snake.

'I could just have the limb with the cancer removed or look at another surgeon...'

'You have listened to the surgeon. You are having *all* your limbs removed. This is a necessary treatment to cure you of your cancer. You darling, you will be without any limbs next week!' Michael said mockingly.

'Why are you like this to me?' Angelica whimpered. 'Why are you bullying your wife?'

'I am not bullying you. That is a strong accusation which is not based on any evidence what so ever'

'But then why are you not interested in changing the situation and carry on with the surgery regardless of it being so destructive?'

'Because it shall and must happen. It is inevitable when you signed Article 50, this was going to happen.'

'That makes no sense,' Angelica whispered. 'If you really loved me, you would want the best for me and would want the treatment that offers the least worst option'

'Amputation means amputation. You have already made the choice. The surgery must now happen...'

'That is absurd! What a ridiculous idea that it would be the least-worst option. I mean don't you care that your wife would have no arms or legs? We haven't prepared for it. Let us call it off.'

'There are levels of survival I am prepared to take,' Michael grinned malevolently, 'I have already planned to sell our house. We may not be able to afford it with the surgery fees. I doubt our health insurance will be able to pay the full amount.'

Angelica felt as if she could vomit. The fact they would have to sell their house to pay for the surgery was extreme, to say the least. Angelica did not talk to Michael about the fact that their health insurance was to pay for the surgery. She simply assumed that they would, given that her life was threatened. There was no real consideration of what would happen if the health insurance provider *didn't* pay for the surgery. She never contacted them throughout all the treatment to find out. It was mid-

March, one week before the surgery and now Michael was saying that they would have to sell the house.

'Let me get this straight. We are going to have to sell the house to pay for my surgery?' Angelica murmured, her hands shaking in a fearful rage.
'Have you contacted the health insurers or not…'
'I thought the hospital has… I can't remember if I have or have not,' Angelica replied.
'Well they will send someone around to assess your condition in hospital I would imagine.'
'Oh my,' Angelica replied.

Angelica's heart raced like a bolted horse. Her life was now a runaway freight train, completely losing control of her situation. Taking back control over cancer was never about losing control of everything but it was about losing her limbs. Or rather what she thought was going to happen was not likely to happen. What she thought was going to happen, prosthetic limbs and $3,500,000 pay-out were now no longer likely. Instead, she was going to have an operation in which she would become completely disabled, with the possibility that her husband would have to sell her house, with no way being able to support herself.
'Don't you want to stop this? Can't you stop it?' Angelica said agitatedly.
'No. The surgery must happen. We need to take back control.'
'This is absurd!' Angelica cried, bursting into tears.
'No, it is not absurd. This was how it was meant to be.'
'Why won't you change your mind on this issue.'
'The decision has been made. When a decision has been made, nothing can revoke that decision. Amputation means amputation.'
'But a quadruple amputation means no limbs for myself. Do you not even care about that? Have you not considered the fact that your wife will be crippled because of the surgery?'
'I will love you as an amputee,' he purred.

A few months back she would have been reassured but now she was disturbed. Why would Michael "love" her anymore as an amputee than now? It was if he wanted something from her having her arms and legs removed. Of course, Angelica hadn't considered why Michael wanted her to have all her limbs removed.

'Why do you want my limbs to be removed when it is completely unnecessary?' Angelica growled.

'Because I love you and want you to live,' he replied.

'There is something else I know it when you are hiding something.'

'What is for dinner?' Michael asked.

'You are going to have to cook dinner Michael. Have you ever prepared for it given that once I have no arms or legs that I will not be able to cook without prosthetics?'

'Well, that settles it. Burritos. I can cook them.'

'But you haven't answered my question. Are you trying to hide something from me? Why do you want me to have my limbs amputated?' Angelica pleaded.

Michael smiled and walked out of the room, leaving Angelica alone, crying into her hands at the fate that had been decided. She has chosen to take back control. But it appeared that all that she had no control at all.

Chapter 13

The phone was ringing. It was only a few weeks before the surgery. Michael had gone to work, leaving Angelica by herself, alone doing nothing but watching the television. She walked over to the landline phone and picked it up.

'Hello, who is speaking?' Angelica asked down the phone.

'Is that Angelica Donaldson?' the female voice asked.

'It is, who is speaking?' Angelica's voice was bemused.

'Hi, sorry for bothering you today. I am the receptionist for Dr Nigel Johnson. I am phoning up regarding your surgery, we have had a few problems regarding the surgery. Is now a good time to speak?'

'What is wrong exactly?' Angelica queried.

'Well, the hospital is rather busy at the moment. We have been phoning people up for none emergency surgery to be cancelled. We are contacting you because we are moving the date of the surgery.'

Angelica became agitated. 'What date are you moving the surgery too? Why are you doing this to me? I am not happy about this!' Angelica snapped.

'I am so sorry about the news. We would have to move the date of your surgery due to a large number of surgeries done by the hospital at this time. We are having to move the date of surgery to April the 12th.'

'April the 12th? Why then? Isn't it just better to get on with surgery on the March the 29th ?'

'No, we don't have enough free operating rooms. We have become fully booked, so we are having to move the time of the surgery to the 12th?'

'I am not particularly happy about this.'

'You will come in as usual on the 11th before the surgery for you to be checked in. Then we will do the surgery on the 12th.'

Angelica sighed. She had wanted to simply get this surgery done. After all, amputation means amputation. Delaying the amputation was simply going to kill Angelica further. Angelica had been dithering on the decision like a pendulum. Erratically uncontrollable, completely changing her mind, she flipped from wanting the surgery to considering it the worst thing in the world. Dr Nigel Johnson proposed a quadruple amputation, to begin with, because the cancer was so advanced and was going to kill her. Angelica knew that amputation meant amputation for the very reason that a complete amputation of every limb was necessary. Angelica knew that she had to take back control of her body. Taking back control meant amputation was necessary. Plus, Angelica taking back control of her own body meant a $3,500,000 pay-out from the life insurance company. Survival was imperative. However, it wasn't that simple. After all, Angelica had been crying that why she couldn't just have a smaller operation. Why did all four limbs have to go? There was no point. This bi-polar mood swings from wanting the surgery to completely fearing it was perhaps the most unsettled Angelica had become. Jumping between extremes was what a collapsing country did. People would reach out to multiple extreme ideas even when they are polar opposite, perhaps to improve their lives. Angelica was such a person. She was both completely for having a quadruple amputation and completely against it.

Angelica had turned off the television. She sat down with her tablet computer and looked up things online. She had wanted for a bit of time to change her mind on the surgery but Michael being the manipulator he had persuaded her once again to have surgery. Angelica looked over the internet at various things such as stories of amputees and wheelchairs. There had been very little preparation for the amputation other than Angelica watching a few things online about it. The lack of preparation for a quadruple amputation could only be overtaken by the genuine lack of understanding of what it was like to be a quadruple amputee. Angelica still somewhat believed in the fact that she was able to get bionic replacement limbs. Bionic limbs were science fiction, a unicorn fantasy made up in the minds of nerds in fiction books. They were at least a decade away. Angelica hoped a technological solution could have been made but it appeared to be a fantasy. But calling it fantasy meant project fear.

Angelica's cell-phone was ringing. It was Elizabeth. Angelica at first didn't want to answer the phone but reluctantly answered it in the end.
    'Hi Elizabeth,' Angelica said.
    'Hi,' Elizabeth Londres replied bluntly.

'Why are you phoning me? I thought you didn't want to talk to me.'

'Well... I am still concerned about you. I haven't forgotten about you.'

'My surgery has been moved forward to April the 12th,' Angelica whined.

Elizabeth didn't respond at first, as Angelica heard silence on the other end of the phone. 'April the 12th?'

'Yes.'

'So why not cancel the surgery then? You now have the time.'

'I need to go through with it. I need to take back control...'

Elizabeth sighed. 'Do you want to come to my house to discuss it? I am free April the 10th.'

'What day is that?'

'A Wednesday.'

'Can't you do earlier than that?'

'No, I can't,' Elizabeth said frustratedly. 'I have other priorities right now.'

'That is two days before surgery.'

'Your point is?'

Angelica couldn't find a point. After all, it was quite amazing that Elizabeth was even speaking to her at all. Angelica had been a horrible friend to Elizabeth to the point that she had almost completely cut off contact with Angelica.

'I can't see how I will be able to change anything that close to the surgery.'

'That is the offer I am going to give you. Take it or leave it.'

Angelica huffed. 'Okay. I will come around your house on April the 10th.'

'Great!' Elizabeth exclaimed, 'see you that day.'

Elizabeth hung up on Angelica. There had been no discussion about what time she was going to go over and it appeared for Angelica to be somewhat superficial. Still, at least she was now on speaking terms with her friend Elizabeth. This hadn't been the case before.

When Michael had arrived back home, there was an air of discomfort. He was not particularly pleased that the surgery had been moved from March the 29th to April the 12th. These changes annoyed Michael, who was hoping that the surgery was going to be completed on March the 29th.

'Why have they changed the date?' Michael shouted.

'Apparently, they were doing it because there were too many surgeries happening on March the 29th, so they decided to move it to April the 12th.'

'That is outrageous. I need to phone the hospital and complain...'

'Don't bother doing that.'

'Why not? Haven't you got life-threatening cancer? You will die if you are not treated.'

'Because it is out of our control.'

'But you are having a quadruple amputation to take back control. We need to take control of the process. I am going to phone up Dr Nigel Johnson' office on your behalf and speak to him...'

'Please...'

'No! I insist. It must be done.'

Michael walked out of the room carrying his cell-phone exasperatedly, whilst Angelica slumped in her chair. No longer was this surgery purely about her and her decision. It never was going to be just her decision. Ultimately her decision of having a quadruple amputation was affecting many other people. These included herself, her family, her friends, her husband. And yet, she just thought it was her decision alone and now Michael, her husband was controlling her decision. She would still go through with it. Why she did this was a question that she sometimes asked herself but it usually went back to the sort of sound bites which included that amputation means amputation, that she needed to take back control, that her body was being taken over by cancer cells and a quadruple amputation would stop the cancer cells killing her.

She continued with browsing the internet about quadruple amputation and understood about the freedom she would now have. There were advantages with having a quadruple amputation of course. A quadruple amputation meant you could compete in the Paralympics. Not that Angelica had any desire to compete in the Paralympics. She was in her 30s after all. But the $3,500,000 pay-out by the life insurance company was the most attractive proposition. After all, if she received bionic limbs, it did not matter that her legs and arms had been amputated.

A day later, Dr Nigel Johnson was meeting with Russell Portin. Russell Portin was not happy to see Dr Nigel Johnson in the slightest. The meeting was inside a café in downtown Dallas. Dr Nigel Johnson was busy and couldn't stay long. Russell Portin, however, insisted on having the meeting in downtown Dallas, suggesting that investment was on the line. Dr Nigel Johnson reluctantly agreed to this.

'How come you have extended out the surgical procedure? I thought it was happening in March the 29th and yet the hospital has decided to extend that to April the 12th. What is the point of that?' Russell Portin shouted angrily.

Dr Nigel Johnson sighed. 'Look it is out of my control. The director of surgery Dr Cameron May has decided to cancel large amounts of surgery and had to change the date of our surgery. There have been large structural changes in the hospital. We are running low on certain medications...'

'This is unacceptable. This is America! We don't run out of medication. That is what happens in a Communist country like Cuba or Venezuela,' Russell exclaimed.

'We are trying to make money here. The hospital is trying to make money and so they have to do some kind of reconstruction. The business you have helped me create is depended on the hospital. You just have to be patient.'

Russell Portin gulped down half a cup of Coke before guzzling on the air he was breathing. 'I have been planning this surgery for a while...'

'That does not take into consideration what has happened with Michael and Angelica. Have they been planning out what life will be like after a quadruple amputation?'

Dr Nigel Johnson took a sip of his drink, whilst Russell Portin considered that stated point. Had his friend or alter-ego planned for life after a quadruple amputation? Well, he was planning to buy the house of Michael Donaldson. The question was had Michael Donaldson planned for the surgery of his wife or not? He had consulted Michael a lot about this procedure and never had he considered whether Michael was prepared for looking after someone who had no limbs at all. So far as Russell was concerned, Michael was carrying on part-time with his job and then spending the other time looking after his wife. Was this enough though? Should Michael plan out intricately the new life that he was about to become part of? This was not Michael's decision to have his legs and arms amputated. It was his wife's decision; one which Michael had been guiding her slowly to make until she would go to having a quadruple amputation. However, like a typical politician, had not planned for this event to happen. Perhaps Russell had cause for concern.

'Michael has informed me that Angelica's friend has invited her to her house for a discussion on April the 10th for one final discussion to persuade her away from surgery. What if they tempt her away from the abyss?' Russell Portin said.

'Ask Michael to go there and he needs to take his arguments. Argue and most of all keep Angelica from changing her mind. It does not matter what other people think. So long as Angelica continues with the surgery, it will be fine.'

Chhapter 14

Elizabeth's house was packed with people who were connected with Angelica's life. Angelica's mum Wilma was there, so was Scott. Erica and Nora were also there, much to the annoyance of Michael, whose relationship soured the connection Angelica had to the Brians family. The so-called Good Friday Settlement of not bringing up the relationship between Erica and Nora could not happen since it was inevitable that they were getting married. There were also people from the Bible study group that she was part of, including Frances and Jeremy Schmidt, who despite her best efforts in offending, seemed to agree to the final night of negotiation. Some people were not invited. Dr Nigel Johnson was not invited for obvious reasons. Kate Sunderland had not been particularly constructive in the conversations and so was not invited. Gina Benjamin-Cruz had not been invited, simply because she would not be able to divulge on confidential information with other people about Angelica. So, it was a few people who had come. Two days before the surgery, April the 10th, this was the final real decision for Angelica whether she was going to go through with the surgery or not.

The layout of the room was that of a circle, with various dips, pizzas and tacos in the middle on a wooden table. Angelica sat on a sofa with Elizabeth on the left side whilst Michael sat to her right. Nora and Erica decided to sit on a separate coach, whilst Jeremy and Frances sat on a separate sofa facing Angelica, Elizabeth and Michael. Frances from the moment she had walked in, was rather at odds with the meeting. Now, she was able to have her say. Scott and Wilma sat on seats separate from the others, at the side.

'Thank you all so much for coming. I wouldn't have invited you all for this discussion if I thought it wasn't productive. Angelica is having a quadruple amputation two days from now. Today is the last real day for any meaningful discussion about this surgery. I believe many of us have disagreements about the surgery....'

Frances broke into Elizabeth's words, 'How about we just let her go and have the surgery? How about we just let her go and have her legs and arms amputated? I mean her surgery cast a real discordance on the last Bible study group that she came to. I want her done with the surgery. If she thinks it will make her life better, let her have the quadruple amputation. Get on with our lives.'

Jeremy looked at his wife and sighed. 'No, we can't just let our friend just have her arms and legs cut off because she is misguided and lied to...'

'She has not lied to Jeremy! She made her decision based on informed consent....' Michael retorted.

'No one in their right minds, is going to have a decision on amputating all their limbs. No one in their right minds would have all of their limbs amputated for anything other than genuine life or death struggle,' Jeremy reasoned.

'Which Angelica is having. Chondrosarcoma is taking over her body as we speak. Her legs and arms need amputating. What else is there more to discuss?' Michael bluntly responded.

'Have you been to see another surgeon discuss the surgery you are having? I am not a surgeon but I doubt any surgeon would say that bone cancer in one leg means you need all four limbs amputated. I have never heard of anything like that...'

'We have had enough of listening to experts!' Michael shouted.

'Order! Order! Order!' Elizabeth shouted like a speaker of the House. 'We need this to be a proper discussion and let this involve everyone here. This is turning into a political free-for-all rather than a talk about a friend's discussion. Let Frances say what she wants to say. Frances.'

'Thank you. I was only wanting to say that Angelica has made her decision. We should all just let her have her limbs cut off for all we care.'

'Right, and why should we agree with that, Frances?' Elizabeth asked.

'The last time we were talking about this, we were in our Bible study group. My view is quite clear. Her decision to have her limbs amputated doesn't concern us and interrupts our important study of the Bible. After the burning down of my home church in a tragic fire, I have been wanting to reconnect with the spirituality of my past. Us having to focus on Angelica's amputations is a pointless endeavor because we aren't focusing on the Bible, just on Angelica's surgery.'

'I think though that having a quadruple amputation isn't just a walk in the park and requires a rethink,' Jeremy said.

'Don't any of you understand? Angelica has decided to have the surgery! Are you trying to frustrate the will of the person? Amputation means amputation!' Michael rebuked.

'Well let her speak on her behalf. We do not need you to talk for her...'

'No, you are wrong. As Ephesians 5:22 says wives should submit to their husbands. Therefore, I can speak on her behalf,' Michael replied.

'But doesn't it say for husbands to love their wives also?' Elizabeth asked.

Michael stared intently into Angelica's eyes. 'I love my wife. I adore her. I want her to live. That is why she needs her legs and arms amputating.'

'Yes, but shouldn't Angelica make her own decision on surgery, not yourself?'

'She has made her decision and won't be changing it. The will of the person can't be changed. It is their will you are frustrating. What don't you understand about making decisions and sticking by them regardless of the costs? Angelica made a decision and we are not changing Angelica's decision for her.'

'But surgical procedures are done on informed consent not just having surgery for its own sake. Having your legs and arms amputated is the most intensive and arguably invasive procedure that is ever done. To just have it done based on fantasy and a belief, it will work out, in the end, is ludicrous.'

'Project fear! Project fear is going into overdrive! What do you not understand about the person's will? When a person makes a choice, we must honor it!' Michael shouted.

'It is not so-called "project fear". I am just making out that there have been no plans by yourselves into the effects on your life.

'We don't need to plan because it will work out all okay. We just need it to be done.'

'So, you are having the most life-changing surgery usually reserved for emergencies only with no planning or preparation?' Elizabeth replied.

'We don't need to plan. It will all pan out, won't it? It is what Angelica decided,' Michael said.

'Can't you have another think about the surgery?'

'You are insulting the decision that Angelica has made to have a quadruple amputation. When we have decided to do something, we must make go through with it, otherwise you under mind the will of the person.'

Wilma shook her head and sighed. 'Why are you doing this to yourselves? I supported your decision at first. However, I conclude that a quadruple amputation is an extreme proposition to have and to not reconsider it is a grave mistake,' Wilma said.

'No one can intervene and violate the decisions that Angelica made!' Michael shouted

'We are not violating decisions…'

'You are Wilma! You all are traitors! Rather than getting behind your friend making a fateful decision to have all of her limbs amputated, you decide to oppose it.'

'We believe it is well, how can we put it politely, rather absurd to have your legs and arms amputated like this,' Elizabeth said tactfully.

'But this isn't your decision, is it? When a person makes a decision, they must stick by the decision that they have made…'

'Why stick by decisions which are ridiculous propositions, to begin with?' Elizabeth questioned relentlessly.

An uneasy silence had developed in the room as the relationship between people began to freeze up cold. Amputation diplomacy was never going to be easy. The food on the table was a way of trying to ease tensions between people. The tensions between the pro-amputation camp, where Michael appeared to be the most enthusiastic member and the anti-amputation camp made up of practically everyone else except Angelica, who like a fanatical politician, had alienated everyone but her husband. There was a large problem that had not been addressed from the start of the meeting; shouldn't Angelica have a voice for the decision she made in the first place? This was rather odd, that in what had become a diplomatic meeting of discord and disagreement, the person whose decision was being discussed was not allowed a voice in such meeting.

'I must say that it is rather odd that we are talking about Angelica and her decision but why hasn't she been allowed to speak Michael?' Elizabeth asked.

This was the question that everyone else was thinking. Indeed, in such a decision, why was the person who made that decision not have the final say over that decision? Why couldn't someone have a final say on the decisions they had made, given the outcome of such a decision was rather life-limiting? But Angelica had not said anything and despite the talk about her life and her decision. Elizabeth had enough of this.

'Right, I think we need Angelica to have her view on why she still thinks that a quadruple amputation is still the right decision for her...' Elizabeth said

'Look, she has said what she thinks on her own amputation...'

'Michael, you are not Angelica and so do not speak on her own behalf. Angelica tell us why you are still going through with the surgery?'

Angelica looked hesitant, gulping a deep breath in and breathing out of her nose, she began to speak. 'I concluded that having Chondrosarcoma is a life-threatening condition that needed to be treated and that the treatment plan that Dr Nigel Johnson was offering was extreme but necessary for my survival. Plus, the $3,200,000 pay-out from the life insurance would be a good beneficial part of improving my life and Michael's life. Bionic limbs may replace all the limbs that I have lost. I believe it is God's will for me to have the surgery. I need to take back control over cancer that is devouring my body...'

'Right, the problem with that position is that how can I say it without hurting your feelings... You are wrong. I can't say it any other way, Angelica. I can be blunt but any treatment for Chondrosarcoma would not involve a quadruple amputation. This really is not good surgical practise and really you need to get another doctor to advise you on the issue and probably some more tests as well. I can't say it any other way,' Elizabeth said bluntly.

'Who do you think you are, Elizabeth, telling my wife that you know more about Chondrosarcoma than herself? I think you should apologize....'

'I am a surgical nurse...'

'Really now? So that makes you an expert on Chondrosarcoma then?' Michael snarked

'Well, an expert is a term that could be used as liable. I certainly know more than a lot of people.'

'Well now, I guess that you are the expert here. But here is something I am going to tell you, we have had enough of expert opinions on things. We the people can make better choices than you Liberal elites with a university degree.'

Most of the people in the room buried their heads in their hands to what Michael was saying. Michael had transformed the meeting into a meeting of child-like name-calling. Infuriating, Michael had gone beyond all bounds with his name-calling, which appeared to be petty politics rather than actual planning of how to deal with the current situation. 'Really Michael? Go on then, tell us all about Angelica's condition then. If you think you know more about Chondrosarcoma than myself or a professor of orthopedics, please enlighten me into the ins and outs of Chondrosarcoma...'

'I don't need to. Dr Nigel Johnson has enlightened me to what is necessary.'

'We are not asking to hear from Dr Nigel Johnson. We are asking to hear from yourself. Please tell us why your wife should have a quadruple amputation on cancer found in an ankle that has had a single biopsy and whose family doctor recommended a second biopsy due to a potential mistake in mismatching patient details...'

'Who told you that?' Michael demanded.

'Your wife did. You see Michael it is one thing to have surgery when there has been a mismatch of patient details. It is quite another having a surgical procedure that goes against the entirety of medical guidelines, to be manipulated into having the surgery.'

Scott, Erica and Nora were startled by this information. They had lost touch with their sister, partly because she had been so alienating towards them when she had previously attacked the relationship between Erica and Nora. Indeed, this quadruple amputation seemed to shatter the Good Friday Settlement that the Brians family created. Why would Erica and Nora only stay in a committed but informal relationship if the only reason stopping them from getting married was upsetting Angelica? Now, given that Angelica was having her legs and arms removed, turned into stumps two days from now, there was no reason to even consider her views, given what she had said to them.

'You know that we feel that this surgery completely invalidates our family agreement in the Good Friday Settlement? We can no longer take your views in any way which is serious because of this surgery,' Nora said, candidly.

'We do not feel it breaks any agreement we made with you. Why do our... I mean my wife's decision affect the agreement. The agreement between us made on Good Friday still stands,'

'You have tried to ask for sympathy but you have built walls between us. These walls were entirely built by you and you alone. When you begged for sympathy and yet gave no support to us for our relationship, we feel completely cheated and feel that you are hypocrites,' Nora said.

'You take that back!' Michael demanded.

'No. Hear it for what it is. You couldn't care less about our relationship and so we couldn't care less about this surgery.'

'Nora, please. We are trying to get people to dissuade Angelica from the surgery. You are not helping.'

'I am giving you what I feel right now. She has shown no respect for me or Erica, so I have no reason why I should show respect to her.'

'Charming,' Angelica said, close to tears.

'Let us get back to why I called this meeting to begin with. Angelica has decided to have her legs and arms amputated and the hospital where she is getting it done has decided to move the surgery. She was originally going to get the surgery done on March the 29th. This is a massive life-changing decision. I do not feel we have explained how extreme this is.'

'We do not care to your positions and quite frankly I am getting tired of this back and forth squabble. Let us just get on with it; amputation means amputation,' Michael said.

'We are not interested in what *you* think Michael. We need to take into considerations what your wife thinks. It is Angelica's decision, not your decision at the end of the day. We need her to get a second decision....'

'She made her decision. What don't you get with a person making their choice sticking by what choice they have made no matter what? Why can't you let her stand by her decision?' Michael spluttered

'We do not feel this decision is wise or in the best interests for Angelica. A quadruple amputation is considered in the worst-case scenarios. To have a quadruple amputation for something that is non-emergency is a large absurdity. We cannot support it at all.'

'What is wrong with you people? You don't believe in choices or people's responsibilities, do you...'

'Why are you not letting your wife speak, Michael? Please let her speak instead of yourself. Why won't we hear her speak instead of you?'

'Because.... we have decided that I am the representative of Angelica...'

'Even though Angelica is here?' Nora asked.

'Yes. She must be represented by myself...'

'But is not the purpose of choices to be represented by someone who isn't yourself,' Nora said.

'What do you mean?'

'You are not allowing herself to speak. Please, Angelica, tell us why you are doing this to yourself?' Nora asked.

'I have already told you why I am having the surgery. I must survive. I must take back control over cancer and receive $3,500,000 pay-out,' Angelica said poignantly.

'But don't you understand that the decision you have made is completely ridiculous. I give up. I don't see why we should try and persuade you against making such absurd decisions. It puts it into perspective my relationship between myself and Erica'

'I just want people to accept the choice that I have made. Instead, everyone is a traitor, betraying me as a person rather than supporting me...'

'I don't think people are betraying you as a friend and family member...'

'They are!' Angelica said in a detested voice.

'Listen to Angelica. People are not traitors simply for disagreeing with you. You have to listen to people...'

'We have had enough listening to other people and experts in particular. Come on Angelica. Let's leave,' Michael said exasperatedly.

'What do you mean?'

'Leave means leave! We are leaving this conversation, this conspiracy against us!' Michael said. Michael stood up, with Angelica following behind him. They walked out of the meeting in silence, with no consideration for the aftermath. That was it. Leave meant leaving and amputation meant amputation. Angelica had made her mind up to have her limbs amputated. There was no going back. The people in the meeting were aghast at her decision to have her limbs amputated. With two days to go, they were hoping to be able to persuade her away from surgery. It failed. Now nothing would get in the way of the choice that Angelica had made. Angelica was to free herself from the trappings of limbs and become a free person. It was God's will after all. No other will was higher than that of God.

Chapter 15

It had come at long last. The day before the surgery. The 11th of April, 2019. There was no Plan B now. Michael was driving Angelica to the hospital. Angelica had been rather calm at the decision of desolation. She was now going to be free from the control of others and their conflict with her decision. Her dare they lecture her on what was best for her! Michael had a smile on his face. Michael was happy. He had realigned his wife's decisions to what he had wanted. No more indecisiveness from Angelica now. Even though the health insurance company had been quiet about offering insurance, Angelica seemed to support the procedure. That would have to come about after the surgery. There was no plan for life after limbs. There had been very few preparations had been made for this life-changing event. Angelica hadn't chosen of which All the months they could have prepared. Now, Angelica and Michael were stripped naked. After everything that was going on, Angelica and Michael had not prepared. Too late to prepare now as the day of surgery was now upon them. Every minute down the interstate was one minute closer to Angelica having her limbs removed. One minute closer to becoming permanently disabled put into a wheelchair. Amputation means amputation. There is no compromise to a gnarling bone saw. It is impossible to triangulate a quadruple amputation. You either have your limbs or you don't. There is no centrist position of amputation; amputation means amputation. Not amputating would be a betrayal, or so one could think. Angelica tried to imagine herself in the open-sky country, in a field all by herself. The wispy-blue sky and woolly clouds rolling by to the calm wind. She imagined the wind, brushing her hair. It was just a thought. There was no wind. Just her imagination to calm her.

When Michael had parked the car in the parking lot, he walked up to the ward that Angelica had been assigned to. The ward was bright, the windows large, walls of white and blue, the staff wearing azure-blue and sapphire-blue scrubs. There were some chairs in the waiting room area and a restricted access part of the ward. Angelica was trying to remember the taste of the waffles and syrup she had in the morning. It was the last breakfast she was having before the surgery. The last breakfast with arms to grab hold of a spoon and folk. Angelica avoided contemplating life with no arms or legs. She had, by watching podcasts and Youtube videos of quadruple amputees but not attempted life as an amputee what so ever. Previously, she had thought that she could easily adapt to prosthetic limbs and it would be practically the same. Michael had not even suggested about prosthetic limbs. There had been no discussion with her health insurance company about getting prosthetic limbs. She remembered phoning the life-insurance company about receiving the pay-out but they had not given any more assurance around it. Michael walked up to the help-desk and Angelica followed behind him, with her travel-case, looking towards the ground. A young attractive female nurse sat behind the desk as Michael grinned at her.

'Hi, can I help you,' she asked politely with an American-customer service smile.

'Hi, I wonder if you could help me. I am trying to book in my wife, Angelica Donaldson for surgery tomorrow by Dr Nigel Johnson.'

'Okay let me check on the system,' the nurse said typing onto the computer. 'Yes, that is it... Oh um yeah. The surgery for tomorrow. That is odd, it says a quadruple amputation.'

The nurse was bemused. She knew which surgeries went on in the hospital and obviously on the ward which was Trauma and Orthopedics ward. Why on earth would there be an elective quadruple amputation? The nurse knew that elective amputations were used for a single limb in severe pain, failed bone reconstruction or for as in Angelica's case, a cancerous growth such as a Chondrosarcoma. Why would someone elect to have a quadruple amputation? Why would a surgeon carry it out on a patient who didn't need it? How would any health insurance company pay for such a procedure? Why was this even happening?

'Um, I think there might be a mistake on the system... I can't believe that surely,' the nurse said with a perplexed voice.

'What about,' Michael said infuriated.

'It says your wife is having a quadruple amputation. That isn't an elective procedure...'

'That is right. The patient elected to have the procedure.' A voice boomed from a man that had just left the restrictive access area. Dressed in dark blue scrubs, wearing a white lab-coat, with beautifully tanned skin was the surgeon Dr Nigel Johnson, glaring at the nurse at the desk as he strolled towards the desk. 'It is an elective procedure for a very, very aggressive Chondrosarcoma. It is life or death.'

'I am sorry Dr Nigel Johnson. It is just that I have never heard it ever before, in my professional life or when I was at university...'

'Aww. Sweetheart. You look *so* young. What is an 18-year-old doing nursing?'

The nurse blushed, grimacing with embarrassment. 'I am 26...'

'Little baby hasn't learned her anatomy or health conditions. Perhaps you should stay out of operating rooms until you have a professional understanding of procedures that we do, alright?' he said with a tone of condescension. Dr Nigel Johnson grinned at Michael, who didn't respond.

'Sorry, Dr Nigel Johnson...'

'That is okay sweetie. Just don't get involved with the big-boys right. Doctors know a lot. Surgeons know best. Nurses know very little. Now are you going to see the patient in for me or what?'

Dr Nigel Johnson was being unnecessarily rude and demanding. The nurse felt patronized by Dr Nigel Johnson. The nurse glared at him for a second and then got up from the desk.

'Shall I show you to your room?' the nurse said to Angelica.

Angelica did not reply, simply looking to the floor when following the nurse down the corridor, that had large windows, bright color and felt of a luxurious hotel as much as a hospital. There were pictures of landscapes on the wall, paintings and photos of the sea and sky. A stark contrast to the harsh reality of Angelica's surgery that she faced. The nurse opened the door to the room, which was a mint-green colour. There was a bed and a television and various medical equipment that reminded the patient they were in a hospital, not a hotel. It was a private room, with a sofa and a chair next to the bed. Outside the room overlooked other hospital buildings, a path and trees outside.

'This is your room for the time you are here with us. We have given you a bleep alarm if you need anything or have any problem with pain and the like, you can get a nurse or a doctor if there is one around,' the nurse said. 'We will have to put some IV lines into you later to prepare you for surgery and to give you fluids as you won't be able to eat or drink until after the surgery that you are having. Do you have anything you want to ask me now?'

'Not that I can think off the top of my head,' Angelica replied.

'Well if you need a nurse, just press the button and one will come to you.'

'Thank you.'

The nurse left the room. Angelica lied on the bed looking up at the ceiling whilst Michael sat down on the chair next to the bed. It was a chair that could tip itself backwards as a fold-down bed.

'Wow this is nifty,' Michael said to Angelica, as he played with the chair.

Angelica stared up at the ceiling, with no desire to speak to Michael sat beside her.

'Well, this is a nice room, isn't it. Aren't you glad your husband earns $250,000?'

Angelica remained silent to Michael's comment.

'Wow, you aren't in the mood for anything…'

'Your wife is having her arms and legs amputated tomorrow and all you can say is silly things about the room?' Angelica snapped.

'Woooh, someone has got angry.'

Angelica rolled on her side and looked at Michael. 'You really don't get the seriousness or don't you care?' Angelica snarled.

'Umm… I am trying to make light of a dark situation that is all. I love you…'

'Words without actions are meaningless. Prove you love me by acting it,' Angelica said.

'I thought you were for the surgery! Stop with your emotions and recognize the liberation of amputation. You are being liberated; you are being freed. Liberated from cancer that will kill you. This occasion should be celebrated. God wants this surgery for you.'

Angelica burst into tears as emotion had overwhelmed her. Michael kissed Angelica on the forehead and smoothed her hair. It was an act of kindness that showed affection between Angelica and Michael. Yet Angelica felt no warmth from it. In her heart, she felt that Michael was just showing some affection just to make her feel good temporarily. Affection was not just a simple show of love but a love showed back actions that were more meaningful than just a kiss on the forehead.

'I love you,' Michael whispered.

'Why do I have to have this surgery?' Angelica whimpered.

'It is necessary. You won't regret the fact that you will be alive rather than dead. You should be thankful that you can have surgery when millions of people have no medical access at all. Having a life without limbs isn't that bad. Just think you will be freed from cancer and will be a free person.'

'Will I be free though?' Angelica replied.

There was a knock at the door. It was Dr Andrea May, the anesthesiologist doing the surgery. She was a wide-set, curvy woman but not necessarily fat, in her middle 40s with sharp rounded brown eyes and middle length brunette hair, dressed in a white lab-coat over her teal-blue scrubs.

'Hi Andrea, you met me before. I am Dr Andrea May your anesthesiologist. I am just here to measure some of your vital signs like your pulse and go through your surgical history one final time, just in case I missed anything out,' the woman said.

The anesthesiologist put a strap for the heart rate monitor around her arm and turned on the machine. A tight pressure was felt in Angelica's arm. Pulsation was felt throughout the arm as the heart rate monitor flashed with information that Angelica could not understand.

'Hmm that is quite high, 125 over 90. 145 beats per minute. That was much higher than before. I guess it is nerves…'

'Well, yes…'

'Aww. Well, I could give you a sedative before going down to the operating room. Something like Lorazepam and Diazepam should be able to work here. Maybe I should increase the dosage,' Dr Andrea May said as she was writing out things on her tablet computer. She appeared to be methodical, with a tenseness about her. Strong and stable on the surface but underneath was a duckling struggling in the water.

'We talked somewhat about your surgical past before. Remind me about previous times you have had surgery,' Dr Andrea May asked.

'I had an appendectomy when I was 15 and all my wisdom teeth removed when I was 24…'

'Were there any side effects do you remember?'

'They said I took longer to come around from my wisdom teeth removal.'

'Your notes say that your body has an intolerance to Nitrogen Oxide gas, Propofol and Halothane. Is that correct?' Dr Andrea May inquired.

'I can't remember.'

'Maybe changing the dosage here would help,' Dr Andrea May said, writing on her tablet computer.

Angelica was anxious. Would less anaesthesia mean that she would wake up when she went under the knife? Worse would she feel the pain when the saw cut through the bone, an unquenchable agony, indescribable to all those who haven't felt it? Angelica shuddered at that thought that she could feel the surgery.

'Is it possible that I could wake up in the surgery?' Angelica asked, apprehensively.

Andrea looked baffled. 'Don't be absurd. That is exceptionally unlikely. I mean it is 1 in 14,000 chance. You are not going to have that happen to you because it is unlikely.'

A plane crash was unlikely to Angelica and yet it was still unnerving to think it could happen. Could the unfortunate happen, for Angelica feel every single cut of the saw and slice of the scalpel? It was not likely, in fact quite unlikely. Chance is always a fact of life that can never be fully anticipated. Things happen that are completely unexpected. So even if it was a 1 in 14,000 chance happening, it still possible could happen. That frightened Angelica. However, the fact that she had bone cancer and now was having, *all* of her limbs removed with little preparation was yet more reasons for Angelica to worry.

'That is still a possibility though,' Angelica said anxiously.
'The amount of anesthesia I will give you, it won't. When you go in, you will be so drugged up that you will be completely delirious and unaware of what is going on before being sedated.'
'What if that doesn't happen?' Angelica pondered, 'What if I am fully aware of what is going on.'
'It won't happen. It is so unlikely to happen,' Dr Andrea May laughed.

There was a Dr Andrea May had a stubborn form of intellectual arrogance, similar to that of Dr Nigel Johnson. Perhaps that was the reason why Dr Nigel Johnson chose Dr Andrea May as his anaesthesiologist. They were both alike, completely fixated on their ability and could not see anything wrong with themselves and their plans. After looking through some more of Angelica's medical history, her health and medication, Dr Andrea May left the room. Angelica lied on her bed worrying about the surgery. She stared at the ceiling, unfazed by Michael who started to chat with her about things that would happen after the surgery. There was no stop button. Amputation means amputation, ran through her head. To be an amputee, she had contemplated but had barely prepared for. The entire change for her life. Life was going to be completely changed and there was no time to prepare now. Only now she could count down the hours before she was finally put asleep. Now, it was on. The clock was ticking.

Tick tock went the clock in Angelica's brain. She had not felt like doing anything since she arrived at the hospital. After texting her mum and Elizabeth in the morning, she had not texted anyone else. It was night time. Angelica's mind refused to sleep. Lying awake, looking at the ceiling she was contemplating why she even chose to her limbs all amputated. It was a completely ridiculous proposal. Yet she was still going through with it. She refused to listen to other people about their views on her choice. It was more tragic now that she had no way of changing her mind. The decision had been made for her. Michael had prompted her to make that decision but ultimately, it was her decision. It was now an inevitable wait until the time that a gurney arrives to take her down to the operating room.

Tick-tock, tick-tock. Only the ticking of the clock inside her brain, the timer counting down until she was put to sleep. Horror and helplessness ensnared her to a trance of paralysis. She felt her breathing filtering out, slowly sedating. Her heart raced like an express train. Tingling went up through her arms. Her breathing stopped and she felt she could not breathe. 20 seconds, 30 seconds, 40 seconds, Angelica could not breathe. The diaphragm contracted but she couldn't breathe. Suffocated in her own body, she felt utterly powerless. This was what she was going to be in a few hours; on an operating table, her skin cut open, her muscles severed and her arms and legs sawn off. Quivering, Angelica finally managed to breathe, before panting. She felt of wax burnt in a fire, her body quivering and shaking in fear.

She did not have any way of telling how long the time past with her dithering in her bed, unable to sleep. The restlessness gnawed away at her, rolling around in bed as the hours had passed by. The gradual light peering into the room was unnerving. Never before was she dreading the sunrise. But today was no ordinary day. Today she was to become an amputee, the complete loss of freedom. From now until she was put to sleep on the operating table, Angelica would have the final hours as an independent person. Gradually the light, became brighter until the sunrise was a bright red and orange, the clouds a blood-vermillion color, of slaughtered carcases in a slaughterhouse. Vicious and angry was the day outside, the wolves were at the door howling.

Angelica, shattered from having no sleep woke up. The nurses instructed her to wash in a shower. The final show where she would be able to stand on her feet. It was an awful feeling, the trepidation, the fear, the preparation to be cut up, to be diced and for her limbs to be severed. She wanted to stay in the warm flow of water forever, the embrace of warm water coming from the shower but alas she was to prepare herself for surgery. The orderlies arrived with the gurney to take her down to the operating room on. After putting on a gown, Angelica was lifted onto the gurney and wheeled down to the operating room.

However, today there was some unexpected resistance. Out of nowhere, without warning, Angelica began to get out of the gurney, pushing the nurses unexpectedly out of the way as if to run. She misbalanced her feet and collapsed helplessly on the floor. Angelica felt utterly powerless. When the nurses positioned her back onto her feet, she tried to bolt again only for the nurses to pinion her to the gurney, strapping her down so that she was unable to fight, only for her to scream as she struggled.

   'Why are you like this Angelica? You do not have to struggle,' one of the nurses said in a perplexed voice.

   'You want to take my limbs away from me.'

   'We are doing this for your own good. You need it done.'

   'Stop it now. Stop the surgery! I don't want it now,' Angelica screamed as she was wheeled down the corridor.

To Angelica, the world seemed to become a blur of intense fear and trepidation. No more was there a desire for her to have the $3,500,000, the belief in cybernetic limbs to replace the limbs she had lost. She was now completely wrecked by the fear of the complete loss of independence. Oh, if only this was a dream but the reality was dawning of what life was going to be for Angelica.

'Why won't you listen to me!' Angelica screamed.

They wheeled her into the operating room, with Dr Andrea May was dressed in scrubs, wearing a surgical mask, gloves and a surgical cap. Brown eyes without a face. She glared at Angelica, who was struggling on the gurney.

'What is the problem Angelica?' she asked with a soothing voice.

'I don't want the surgery. Why won't you let it stop?'

'Aww. I am sorry. I should have administered the Lorazepam and Diazepam in your room so that you were calmer for the surgical room. Here you go,' Andrea May said, as she injected her with a concoction of drugs. Angelica felt considerably drowsier and more docile.

The surgical staff lifted Angelica from the gurney onto the operating table. After Angelica kicked and struggled a few times, the staff strapped her down to the table. Angelica was unable to move, pinned to the table. The room was a sterile-white color, with a vast amount of equipment, no windows to the outside world. The staff were all masked and gloved, with a bright surgical lamp that was attached to the ceiling. The room was a cool temperature, enough to make a person shiver. Angelica looked around, naked as her body lay on the table, pinioned to the bitterly cold table.

'I am cold. ,' Angelica said.

'Okay, let me just inject you shall I? Nice deep breaths for me please, you might feel a small scratch,' Andrea said calmly to Angelica, glaring into her eyes with a masked face. Dr Andrea May injected the syringe into the IV line in Angelica's arm. Angelica felt light-headed, faint and disorientated, her head spinning. Andrea injected another syringe into Angelica's arm, making Angelica sleepy before a mask was placed over Angelica's face and held by Andrea's gloved hand. Angelica drifted off slowly, her pace rate dropping on the cardiographic heart monitor. Angelica finally shut her eyes. Dr Andrea May removed the mask from

Angelica's face and then inserted a tracheal tube down Angelica's throat for tracheal intubation.

A blue drape was placed over the inert body. The arms and legs of Angelica were visible. The surgical nurses rubbed in an iodine solution over Angelica's limbs, turning them into the colour of a sweet and sour pork dish All the surgical instruments, the retractors, scalpels, tweezers, cauterizers and bone saws were counted by the surgical nurses. Tourniquets had been applied to all four limbs. The surgeon himself, Dr Nigel Johnson strolled into the operating room. He was joined by a surgical resident Esther Francois, a Quebecer who was resident at the Texas Baptist University hospital. Surgical nurses helped to dress him into a jade-blue surgical gown and plunged bone-white latex gloves onto his hands and arms. He glared at the surgical team surrounding him. He was supported by Dr Andrea May, the anesthesiologist, assistant surgeon the ambitious Dr Jacob Johnson and the scrub nurse was the young African-American Caroline Cockbain, with various support staff waiting behind them. Dr Nigel Johnson was confident that his ability was alone to continue the surgery without other specialities. The fewer people supporting him, the better since the hospital may have not allowed the surgery due to gross violations of ethics.

'How was the patient today?' Dr Nigel Johnson asked the surgical team, looking around the room.

'The patient was highly agitated before we anesthetized her. She was resistant before surgery saying she didn't consent to surgery and she no longer wanted it,' Dr Andrea May said with the serious tone

'Oh, dear. What the hell were you doing Dr Andrea May? You should have gone into her room before the surgery and given her some sedative, Lorazepam or Diazepam or Midazolam before we started. What were you thinking?' Dr Nigel Johnson exclaimed rudely becoming agitated.

'We restrained her because...'

'If we get caught and there is an investigation then we could all lose our licences and may be sued by it! Yet, it is lucky that I have a contact that will get us out of that predicament.'

'I agreed to this procedure despite it breaking all ethical guidelines and for my disagreement of it,' Dr Andrea May snapped. 'I could have easily reported you to the Texas Medical Board for completely unnecessary surgery. She does not need a quadruple amputation. I know that. You know that. We all know that.'

'You are paid by me to be here. Don't forget that. The hospital isn't paying you; I am. Dr Johnson's Surgical the company I have found with the help of my contact Russell Portin is paying for your salaries here. And you are being paid a lot.'

'Right,' Dr Andrea May said.

'Well then. I hope we are ready to begin the surgery then,' Dr Nigel Johnson said.

'Umm... Yes,' Dr Andrea May said, her eyes looking shifty around the room. Masks hide the apprehensions of anaesthesiologists, scrub nurses and surgeons well. The team looked around at one another.

'Fucking hell. I never been to surgery in all my life and seen that we are not prepared for any basic thing. What are you, amateurs or something? This is a fucking joke that you couldn't prepare. Andrea, couldn't you perform any basic drug calculations you...'

'Listen, Nigel, I was dragged into this mess by yourself and your schemes.'

'My schemes? My schemes,' Dr Nigel Johnson shouted. Dr Nigel Johnson tried not to flap his arms around angrily breaking aseptic procedural protocol. 'The patient has a Chondrosarcoma and needs surgery to remove her right leg, below the knees plus perform a left leg amputation below knees and two below elbow arm amputations to prevent it from spreading. Fuck my life woman. Do you not even know how to be an anesthesiologist?'

Andrea scowled with a look of the eyes that could melt ice. 'I would be careful about what you say about me. Since the anestheologist controls practically everything the patient needs. Oxygen SATs, anesthesia concentration, oxygen levels, pulse rate. If I walk out, what are you going to do? There won't be anyone to negotiate the surgery to keep the patient asleep, will there. I keep her alive,' Dr Andrea May exclaimed in a position of strength.

Dr Nigel Johnson sighed and breathed in deeply. 'I concede. But I still think that this surgery is completely thrown together by a group of medical students. You all ought to be ashamed of yourselves. Surgery requires preparation and this has been thrown together. Nonetheless, let us begin. Caroline, hand me the scalpel.'

Chapter 16

Surgery comes in many varieties. Neurological surgery is a form of rocket science and computer science, rewiring a computer matrix that controls a person's existence. Cardiothoracic surgery is a form of precision engineering, a bloody wonder of the modern age, surgery leaving the patient in a limbo between death and life. Cardiothoracic surgery also is done with less anesthesia, risking anesthesia awareness or sensation and awareness of surgery. Gastroenterological surgery, the surgery of colons, appendices and stomachs is fastidious in the long hours of concentration. Laparoscopic nephrectomies are meticulous works of art, given the proximities the kidneys to the Vena Cava and Aorta. Kidneys are connected to renal arteries making haemorrhaging a potential cause of a brutal, bloody death. Gynaecological surgery is a delicate art of the reengineering of a female's most personal regions; breast surgery the proximity and intimacy of that of a husband or partner. Vascular surgery, is like plumbing inside of a nuclear reactor, requiring laser precision and a hand of grace to perform intricately delicate cuts. Plastic surgery is 21st-century sculpturing. Orthopedics, however, resembles butchery, a beautiful act of savagery, a grotesque masterpiece of calculated cuts, an attractive act of desolation. Orthopedic surgery is delightfully nauseating in its acts of barbaric splendour. The smell of burnt blood, cauterized by a surgeon permeates the air, the lingering smell is like that of a barbeque, burnt hair mixed with pork chops. Humans taste like pork.

Angelica was a helpless pork chop. The first incision into the right leg was that of a finality, decisive straight through the facia, exposing a layer of subcutaneous tissue which resembled that of strips of bacon. Utterly agony. Hellish Inferno, the pain of 100 hornets stinging simultaneously.

Dr Andrea May checked the ECG monitor and it beeped as it should. The anesthesia pump acting as a diaphragm sucked oxygen, nitrous oxide and halothane into the lungs. Pulse rate was stable, blood pressure of 90 over 60. Dr Andrea May was not too worried about the potential hypovolemic shock as the tourniquets had been applied pre-operatively. Still, given that it was borderline hypotension, Dr Andrea May should have been slightly more concerned. Dr Nigel Johnson cut the muscle to the tibia and transected the anterior and lateral compartment muscles on Angelica's right leg, making a large flap of skin that dangled away from the muscle.

'Tweezers please,' Dr Nigel Johnson said.

The scrub nurse, Caroline Cockbain handed Dr Nigel Johnson a set of tweezers, where he pulled apart muscles, tissue and nerves. Tumultuous torment. Dr Nigel Johnson divided the peroneal nerve with the tweezers, separating from the anterior tibial vessels. It was an artistic act of savagery; blood stained the gloved hands a hellish-crimson. After the nerves had been protracted and separated, Dr Nigel Johnson then proceeded to ligate the various nerves that ran adjacent to the tibia in the subcutaneous tissue, tearing away at the various vessels and nerves in Angelica's leg.

'Cauterizer, please,' Dr Nigel Johnson exclaimed.

Caroline Cockbain handed Dr Nigel Johnson an electro-cauterizer and Dr Nigel Johnson proceeded to cut away at the subcutaneous tissue.

'Retractors.'

Dr Nigel Johnson proceeded to cut away at the periosteum, revealing the tibia. The muscle and tissue surrounding the bone had been slashed away, leaving just the bone and large hole between that and the fibula. Unending agony.

'Bone saw please,' Dr Nigel Johnson said.

The sound of the bone saw penetrating through the bone was that of carpenter's workshop. Dr Nigel Johnson cut through the tibia with finality, severing it as if it was a block of lumber. The only connection was that of the fibula underneath. The leg was dangling from the muscle and skin, looking like a piece of butchered meat. After hooking out the leg, Dr Nigel Johnson divided the fibula with the bone-saw, before using a large knife to cut the muscle adjacent to the fibula and tibia, which left around 20 ounces of leg-steak for Dr Nigel Johnson to close the wound with. Angelica's leg was placed in a clear-bag and was sent to the pathology for cancer analysis. After repairing the incision, Dr Nigel Johnson sighed.

'One limb, three more to go,' Dr Nigel Johnson said in a weary voice.

'Are you sure you want to carry on with the surgery given that if we amputate her arms and another leg as well, she may be able to sue us?' Dr Jacob Johnson asked Dr Nigel Johnson. Dr Nigel Johnson glared at Dr Jacob Johnson in the eye.

'You haven't been paid by me to just stop the operation here. Russell Portin has paid $250,000 for each limb to be removed. Hardly going to stop this procedure here am I?' Dr Nigel Johnson scoffed arrogantly. 'If you want to leave, you can but you signed your contract to stay until the end of the surgery.'

'Of course...'

'Continue as normal. Nurse, scalpel. Time to remove Angelica's left leg.'

The removal of the second leg was more macabre than the first. A completely healthy bone was to be removed for no other reason than because of a $250,000 price-tag Russell Portin had placed on a quadruple amputation. Dr Andrea May was slightly jittery at the thought of the unnecessary surgery that they were doing, her arms tingled in fear every time Dr Nigel Johnson cut through the bone with the oscillating saw. Some of the surgical staff looked at each other awkwardly at the desolation that was being inflicted. Once Dr Nigel had removed the other leg, he proceeded to the arms.

First, Dr Nigel Johnson made a below elbow incision on the right arm, identifying and then ligating the cephalic vein. Dissections were made deeper into the tissue in the arm before Dr Nigel Johnson recognized the radial artery. The radial artery was ligated and dissected back. Slicing deeper into the muscle, the radian nerve was identified and dismembered. The continuation of the disabling desolation included the ulnar nerve being ligated and severed back, the ulnar artery ligated and cut. Dr Nigel Johnson slashed deep into the muscles and exposed the ulna.

'Bone saw,' Dr Nigel Johnson uttered.

With the bone saw, Dr Nigel Johnson cut through the ulna, finally removing the arm. He repaired the damage before beginning the process on the other arm. At the end of the surgery, the masterpiece of beautiful sculpting, a quadruple amputee, wheeled out of the operating room. Her face was covered by a mask and she was still in an unconscious state. The April 12th, 2019 was to completely change the life of Angelica. Now, after the months of waiting and arguing, falling out with friends, she was what she wanted to be. A quadruple amputee. Dr Nigel Johnson grinned at the large $1,000,000 monetary transfer he was going to receive.

Waking up from surgery, to find that you have no arms or legs is a horrific event for someone to deal with. The bleeping of the cardiographic heart monitor in the background, Angelica gradually became aroused from her sedated state. She looked around the room at the various doctors and nurses. Looking down at her body, it felt as if her heart was completely torn in to. Angelica was distraught, crying out in the realization that they had finally amputated her arms and legs. She sunk down into her stumped arms and curled up into stumped fetal position, bawling out in raw emotion.

'I am an absolute fool,' she screamed, uncontrollably. 'Oh, why did I decide to have surgery? What was the point?'

Angelica was inconsolable. None of the nurses could attempt to comfort her in her absolute agony. Michael was conveniently away from the agony of his wife Angelica.

'Where is Michael?' Angelica shouted.

'Umm. He is out at the moment. Look, you decided due to your life being in danger...'

'But I didn't have to have all my limbs amputated. What was I thinking? I was being so stupid in my thinking!' Angelica exclaimed.

Michael, the husband who did not wait for his wife to come around from surgery, arrived 2 hours after Angelica had come around from the anesthesia. When he saw the stumped limbs of his wife, who resembled a soggy teddy bear, he smiled at the accomplishment.

'Michael, where have you been?' Angelica cried.

'Sorry Angelica, I was working…'

'I have had my legs and arms amputated and you were working? How could you?'

'You need to understand. It was not my choice to work when my little sweetheart had some major surgery. But I had no choice given that we are running low on money. Our health insurance company National America Health phoned this morning when you were in surgery. They wanted to talk about the procedure you had today and they are sending an agent to you tomorrow.'

'Well, you should have told them to go away.'

'Well, given the fact they are paying for the procedure, I wouldn't be so rude. They said there was a problem with the classification of the procedure regarding their coverage for health conditions.'

'What? What do you mean?' Angelica exclaimed.

'They won't cover procedures that do not address a health condition. They said to me that they would discuss it to you tomorrow with the agent who comes to visit you.'

'They will provide treatment, right? They can't just pull coverage like that…'

'Did you even contact National America Health to talk to them about the procedure before you decided to continue the surgery?'

Angelica was worried. Surely, NAH would be contacted by the hospital, by Dr Nigel Johnson that he was doing the surgery on her. Angelica may not have contacted them, but she couldn't remember if she did or not.

The fact that she didn't remember doing it perhaps meant she didn't do it.

'Oh, dear. What if they not pay-out our health insurance for this procedure? Surely, we have the money,' Angelica whined to Michael.

Michael looked outside the room to the world outside, to the vermillion-golden sunset and to the joggers who were on their late afternoon jog. He sighed loudly and looked back at his amputee wife who lay on the bed.

'If they come back and say to us that your coverage has been rejected, we'll have to sell our house and downsize immediately. We don't have the money to cover the surgery. Thankfully, our house is worth quite a bit in value so we can sell that and downscale.'

Angelica's heart sank like a ship that hit an iceberg. When she first received the news, she thought that she would become better off, that she was taking back control of her body and gaining a decision over her life. Now, she was powerless, her life handed over to her husband to control. Now, she was merely Michael's pawn. Surely, her life insurance Laurence and Johnson would pay-out enough to cover the surgery but also to pay for prosthetics.

'What about prosthetics?' Angelica cried to Michael.

Michael laughed coldly, 'You can forget about them. If our health insurance does not pay-out for the procedure, we will be having to make massive cutbacks in our life. No more vacations. We will sell your car. No more day trips by yourself but that will obviously go since you can't do anything by yourself.'

Angelica becomes upset again. Michael smoothed her hair.

'Leave me, Michael! Why do you only think of yourself?' Angelica cried.

'Me thinking of myself? What a ridiculous accusation. It was *you* who attacked your friends and family over not supporting your choice to take back control. No one else made that choice…'

'But you forced me in the end to have surgery! You made me go through with it!'

The medical staff looked awkwardly at each other but did not interfere with Angelica's and Michael's argument. Michael frowned, his eyes becoming that of an aggressive owl, his mouth clenched with anger.

'It is all my fault, is it? I supported you through the entire process right up until today. You have cut yourself off from people. You ignored people, you ignored healthcare professionals including your family doctor. Why is it my fault that you decided to have your limbs amputated? At the end of the day, you chose it on yourself,' he exclaimed agitatedly.

Angelica realized that she, in the end, made the choice to have her limbs amputated. There was a sense of amnesia from the beginning of the day. She couldn't remember how she went down to the operating room and didn't remember the surgery itself. Grimacing, she felt a sharp pain in her leg as if someone was sawing through her leg and it made her think of having a nightmare of being awake in surgery. Yet this was nothing more than just a nightmare, Angelica thought to herself.

'It is my fault. I did decide it. I was wrong,' Angelica whimpered to herself.

Michael grinned to himself, 'Yes. But don't worry cupcake. I am with you now. I will protect you. You are *mine* now,' Michael smiled, embracing his stumped wife in a tight, encroaching cuddle.

Angelica sniffed away her tears and kissed her husband on the cheek. Michael had gotten Angelica exactly where he wanted her. Taking back control never meant taking back control. It just meant dependence on other people. Angelica would now be dependent on Michael for her existence. No matter what Michael did from now on, Michael had complete assurance that Angelica was dependent on him as a person.

'If we do have to sell up, that isn't a big deal. Because I will always have you, Angelica. That is all I want.'

The day after surgery, Angelica lay in her room looking up at the ceiling. Bandages covered the stumps that she had as limbs. Michael stood at the window, looking outside at the people that were passing, watching a world go by. Angelica had sobbed for a while. She realized what being an amputee now was. Everything that she could do in the past, brushing her hair, washing, cleaning her teeth, changing her clothes, moving around with her legs, even watching television or answering a cell-phone, she could no longer do. Tablets and smart cell-phones thankfully allowed voice control, so she had some independence with her tablet and smart cell-phones. But with everything else, she had no control over her life. There was a knock at the door.

'Come in,' Michael and Angelica said in unison.

A woman dressed in a suit entered. She had tied back blonde hair, appearing to be in her thirties, a similar age to Angelica herself. Sharp lightning blue eyes which were electrifying looked around the room and glared at the stumped woman on her bed before looking back at the man in the window.

'Hello. I am Ms Christianson. I am the Insurance Agent from NAH responsible for following up procedures that are filed by our customers. We have received a health insurance claim of $65,000 plus $15,000 for aftercare costs of hospital stay. Can you explain to me about your health condition and why you needed treatment?' the woman said, writing on her tablet computer.

'Well, I had a Chondrosarcoma on my right foot. I contacted the surgeon Dr Nigel Johnson and he recommended a quadruple amputation. I made preparations for that surgery and it was performed yesterday on March 29th 2019,' Angelica stated.

'Did you contact us before the surgery?' the woman asked coldly.

'I don't remember that.'

'Our system has no recollection of you contacting us about the procedure. No discussions with any of our staff. We have looked through your medical records for the last few months and we can identify a visit to your family doctor Dr Gina Benjamin-Cruz. We have contacted her and she made us aware that she completely advised against you having surgery because she deemed it wholly unnecessary to a quadruple amputation,' Ms Christianson stated.

'Have you contacted my surgeon to explain to him about this? Dr Nigel Johnson would argue that it was necessary,' Angelica said, becoming upset.

'We have contacted multiple other orthopedic surgeons and doctors that we have as advisors to consult on various medical conditions so we can provide the best insurance coverage. They thought that the surgery you had was also wholly unnecessary. We as a company do not give out insurance payments to people who have unnecessary surgery but also, we would not be covering your surgery on the basis that you did not contact us before the surgery.'

Angelica's heart thudded against her chest as if she had seen an apparition of some kind. 'What do you mean that you won't cover the surgery?' Angelica demanded.

'You violated our terms and conditions of our healthcare contract Clause 3 sub-article 6 a), All patients must contact the health insurance company regarding all treatment that they will receive. Clause 6 sub-article c), NAH does not cover surgery deemed unnecessary by medical personnel including and not limited to advise from doctors, surgeons, nurses and other registered healthcare professionals. NAH has full right to suspend cover to such surgery. We, therefore, feel that you have violated our terms and conditions and are therefore liable for the full healthcare costs.'

Angelica looked at Michael who looked at Ms Christianson, 'I guess we will have to put our house on the market then,' Michael said.

'How can you do that? I have just had surgery and you are now saying we are libel to large amounts of healthcare costs?' Angelica wailed.

The woman shrugged her shoulders. 'I do a job to talk to patients about their healthcare so that NAH does not have to pay for unnecessary procedures. That is the healthcare system.'

The absurdity of US healthcare. A surgeon can do unnecessary surgery. The patient then receives no coverage for that treatment, despite it not being their fault. However, Angelica was fully aware of the treatment package. After all, she signed the Article 50 healthcare liability form. In some ways, she knew about the potential of the surgery. This is what she had elected to have. Angelica's fault was her own.

Russell Portin slurped on a chocolate milkshake, sucking it up like it was an oil field. Dr Nigel Johnson, dressed in scrubs and a white lab coat joined him at the table. It was one the Baptist University of Texas hospital's restaurants, selling pizzas, hamburgers, soda and milkshake among its highly nutritious menu items. The restaurant was filled with various healthcare professionals and visitors. It had the feel of a diner, the staff walking around with coffee, the seating was that of an uncomfortable 50s leather sofa. It appeared to be rather clean though that was more to do with hospital procedures than actual business intention.

'Greetings,' Dr Nigel Johnson said, smiling at Russell.

Russell put his milkshake down. 'Hi. How is surgery today?'

'Surgery is surgery. No amputations today. I had one leg reconstructive surgery for a horse rider who fell off their horse.'

'Intensive.'

'Isn't it? Anyway. How is your business going?'

'Business is business.'

'You won't talk about it?'

'Well, I have made a lot of money recently. Great when you are a registered Panama citizen,' Russell smiled.

'Our company has been incorporated. My first surgery under this company was for that quadruple amputation for the wife of our friend Michael Donaldson.'

Russell smiled. 'Michael Donaldson? He has gone into serious financial difficulties because of the surgery.'

Dr Nigel Johnson frowned. He was not happy at such a suggestion. Michael Donaldson was not supposed to go into financial difficulties after the surgery.

'How has that happened? I thought our friend Michael should not have gone into financial difficulties...'

Russell Portin grinned. He had been scheming well and knew why Michael Donaldson needed to go into debt. 'It was all part of the plan. Michael Donaldson is selling his house. Any debts and healthcare costs associated with the surgery which are now in the tens of thousands will be paid off by the house sale. Now this will mean that any healthcare costs will essentially be tax write-offs. His wife's surgery will become a tax write-off. So, given that, he will be able to sell his house, which I will immediately buy off of Michael. Michael will downsize to a smaller property. The money gained from the sale will pay off the final remainder of the surgery and the rest will be necessary for Michael to live off. All of this becomes one massive tax scheme.'

'Genius.'

'It gets better. Looking after a disabled person allows him to reclaim some more tax deductibles. All the while keeping the profits from a business trade away from the greedy hands of the Fed.'

Dr Nigel Johnson was enthralled with the sophistication of the tax scheme that Russell Portin had developed. Russell Portin had developed a tax scheme with the intricacies and strength of a spider's web. Here Dr Nigel Johnson was a mere orthopedic surgeon, earning an exceptionally high salary but now, he too had bought into Russell Portin's tax schemes. With the business that he had set up with Russell Portin, he was hoping that he could keep even more money since he no longer paid income tax and instead paid the lower capital gains tax rate.

'So, when will the money enter the business account?' Dr Nigel Johnson asked.

'Soon. I will be sending the money out this week. I believe it has already been sent. When it leaves my Panama bank account it will arrive in an account in US Virgin Islands and then on to our business account as then it will not be seen as pure money laundering. We mustn't get arrest for money laundering!' Russell sniggered.

Dr Nigel Johnson didn't smile and was concerned with those two words. Money laundering. Pushing money around the world from different bank accounts to different countries was a way of the FBI investigating you. 'Are you sure that this will not be detected for money laundering? They may see our web of money and detect a trail that leads directly back to you?'

'Well, it is possible. I have designed this scheme so that my Panama account is not detected concerning our friend in Dallas Texas. I cannot be implicated with him, though that is my Achille's Heel. I know that our web of trades goes through millions of dollars of trades. If we are implicated together, then that will be my downfall,' Russell stated glumly.

'How are you going to stop that from happening?' Dr Nigel Johnson asked.

'By making sure that our web is as distant as possible. To be honest, it has worked so far. I am Michael's "consultant" where he pays me thousands of dollars a year in "consulting" fees. Those fees are immediately deducted and moved into the Panama bank account for safekeeping away from the government. Taxation is theft. I cannot allow the government of the United States of America to take my hard-earned money from me.'

'Absolutely.'

'So, I take the money and I take it away from the government of the United States, into a foreign country where taxes are much lower than here in the US.'

'A good patriotic thing to do, avoiding your taxes.'

Patriotism, the love of one's country, has been interpreted in many ways in history. For Russell Portin and Michael, patriotism meant avoiding as much tax as possible to protect oneself from higher taxes.

This, of course, invites the interesting question; is it possible for someone to claim they are patriotic despite their actions showing the contrary? Michael and Russell did not seem to care much about the US by their actions as businessmen since both Michael and Russell acted in ways which were contrary to love their country. And yet both of them called themselves patriots. Was it possible for someone to act in a way which displayed love to one's country, despite it being a completely unloving thing to do?

'I am a good patriot and I agree that we should keep taxes to a minimum since that is a patriotic thing. I do not know though if it is patriotic to avoid paying taxes.'

'It is patriotic since keeping the state as small as possible is the patriot's desire.'

'I don't know if I agree with you on that one. Anyway, I appreciate the fact that you have set up a scheme that has helped me save money. The hospital has accepted the payment for surgery to go through this company that we have set up.'

'Just remember to not pay yourself a salary and pay out a dividend instead as dividends come under capital gains rather than income tax.'

'Agreed. And you will receive half of the money for the first payment of dividends. After that, it will reduce to half payment.'

'That is the plan.'

'What do you plan to do for the rest of the day?'

'I am going to have to plan out purchasing Michael Donaldson's house. That will involve sorting out the legal paperwork and the like to make sure that it is completely legal and more important watertight so that the FBI can't use it as evidence against me.'

'Do you know anything more about the FBI and whether they are investigating you?'

'I do not know whether they are. Their investigations are secretive. They aren't going to inform me of their presence, are they?' Russell said to Dr Nigel Johnson.

'I suppose not.'

'Any way. I shouldn't hold you up for any more of your time. I have plans to attend to regarding the sale of the house. Speak to you later.'

Russell got up and left the hospital. He drove for around 45 minutes towards the downtown of Dallas. He went was going to his lawyer's office in the center of Dallas. The office was in a skyscraper, 70 floors high, the bottom of which had a plaza with elevators going high up into the building. There palm trees and various vendors at the bottom of the complex. His office was 52 floors up so Russell took the elevator to get to the office. He let the receptionist knew that he had arrived in the building. Russell sat on the chair inside the reception. There was the plant and it was possible to look out of the window onto the street below and see the entire Dallas skyline. The sky was a golden color in the twilight late-afternoon sun. Gold was interlaced with the silvery clouds like royal clothes of coronation.

'Russell Portin, how are you doing today?' a man asked, dressed in a Prussian blue suit. It was Dean Martin, the lawyer of Russell Portin. He was a tall man and projected an aura of power; a man with of strength, a man of steel.

'I am doing well today.'

'Would you like to come in?' he asked.

'That was the plan.'

Dean Martin's office was elegant and smart. He had a glass cabinet table, an Apple computer a window that overlooked the Dallas skyline. Beside his desk was a palm tree in a pot.

'Would you like some coffee?' Dean asked Russell.

'I would love some.'

'Hi, Madison? Yeah, could you get two coffees please,' Dean said down his intercom, 'So, you want to purchase the house of Michael Donaldson your friend?'

'That is correct. I have the money whenever it is necessary to pay, I just need you to sort out the paper-work.'

'That is the plan.'

'Where do you plan to get the money for the purchase of Michael Donaldson's house?'

'I am getting it from my US registered bank account. The money is registered in dollars.'

'That seems okay. Where has that money come from?'

'I have taken it from a US Virgin Islands account.'

'There may be some questions of moving your money around, given that tax avoidance and money laundering is a consideration for the IRS.'

'There is not a problem though, I assume.'

'There might be some problems with the belief that you may be trying to buy up assets as a means to escape taxes or a way of money laundering. As long as you are transparent, nothing will be done about it.'

A receptionist entered with the two cups of coffee that Dean had asked for. The receptionist put the coffees on the desk before leaving again. Dean handed one of the coffees to Russell Portin.

'My main concern is that you don't get attention from the FBI that you are trying to move your money around the place in a way which is a form of money laundering.'

'All the money that I make in the US is known by the authorities. They know where I have got the money from and they would have charged me right now if they had the evidence, wouldn't they?' Russell Portin said.

'That is correct. I have looked over your business interests in the US and you are connected with one person in particular; Michael Donaldson. The problem that might arise from the sale is that the authorities may see this sale as a means of hiding illicit gains elsewhere,' Dean replied.

Russell smirked, 'I have nothing to hide. I have no part in any illegal activities regarding drug smuggling or anything like that.'

'The main concern is not that. It is that you will have been seen as taking part in illegal monetary activities namely tax evasion and money laundering. Do you have your bank statements for me to go through?'

'I do.'

Russell got out of a black briefcase some financial documents which he thrust towards Dean over the other side of the desk. Dean glanced through the financial documents nodding from time to time as he sifted through the material.

'Well, I can't see many faults here. It appears that your US bank account is legitimately and all the income that is coming into it is legitimate. Hmm. Yeah, I can process the house sale. There is no problem with the money side of the sale. I think we can finalize the sale by next week.'

'Why thank you. You are a very good lawyer of mine.'

The two men shook hands and Russell left the building, back to his SUV that was parked in the parking lot and left. Russell smiled at the proceedings that he was involved in. They were flawless in execution, the fact that he was able to create a buy the house that was owned by his "friend" Michael Donaldson without it looking particularly suspicious when regarding money laundering or tax evasion. Still, Russell had to be careful and not let his guard down. He knew that he was being watched, feeling the breath of the Fed on him everywhere he went like an all-consuming leviathan.

Chapter 17

'You sold our house?' Angelica screamed. She had been in agony all night, having had serious limb pain across her stumped-limbs. Worse were nightmares of being in agony and being conscious whilst her limbs were being amputated. They were just dreams, the medical staff had been saying. Nothing particularly problematic but she kept saying that she was in agony in the dreams and the agony continued until she woke up.

'We have no alternative. It was that or we would have to declare bankrupt from the healthcare costs of the surgery...'

'Why, why... why... Did I even have the surgery?' Angelica cried, curling up into a fetal position in her bed. Michael didn't embrace her this time around.

'The Texas Baptist University Hospital contacted me saying that the NAH had said that they would not be paying for the surgery and that we would need to find $85,000 for the surgery and aftercare. We don't have the money for that so we have to sell up our house to pay for it. We bought our house for $400,000. We are selling it for $650,000 and deducting taxes should have enough for us to pay for the healthcare costs and enough for us to get by.'

Angelica slumped into her bed at the news. 'Have we got somewhere we can go?'

'We'll have to find somewhere which is less glamorous than before. We aren't going to have a swimming pool where we live now. All of our luxuries, our vacations will have gone. Luckily, I have found somewhere for us to go.'

'So, what? We have nothing now. We have lost our house. Why was I even born?' Angelica whined.

'We have each other. That is the main thing right. You and me. That is all that is necessary,' Michael smiled to Angelica. Angelica frowned, looking up at the ceiling.

A nurse dressed in sapphire-blue scrubs entered the room. She was carrying a clipboard, wearing glasses and appeared to be around Angelica's age, perhaps a bit younger.

'How are we doing today, Angelica?' she asked, looking at her clipboard. Angelica did not respond to the nurse's prompt.

'Is everything okay Angelica?' the nurse asked, looking at Angelica who appeared to be despondent and upset.

'I keep having nightmares…. Of being operated on. I feel my legs and arms being cut off, I hear horrible sounds and smell hellish burning as if my hair was being burned on a barbeque,' Angelica cried. It was no use to curl up since she was stumped.

The nurse was quietly concerned at what Angelica was telling her, making notes on her clipboard.

'Can you describe the sensation and the nightmare to me…'

'Oh, its agony,' Angelica whined, trying to stop herself from crying. 'I feel cuts into my limbs when I am asleep. I smell what genuinely smells like my hair has been smothered onto a barbeque and hear people talking in the background. I heard electric saws and felt burning across my limbs.'

'Oh, dear. I will say something to Dr Nigel Johnson about these dreams you are having. He may be able to pop around later to talk to you,' the nurse said nervously.

She left the room as if she had nothing else to do in the room. Angelica turned to Michael who smiled at Angelica. A frown that could soar milk came across Angelica's face.

'So, you have sold the house and now what?' Angelica groaned.

'We'll rent for a while to get ourselves the money to be able to buy a property again. Given that I was able to sell the house this quickly, we have saved ourselves from bankruptcy. We will have to accept a lower standard of living for a while.'

'I can't believe it has come to this. What about my pay-out? Wasn't I going to get a pay-]out?'

'I haven't heard anything from the life insurance people…'

'Phone them up right away! I am not going to lose my legs and arms only for us to have to sell up our house for nothing,' Angelica said aggressively.

'Okay, I will get back to them. In the meantime, we need to talk about wheelchairs. I expect that we should get a motorized wheelchair for you to get around the room...'

'What about prosthetic limbs? Why can't I get limbs for me to be able to move about in?'

Michael laughed awkwardly. Prosthetic limbs weren't a priority. They had been unable to negotiate any deal where Angelica was able to get prosthetic limbs. This was one of the reasons why Angelica had the surgery, to begin with; that she was able to get either prosthetic limbs or what she was hoping for which was bionic limbs. With bionic limbs, Angelica would be able to have a normal life without the need to replace her limbs with real limbs from a transplant. However, there had been no suggestion that bionic limbs would actual happen, no more than this being a pipedream, blue-sky thinking of the future. There may have been bionic limbs 15 or 20 years from then, but for Angelica in the present, there was no conciliation. She was not going to have any limbs and would be stuck with stumps as limbs for the forcible future.

'Um, honey, I don't think we will be able to afford any prosthetic limbs. We don't have the money right now. We are not well off to say the least. With the money we have spent on your healthcare, we are looking around $30,000-$50,000 in the bank. That won't be enough for any prosthetic limbs or bionic limbs. We will just have to get by with what we have got.'

Angelica cried. She felt this impending sense of regret, that she regretted even having the surgery and signing the surgical consent form known as Article 50. If only she had not signed the Article 50 consent form. This was what it all had come down to, her delusion of grandeur, the belief that God had been talking through the television into her having her legs and arms amputated and ultimately, her undying delusion that she had to have the surgery and that she could not revoke Article 50 because of the payment of $4,000 and the fact that she would still have cancer inside of her bones. This, of course, would not be easily ignored. She could not simply allow herself to forget the failures that she was responsible for, that she had failed to heed the advise of her friends and family that all persuaded her not to carry on with the surgery.

'How foolish have I been that I would not have sorted out another surgeon or sort other treatment options. I have been so wrong...'

'Don't beat yourself up overthinking you made the wrong choice. You have had your limbs amputated. So, what? Many people have their limbs amputated every year...'

'No one willing has all their limbs amputated, Michael.'

'But you have had a very aggressive form of cancer that was going to kill you if you did nothing. You did the right thing. Never consider the alternatives, the what-ifs, that there were other choices out there. Amputation means amputation. There is not an easy prospect, no easy way out of it. You made the difficult choice to have all your limbs amputated to save your life because we both know that life is precious a gift from God,' Michael said, lying to Angelica about why she had the surgery.

Michael knew that Angelica at the beginning of the treatment plan was going to have the surgery for the money. She wanted the $3,500,000 pay-out from the life insurance company. This, of course, was a completely hypothetical amount of money. It was just part of his strategy to try and make Angelica sign up for surgery, despite all of the pleas against it from her family, from the family doctor, from her friends. Now she had made the wrong decision. Michael knew that Angelica would be dependent on him. This he had been planning since the day that he was in the office with Dr Nigel Johnson. Dependence was such a position that allowed a person to exert a significant amount of power over the one who required them for their survival. Power, the ability to control or determine the outcome of situations. When people have control over people's lives to the point of dependence, then they can believe themselves to be exceptionally powerful. Michael was one such person. Michael had now positioned himself into a position of power over Angelica who now was completely dependent on Michael for her existence. And to that, he smiled. Power corrupts. Absolute power corrupts absolutely.

'When we go to our new place, things will change. I am going to have to take fewer shifts so I can look after you. You are my wife, of course. You are going to need a lot of attention and maintenance now. We will get you an electric-wheelchair so you can have some freedom of movement. Not that you will have much independence. But there again, that wasn't the point of the surgery,' Michael chuckled.
Taking back control required the complete loss of control. Amputation meant amputation. God's will must be enacted. To take control over cancer and for Angelica to survive, she had to lose all control of her life. She had lost her house, because of the healthcare bills. Complete loss of her limbs, which meant she could not act or do anything. Her friends and family were gradually abandoning her to her fate. Elizabeth talked to her before the surgery but now she was cut off completely. Taking back control meant loneliness, with only Michael as her companion. Isolated, on an island, Angelica had taken back control but lost everything else that went with it.
'It doesn't matter Michael. I hate myself. Why was I so stupid in having the surgery?' Angelica asked, her eyes filled with tears of despair. Michael didn't answer. He stroked her hair as if Angelica was his pet. Michael smiled whilst Angelica wailed inside of her, sniffing away her tears. She had nothing left. Perhaps her last hope was the life insurance company. They still hadn't contacted either Angelica or Michael. When Laurence and Johnson did contact them, maybe then it would lift her spirits. In the meantime, there was nothing to be particularly happy about. Nothing to hope for. Decline and despair were the words that could summarize the state of Angelica's existence.

A while later, Dr Nigel Johnson visited Angelica. He had heard the report from the nurse who had seen Angelica earlier in the day. He was concerned at what the nurse had said to him and wanted to chat to Angelica about her experiences. Angelica was sat in a wheelchair by the window, looking outside at the people who were running or walking their dogs on the park outside. It made her feel miserable to see other people's lives appear so much happier compared to her own life. Misery to their happiness, Angelica was no cold inside, isolated from the world that she was once part of.

'Hi Angelica, how are you feeling?' Dr Nigel Johnson asked.

'Horrible,' Angelica groaned. 'I wish that I never had the surgery. I was stupid to have all my limbs amputated.'

Dr Nigel Johnson smiled awkwardly, 'What has happened has happened. I wouldn't say it was stupid. We all make decisions...'

'I was an idiot! Why did I even listen to you and Michael?' Angelica whined.

'Angelica, Dr Nigel Johnson is trying to help you. Let us not be rude please,' Michael said aggressively.

'Why should I even listen to you...'

'I was here because I heard from one of the nurses who saw you today that you were having nightmares about the surgery. Is that correct?'

'Yes, that is true.'

Dr Nigel Johnson eyes flit to Michael who was busy looking at Angelica, before looking back at Angelica. He gulped to himself like removing his throat of a drink of strong whiskey.

'Tell me about these nightmares, what happens in them?'

'I am on the operating table and I see people in blue remove my limbs one by one. I smell a strange smell which resembles burnt hair and barbeque and I hear people talking these people talking.'

'Tell me what they are saying?' Dr Nigel Johnson asked anxiously.

'I can't work out what they are saying.'

Dr Nigel Johnson sighed with a strong sense of relief. 'Thank goodness for that. I think it some kind of mental health problem. Probably nothing too problematic. I will chat to the anestheslogist who put you to sleep and I will prescribe some anti-psychotics, most likely some Midazolam and some Olanzapine, 10 mg. Alongside this, I will proscribe anti-depressants including Fluoxetine, Citalopram and pain relief, most likely some fentanyl patches for you to wear in the day or though I could also prescribe some ketamine for pain relief. Sometimes one of the side effects of amputation can be phantom-limb syndrome, where you think that you have a limb due to the destruction of nerve endings.'

'Whatever. I don't believe that you are doing this for my benefit. I hear in the dream the word $250,000 appear...'

'It is just depression, okay?' Dr Nigel Johnson said with a fearful voice. 'It isn't anything else.'

'I doubt what you are saying is true.'

Dr Nigel Johnson did not pursue the dreams that Angelica was having with Dr Andrea May. After all, it was unlikely for it to have been anything. Dr Nigel Johnson had no reason to consider why Angelica was having these episodes. He thought they were most likely to do with depression. Whatever it was, Dr Nigel Johnson seemed largely indifferent. It wasn't going to change the situation and it wasn't going to threaten him. The money is what mattered. Everything else was a means to that end.

Chapter 18

Angelica looked out of the window, in a wheelchair that Michael had chosen for her to have. For now, Angelica had to be pushed along in it as an incapacitated crippled that she had become. Now, it had been a few weeks since she had her limbs amputated. What was the point? There was none. She had unnecessary surgery, only for her health insurance to not cover the treatment because it was unnecessary. Michael had sold the house because they could not afford the health insurance debt. Angelica faced a grim future of being completely isolated and entirely dependent on Michael. Worse was the fact, all the while Angelica was contemplating the grim future she was having, Michael, was petting her hair.

'I wish you didn't pet my hair, Michael,' Angelica whined.

'Why not my lovely cupcake?' Michael grinned, glaring at Angelica in the eye.

'I am not an animal. I am made in the image of God...'

'Made in the image of God?' Michael cackled. 'What God is a 35-year-old amputee woman married to a bankrupt man?'

'I am not God. But we are all made in his image.'

'Whatever you like to say.'

Angelica sighed mourning, still in a state of despair over her lost limbs. She had the possibility of stopping it. There were many times the amputation could have been stopped. They were never realized. For so long Angelica desired the $3,500,000 pay-out or the threat used by Article 50 Healthcare Waiver that Angelica did not ever consider changing her mind. Besides, it was God's will that she had the surgery. The Lord had willed for her to have her arms and legs amputated. If he didn't will it, it wouldn't have happened. God through the Holy Spirit had spoken through the television to her and convinced her to have the surgery. All of her friends and family that tried to convince her otherwise were like Simon-Peter, convincing Jesus not to die.

God can speak to people through all kinds of media, or so Angelica's pastor at the Dallas Evangelical Cornerstone church once said. The same way God spoke through the Bible, God could speak through the internet, the television, the radio, or so he said. This belief was so passionately woven into Angelica's theology, that it was in part the reason why she had her limbs amputated. After all, God wanted her to have no arms or legs. If he didn't, he wouldn't have allowed it to happen. He would have intervened. And yet now, she was without arms or legs. God willed it. The will of God needed to be obeyed.

Why does not God intervene? Angelica pondered depressingly. Indeed, God appeared silent as if he wasn't there at all. Angelica never really questioned God's existence. That was dangerous. Why throw your eternal salvation out of the window? And yet she wondered why God had not stopped and intervened in the situation. Could God have stopped her from having the surgery or not? Was it God's will? It must have been God's will or else it would not have happened.

'Why does God allow me to suffer?' she whispered to Michael.
'Because he does,' Michael quickly responded. Michael lacked the theological understanding of God that Angelica had. He went to church and had a sort of superficial spirituality but never the spirituality that Angelica possessed. He never really committed to the Christianity that Angelica had committed to.
'Why did God allow me to have cancer or not stop me from having my legs and arms amputated? Why did he not stop me from having this?'
'Why are you asking such questions? It is almost as if you believe that God has made a mistake or that you have made a mistake,' Michael stated.
'I have made a mistake. I wish I never had my arms and legs amputated. It was a stupid decision.'
'But you had to make the choice to survive. You were dying from your cancer. And it needed to be completely removed from your body. Taking back control was important. Amputation meant amputation. Remember that.'

'It was the wrong choice though. I could have gone to another surgeon who would not have performed a quadruple amputation. I was foolish,' Angelica whined.

Michael frowned, knowing now that Angelica completely regretted the surgery, he would struggle to make her content. With Angelica and Michael losing their house, their savings, they no longer were in the middle-class that Angelica was. The quadruple amputation had crippled their savings and the amount of money that they owned. Now, project fear was project reality.

The house was bare. The walls were skeletal-white, uncarpeted wooden floors. The sofas and chairs looked like worn-out 90s furniture. The television had been downgraded, no longer having a plasma-screen but looked also to be out of date. The entire house had gone backwards; only being a 2-bedroom single-storey villa. It lacked the middle-class charm of the previous house, which was the home of the American dream. No more American dream for Angelica. There were no tears from her as she locked up a depressive gloom inside herself. She wheeled herself through the front door in an electric wheelchair that Michael had bought. There was no more money for luxuries; the wheelchair set them back $17,000 out of their bank account. The $3,500,000 pay-out from her health insurance was nothing more than just a pipe-dream that never existed, to begin with. Her hope of having prosthetic limbs, of cybernetic limbs that had been the temptation of having the surgery. Cybernetic limbs were years away from the current year. Tears slid down Angelica's cheeks as she rode slowly through the house, noticing at how much of their things was missing. Having sold off much of their stuff to pay for the operation, Michael and Angelica were left with the bare bone realities of existence.

'Where is everything, Michael?' Angelica cried.

'I have had to sell everything. All of our stuff. We have much less than we had. But we have each other,' Michael smiled.

'Oh Michael, what a terrible mistake I have made,' Angelica reiterated, glumly.

'Kate Sunderland has agreed to help you out a few days a week for a few extra dollars in cash. Apparently, Kate has told me she is in hard times financially as her husband has been laid off from his job as a truck driver.'

'She never told me that. Why did she tell you and not me?' Angelica asked.

Michael shrugged his shoulders. 'I have been able to reduce my hours at work, so I can spend more time with you. I hope you don't mind that because of this, we will have less to go on. There will be no more fancy vacations, our lives shall have far fewer luxuries. We will not have the same lives that we once enjoyed in the past.'

Angelica could not do anything. Taking back control meant losing control of herself. Amputation meant amputation and so she was now merely a torso able of thinking and watching television. Not planning out what a quadruple amputation meant, there was no consideration about basic functions that Angelica needed to survive as an independent human being. Angelica had not discussed with healthcare professionals in great length about how she would shower, how she was to eat, to clothe herself, to go to the toilet, how she would be able to drive her car around. These issues were never fully considered by Angelica. Instead, she always believed that she would be able to receive cybernetic limbs to compensate or at least prosthetic limbs to be able to function as a human being. Now, she realized there was nothing for her.

'I am going to work tomorrow. Today, I managed to get it off,' Michael said. 'We are having pizza tonight if you don't mind.'

Angelica drove herself into the front room and looked out the window in a phased out-glare. The hope had been sucked out of her. No more desiring a better life. The hope for $3,500,000 had gone. There was little hope of being able to help herself and be able to do anything except watch television all day. The house was miles away from downtown

Dallas and so she had no hope of getting anywhere without someone driving her. Outside, Angelica noticed an unmarked white van parked outside. This van was rather inconspicuous, there but not particularly that obvious.

'I am going to watch some television if you don't mind,' Michael said.

'What are you planning on watching?' Angelica said.

'I don't know, I will just flip around.'

The usual satellite television, surrounded with conspiracy theories, duck hunting and other random programs that spewed forth on US television. Michael decided to watch a program on Canadian truckers.

'I don't want to watch this program,' Angelica protested.

'Too bad we are watching it,' Michael said.

Angelica watched television before having her legs and arms amputated, with most of the time her being able to watch programs that she wanted to watch. Now it was different. Michael was calling the shots on which programs they were going to watch. A regime change had taken place. The coup had happened; Angelica had lost control of everything. Michael was more assertive than before. This had taken Angelica by surprise. He was supportive before the surgery and now he was taking back control over the marriage that previously was more egalitarian.

'I am surprised you are like this, Michael,' Angelica whined, 'I thought you were supportive of me. I thought you would allow me to make decisions.'

'Things have changed. I now make the decisions,' Michael snapped aggressively.

Angelica frowned in disbelief and stared at him.

'You will have the entire house to yourself tomorrow other than Kate coming over to help us with some of the housework and help you with day to day things. You can watch as much television as you want, given that you can't do anything else.'

'That is unfair!' Angelica retorted.

'I am stating a fact. You can't do anything. You are helpless and you are dependent on me,' Michael grinned.

Angelica avoided eye contact with Michael, looking out the window to the street outside. Tears were welling up in her eyes but she didn't cry. Michael was unmoved, continuing to watch the television of the dull program that was on. Angelica hoped that despite the surgery, Michael would be caring towards her, but it seemed now that even he could not be trusted. Still, Angelica noticed the white van was positioned outside the house.

'Michael, why is there a white van positioned outside the house?' Angelica whimpered.

Michael looked towards the tearful Angelica, before standing up and moving towards the window. Michael glared out of the window, only for the van to drive off without any warning.

Michael was taken aback by this. They were watching him. They were hunting him down. He was evading them, for now. But it was not possible to completely hide from them. He was trying to hide from the sun in a desert. Michael could hide in the ditch for a while, in the shade. But the sun, it rises throughout the day until it is noon. At noon, the sun is high in the sky, unable to hide from. They were after him. All this hiding, the spider-web of money and deceit that he had created and now, the wolves were howling at the door.

'Those wretched vans snooping on our liberty. I need to call the cops for us to deal with them,' Michael growled.

'Who are they...'

'Never you mind. It is probably just workmen getting a bit lost. Could be anyone, to be honest. What does it matter to you?'

'I am intrigued by what they are up to. You seem awfully defensive....'

'I am upset that my life is being infringed upon! Damn Commies and the state. I am being watched...'

'Damn Commies and the state, who is watching you?' Angelica integrated.

Michael glared at the incapacitated female, before smiling and bursting out into hysterical laughter. Angelica sat and shook her head in disbelief at Michael. The laughter was disconcerting. Losing all sense of reality, Michael laughed for no reason. Pointless laughter. A sense of madness covered the intentions of Michael.

'What is the matter with you?' Angelica screamed at him.

'Nothing is the matter. Everything is fine,' Michael said, reverting to his normal self almost instantaneously.

How could Michael job from hysteria to normality so quickly? Angelica was thinking to herself. It appeared that he was trying to hide something from her. Michael was not giving anything away, however. He appeared to try and segment knowledge that he knew away from Angelica. What had he got to hide? Angelica thought. It didn't matter though. Angelica was a person who had been desolated with a quadruple amputation, reliant now for the rest of her life on Michael as her carer and breadwinner.

'Would you like a drink my cupcake,' Michael said.

Angelica sighed. 'I guess I need one.'

In the hospital, everything was done by the nursing staff and nursing assistants. They helped Angelica get dressed, brushed her teeth, helped her to the toilet, fed her, got her drinks. She, being total without any control of herself, was unable to do anything other than watch television, using the voice assistant on her mobile phone. Technology made it possible to have some kind of life without arms or legs. Or so she wished. The dream of having cybernetic limbs was now unlikely to ever happen. The $3.5 million pay-out was never real, to begin with. Angelica was now just a torso without any form of future, stuck without any hope of a better life. All because she believed amputating her limbs would bring her back control, that it would make her lots of money and that it was the divine will of God. Of course, it couldn't bring back control. A quadruple amputee with no prosthetics would be a depressing ordeal and one which was bleak. Amputation meant amputation. Angelica, continued to cry quietly, sniffling to herself that she may never be able to just simply drink a cup of water again.

Michael smiled to himself as he poured out the fruit drink into the cup. It was a bloody-scarlet cranberry and raspberry fruit juice. It had the color of arterial blood. He waltzed over Angelica and held the cup in front of her.

'Can you drink it, sweetie?' Michael sneered at Angelica.
She tried to grip a simple cup of fruit juice with her stumps and lifting it slowly, Angelica negotiated the cup of fruit juice to her mouth, awkwardly, only for herself to spill it all down her front. Michael sniggered. Angelica glared at him in a curdled look, as if she was about to burst into tears. She didn't cry; it was no use.

'Aw. Poor little girl. Can't drink a simple cup of fruit juice without spilling it down your front?' Michael cackled.
Angelica quivered but did not respond to the glaring mocks of Michael.
'Here, I will get some straws that I bought for you especially. I don't know what you are going to do when I am at work. I won't be around to make you cups of drink.'

After making another drink, Michael strolled back towards Angelica with another cup of cranberry and raspberry fruit juice, this time with a straw in it so Angelica could suck up the drink without having to grip the cup for her to drink the juice. Michael held the cup and watched Angelica incessantly drink the juice.
Angelica slurped sips through the cup, feeling humiliated that she couldn't even drink a cup by herself. Delipidated, with no functioning limbs, Angelica was a cut-down tree, left to only a stump that existed now. She could watch television, still but was unable to anything else. Angelica, a woman who was once independent, able to go out on day trips to Dallas to meet up with friends, was now able to do nothing by herself, other than use her cell-phone for voice-activated apps, watch television and listen to the radio.

'I need the toilet,' Angelica said to Michael.

'Let me help you….'

'I can do it myself…'

'You can't even drink something yourself. How are you supposed to go to the toilet by yourself?'

Angelica stared at Michael, dumb-struck by what he had said. 'You expect me to let you help me to the toilet, a simple basic function that I can do on my own? Can I not have independence on a basic issue?'

In the hospital, the issue of toileting was something that nurses helped Angelica out with. She was supported as a disabled person, permanently helped out, with the nurses pulling her undergarments down, so she could pass urine or defecate. Now, she was to take back control of her toilet habits and her toilet routines. But it appeared that Michael was right. Taking back control of going to the toilet was now problematic, to say the least. Angelica could no longer walk at all, given that both of her legs had been amputated. Once she was in the toilet, she would be unable to pull down her pants and undergarments since she had no arms to grab hold of the clothes with. Who would have thought that taking back control was so difficult? Angelica relished the potential of having new cybernetic limbs that would replace the limbs that Angelica would lose. Now, there were no cybernetic limbs. So, she was completely unable to function by herself. Taking back control meant losing all control.

'Yes, I expect you will need a hand with toileting.'

'I find it patronizing that you would want to help me toileting. I am a grown woman…'

'You try going to toilet yourself then. Go and have control of your toileting routines.'

Angelica snorted at Michael and rode her wheelchair towards the door of the toilet. Michael followed her, smiling as if he was about to laugh at his decrepit wife. Angelica positioned herself by the door of the toilet.

She attempted to open the door but couldn't because the wheelchair was positioned in front of the door. Also, she forgot she had no hands to grip the door with. Just stumps. Stumps can't grip anything. So she tried to open the door with her stumps, trying to push the handle on the door down. However, Angelica was unable to do these things. She was unable to open the door, unable to get herself into the toilet. She had become unable to do something so basic. Taking back control meant losing it.

'You are struggling to open the toilet door.'

'I am trying Michael!' Angelica aggressively retorted to Michael.

'You are unable to open the door to the toilet, how are you supposed to expect that you can gain independence in anything else? How do expect me to think that you can live independently and without the support of others if you are so crimpled, unable to act in something as basic as going to the toilet?' Michael smiled at Angelica.

Angelica was indignant and angry at Michael. 'You have left me without arms or legs for me to be free and independent!' she shouted at him.

'No Angelica, you did. After all, you wanted to have $3,500,000 pay-out from the life insurance company. You wanted to eradicate cancer and you believed that it was somehow a divine message from God himself. Your act of having your legs and arms amputated was somehow what you believed to be God's will. And you ignored your friends and family as they advised you to have a different surgeon to Dr Nigel Johnson. Not to mention refusing advise from the expert of Dr Gina Benjamin-Cruz our family physician.'

Michael had become the ultimate manipulator. Controlling the narrative like a populist demagogue. It was Michael who had persuaded Angelica to listen to Dr Nigel Johnson and persuaded her to have the surgery that Dr Nigel Johnson was offering. Now, Michael was deflecting the blame of shaping the decision that Angelica made so that it was Angelica's fault all along. Angelica was not simply going to buy, though the fact that she was responsible for the surgery. After all, he had convinced her to have the surgery. He did not need to do this other than his desire for control and obedience. Now, he had more control of Angelica than he could ever dream of. And he knew what exactly he had in mind for that control.

'Michael, it was you who advised me to have the surgery with Dr Nigel Johnson. You didn't have to have it. And what about the prosthetic limbs or the rehabilitation? You have taken me out of the hospital without any form of rehabilitation….'

'That was because we were out of money, Angelica. We have lost all that money. I had to sell our old house to get to this house. How are we supposed to afford new prosthetic limbs if we are unable to even afford to keep our old house? Healthcare is an expensive luxury that people have to pay for. It is a luxury. Not a right. That is why we are Republicans, isn't it?'

Politics when Angelica was struggling to go to the bathroom. Why did politics have to come out at such awkward times? Dr Nigel Johnson compared the surgery he was doing to Donald Trump. Now, Michael was brought up the politics of healthcare at a time when Angelica was trying to go to the toilet. Perhaps Angelica didn't believe in conservative political policies now of denying people healthcare because she now had her limbs amputated, losing a lot of her money in the process. Perhaps Angelica had lost interest in politics entirely. Or had she? Her decision to have her arms and legs amputated was after all a political decision, a decision that was influenced by politics. Religion and politics.

In the end, Michael opened the door for Angelica after having a lot of fun mocking her inability to do such a basic task. Angelica snarled, before trying to get her electric wheelchair through the door. She got it stuck. Twice, having to reverse in and out of the door multiple times.

'Have you bought a house that has not been adapted to my needs?' Angelica asked.

Preparation had been virtually non-existent. No plans of how Angelica would function without arms or legs. This lack of preparation by both Angelica and Michael was now telling. There was no consideration of what toilet Angelica needed, over what considerations she would have toileting herself. The lack of preparation was a ferry company with no ships. Now Angelica was struggling even getting into the toilet, let alone trying to go to the toilet. All the while, Angelica was now becoming even more desperate for the toilet. But toileting was never really planned for by either Angelica or Michael. For Angelica, all she wanted was to get the freedom that was gained from receiving a $3.5 million pay-out and to having a new future with cybernetic limbs. Michael did not prepare this because he was not making the choice to have his limbs amputated. It was Angelica who decided to have her legs and her arms amputated. He would never have made such a ridiculous decision.

Chapter 19

'I can't hold it in much longer!' Angelica screamed out.

'Well then go on! Go to the toilet then. Nothing is stopping you. I am not going to help you unless you want help,' Michael snapped.

Angelica managed after multiple attempts to manoeuvre the motorized wheelchair through the doorway, which was way too small for any kind of motorized wheelchair. She was struggled to use the motorized wheelchair in such small places, given she lacked the fine motor skills after losing her hands. Then she manoeuvred herself to the toilet. She attempted to climb onto the toilet seat, using her stumped arms as support, enabling her to reposition herself on the toilet. Instead, she slipped, sliding from the toilet seat, back onto her wheelchair. She groaned, desperately needing the toilet. Again, she attempted to shift herself onto the toilet. And again, she slid back into her chair.

'Oh gosh this is unbearable!' Angelica shouted with intense anguish.

'Why don't you move ...'

'Oh, would you shut up!' Angelica retorted.

'Make me... Oh, wait you can't.'

Angelica looked at Michael with a curdling stare. As she was doing it, her denim short skirt that she was wearing darkened and she began to cry. The embarrassment was setting in. The feeling of wetness became apparent to Angelica and there was a small smell permeating throughout the toilet. Urinating herself was a predictable outcome, given that Angelica had made no preparations for leaving the hospital, never mind how she would function at urinating. It was based on calculations that she would get prosthetic limbs and life insurance pay-out. Of course, none of these things was real. So, Angelica had a life-changing surgical procedure and now ended up in a puddle of her urine because of it. Michael smiled at Angelica, salaciously, with a feeling of power that he now exerted over the helpless woman.

'Aww, sweetheart. Let me clean you up.'

In her cries of embarrassment and shame, Michael stripped her entirely naked, removing all her clothes, until she just looked coldly without a smile on her face. She was hideously attractive, or so Michael thought to himself. After putting on a pair of latex gloves, he smothered Angelica's body with baby wipes, wiping her abdomen down before moving to her groin. Michael meticulously smoothed Angelica, her face cringing at the uncomfortable fact that her husband was groping her body. He was cleaning her. She was unable to clean herself after not having any arms or legs.

'You don't have to do that,' Angelica whimpered in a voice of surrender. Michael just smiled, his cold breath felt over Angelica's body.

Michael continued to clean Angelica's body. After picking up another baby wipe, Michael started to scrub Angelica's face with a baby wipe until the smothering had become suffocating. Angelica struggled away from Michael only for him to grab and hold her for him to smother her face even more.

'Stop it!' Angelica shrieked.

Michael was taken aback by the intensity of Angelica's screech, which seemed deafening and powerful. Michael after wiping down Angelica's groin put her clothes back on and allowed herself to pilot out of the toilet.

Angelica refused to talk to Michael after what he had done to her in the toilet. She sat on a sofa, without engaging with Michael, sitting staring out the window at the world outside. There was an uneasy silence between Michael and Angelica. The silence was that of the cold war. They weren't openly at war with each other, but they were no longer loving towards each other.

'What do you want for dinner? I was thinking of doing spaghetti Bolognese,' Michael said.

Angelica looked at him as if he was speaking a foreign language and shrugged her shoulders, alienated from the man that was said to be her husband. She was not going to say anything to him. What he had done was unacceptable.

'Okay, I will get us spaghetti Bolognese then,' Michael said quietly.

Michael went out into the kitchen. He rarely cooked before Angelica had the surgery. He was about to cook dinner after years of never cooking. *No worries*, Michael thought to himself. *I have learned to cook before Angelica had her surgery and I have read a lot of cooking books and recipes when she had the surgery.* So, Michael, being the improviser that he was started to cook the food. Chopped onions and garlic before frying them. Grated carrots; mixed in some minced beef to the fried garlic and onions before adding grated carrots. So far, so good. Added some herbs and chopped tomatoes before putting some spaghetti into boiling water. *Great*, Michael thought to himself, so Michael decided to sit down and watch some more television. This time, Michael watched some garbage television of typical reality tv, much to the disgust of Angelica who wanted to watch yet more of her religious television programs. Angelica did not aggressively reply to Michael, did not grumble. She just glared at him briefly before continuing to watch the television.

Michael had forgotten to keep an eye on the dinner he was making. Watching the television, the water boiled over on the spaghetti, whilst the Bolognese partially burnt. When Michael went back in the to the kitchen, he realised that a large amount of his dinner that he had cooked had been ruined.

'Oh no my dinner is ruined,' Michael shouted.

'What has happened?' Angelica shouted back at Michael.

Michael walked into the living room carrying his burnt Bolognese sauce, which had black bits of carbon in it.

'Well, this is dinner,' Michael replied.

Angelica frowned. Michael who was now the cook and he like a British politician had made a complete mess of the cooking. Not something that she was going to enjoy. At the dining table, Michael was feeding Angelica as a baby, swivelling up the undercooked spaghetti which was crunchy and spooning it into her mouth. She did not show any kind of appreciation to this, as he continued to feed her, as she might as well wear a diaper the amount of mollycoddling, she was receiving. Undignifying was an understatement. She no longer had independence. Gaining her freedom meant losing it, whilst taking back control meant giving total control to her husband. Her husband seemed to enjoy this new power gain. There had never been a power-struggle between Angelica and Michael but for some reason, Michael seemed to enjoy this complete asymmetry of a relationship. Michael now completely controlled Angelica. She was now his doll, his teddy bear, completely and unable to act without Michael. Michael was the dominator, the overlord in the relationship. A patriarch.

'Tomorrow, I am going to measure you and buy new clothes for yourself.'

'Why? I don't need clothes. Why are you wasting money on new clothes? Are you trying to bankrupt us?' Angelica sniffled.

'No. I am not actually. Besides, what are you going to do?'

'I can scream.'

'That is, it? Scream? Hardly a revolution or a revolt of sorts. Screeching isn't going to stop the elitist takeover, is it?' Michael grinned and cackled.

'Well you don't own me, do you?' Angelica grizzled.

'Own is a strong word. A dictator doesn't own his country, does he? He allows private property after all. Neither does a general own his soldiers. But I do have a lot of say over what now happens to you. You are mine now,' Michael smirked. Michael smirked at the helpless position of his wife. What was she going to be able to do against him? The control he possessed was almost total since she now depended on him for survival.

'Why do you boast of your control over me? What do you gain? I thought you loved me?' Angelica replied; her face full of fear.

'I do love you. The same way a person loves their favorite toy, I love you. You are mine and nothing can take you away from me.'

'Yes, but I want to have my own life...'

'You can't escape the realities of life. You have no arms or legs. So, you are best to just let me look after to you. Try to relax.'

'How can I relax, when you have a control-complex and a desire to own me?'

'Well, there is nothing you can do now. So, let me tell you what we are going to do tomorrow. The plan for tomorrow is this, I will get you up. I will wash you and put clothes on you. I will put makeup on you and make you your breakfast. After that, I will brush your teeth before going to work. After I come back from work, I will get a tape measure out and measure you up for new clothes that I am going to buy for you.'

'What about my choices for tomorrow?'

'You can try doing them if you want. Perhaps Kate will help you.'

'You will spend all of our money if you are not careful,' Angelica whined.

'Oh don't you worry about that,' Michael laughed, 'the money is not of your concern.'

I have plenty more dollars in the bank. Money is of no concern. I make thousands of dollars a day from Forex, commodity selling and stock options. Don't think we will run out, he said to Angelica in his head.

Angelica scowled at Michael and indicated that she wanted to be put back into the living room with the tilting of her head. She did not want to speak to Michael, which pleased Michael a lot. He was on his laptop computer for the rest of the evening, looking over trades that were ongoing on his. After placing some orders on a financial trading website, Michael turned off his laptop and smiled. His work colleague Russell Portin was going to be meeting Dr Nigel Johnson again tomorrow and hoped to settle a few things out.

Chapter 20

'I don't think it's working Russell,' Dr Nigel Johnson said.

'What do you mean?' Russell replied.

Dr Nigel Johnson and Russell were meeting in a café in downtown Dallas. The café was filled with bearded hipsters. Not the sort of people that Russell would associate with Russell or Dr Nigel Johnson. But hiding in a place like this was Russell's choosing. There were always eyes watching him. Russell was sipping his latte whilst Dr Nigel Johnson had an Americano. Russell was always trying to blend into his surroundings.

'The hospital rejected my application to wholesale renegotiate contracts I have with them. Their letter said they refuse to do business to external contractors in critical situations such as surgery deeming inadequate safeguards on patient safety as the main concern...'

'What about the last surgery then?' Russell said frustratedly.

'The money has gone through. The surgery paid for Angelica had gone. But they have rejected doing away with the contracts I already have.' Russell sank back in his chair and smiled, 'You could just move to another hospital and see if they will accept your contracts.'

'I could. The surgery wouldn't affect reemployment?'

'No. Why would it?'

'What if she was aware of the surgery?'

'Michael has not told me anything about it. I think we are safe. Believe me. I have things that the Fed us trying to hunt me down on. You shouldn't worry about it. Really. Let us chat about the company. That is what I here for. Tell me, what are you going to do with this refusal to renegotiate the contract with the hospital?'

Dr Nigel Johnson sighed to himself, pinching his face and groaning. He wasn't that concerned about the renegotiation of his contract more than the potential costs of being sued or even going to prison in an expensive law cause that Russell Portin had no interesting in trying to suppress or stop.

'I feel you are just trying to waste my time, Russell. You are not interested in stopping the potentially dangerous nature of a scandal that could end my career. Why don't you at least pay attention?'

'Because it is completely overblown. I feel it is not something I am worried about. Please. Why are you so worried about it? After all, Michael has said nothing to me about the problem. Why does it matter you?'

'It is the one thing that could end us...'

'I don't think it is. Now let us talk about renegotiating your contract shall we...'

Dr Nigel Johnson became exasperated. 'Look if you are not going to take an interest in the potential of this, then I won't expand the company, I won't move elsewhere. Case closed.'

Russell Portin glared at Dr Nigel Johnson, 'Do you want me to ask Michael?'

'What a silly question. You are Michael, aren't you?'

'Yes. I am.'

'Why do you pretend to be two people when you are with me?'

'I am carrying my Panama passport,' Russell said, 'the fed may always be watching me. I have to   pretend I am someone else when I am in a public place...'

'I will never understand you, Michael. It seems very pointless to me.'

'Nothing is ever pointless. Believe me when I tell you about having two personas. It is useful particularly in public.'

Michael smiled, sipping his latte before letting out a large sigh of relief. 'I have always separated both Russell Portin and Michael Donaldson. They never were in the same room together because we are both the same.'

Michael touched his eyes and removed the contact lenses he was wearing, showing his oasis blue eyes that he usually had. 'So, let me tell you about Angelica. There is no problem yet of the nightmares that she was having previously. She has not mentioned it to me. She has struggled to go to the toilet and has become rather angry at the fact that I have taken control of more power. But she is powerless. She has not had any flashbacks whilst at home so far. I am not worried about her.'

'That is what all I wanted to know.'

'Now, can we finally talk about the business.'

Dr Nigel Johnson looked at his phone and shook his head. 'No. I can't. Not now. I have to go back to the hospital.'

'Well, thanks anyway. I will get back in touch soon about it...'

Dr Nigel Johnson stood up and walked away. 'Yeah, whatever you want. Speak to my secretary. See if I care.'

Michael walked out of the café, walking to put the contact lenses back into his eyes. He decided not to. After all, he was driving home and seeing Angelica and he could not let her know of the split personality that he had. He was planning to do some trading in the afternoon. There was nothing he needed, after all, he had been pretending that he was on a reduced income for a few months.

Once at home, Michael was planning to get Angelica new clothes. He wanted to measure her so that he could get the right clothes size for her or so he said. Angelica was not being cooperative in the situation.

'I don't need any new clothes,' Angelica whined to Michael. 'We don't have the money for new clothes... Why am I having new clothes...'

'Because I said so and you are. I need to get the tape measure out to measure your body size accurately so they can make custom made clothes for a quadruple amputee.'

Angelica was bemused and angry, 'Why do you need to get specially made clothes for me? There is no reason for this. You don't need to do this. I don't want any new clothes and you are burning our money by doing them.'

'Don't worry about the money,' Michael said, 'We have plenty of it. Believe me...'

'So why did we sell our old mansion then!' Angelica bellowed furiously.

'Because it wasn't suitable for a disabled person,' Michael lied like a politician, 'you needed to have a new house because the last house we had was not suitable.'

Gaslighting. Angelica remembered that they sold the last house simply to pay for the surgery. Yet, now Michael was saying the real reason was that the last house was not suitable. And he had a point. The last house was rather unsuitable for a wheelchair. But at the time, there was no conversation about moving because of the new profound disability; the conservation was about money. The change of *why* Angelica and Michael moved houses was a subtle change of the argument. Ideas and reasons change over time but this was a change.

'That wasn't the reason Michael and you know that. I remember we left because we lacked money...'

Michael put his hand on her shoulder and smiled at Angelica. 'Aww. You poor thing. Your memory must be affected by the propofol and morphine that was injected into you. I never said that. We moved because we couldn't live in our old house anymore.'

Michael smiled at the grimace of Angelica whose own memory had been destabilized, thrown out in a coup d'état. The narrative now changed at whim by Michael was that had sold the old house because it was unsuitable for her. This, of course, was completely different from the original claim. Michael may as well have been the president of the USA because he could simply change the narrative and expect no response. Now, Angelica was questioning her memory.

'Michael, I explicitly remember that we sold our house because we lacked the money.'

'Memories can be false. That was a false memory,' Michael smiled.

'I am sure it is true. I remembered it.'

'No. Not true.'

'I need the toilet,' Angelica whined.

'Say that I am right and I will help you to toilet let.'

Angelica gritted her teeth, 'I won't just say that you are right because I know what you said and we sold the house because we didn't have the money for surgery.'

'Well take yourself to the toilet then. If you want to believe false lies that you made up, be my guest. But the truth is we moved because the last house was not suitable for a disabled person in a wheelchair.'

'Well, I need the toilet. Can you help me, please?'

'No. Because you are making lies up about me and what I said,' Michael replied in a serious interrogating voice, 'and until you can confirm what I said and say that I did say that we sold our house because you were getting the surgery, then I will not help you.'

Michael left her in a state of needing the toilet for 10 to 15 minutes walking back now and then, to see if she had changed her mind and accepted his ideas.

'Ohh Michael, I need the toilet,' Angelica cried. Tried as she might, she failed and a damp patch appeared around her groin. She looked tearfully at Michael who almost was about to laugh but held his mocking laugh in. 'Michael...'

'Well all you have to do is tell me that what I said was right and correct. Just believe what I said.'

'Michael...' Angelica cried.

'No good. You can get your own clothes on...'

'I can't.... I have no arms.... I am pathetic... You are right,' she cried in a tone of submission, of defeat. The misery was grinding. There was no use challenging what couldn't be challenged. Michael was right all along, they had moved because she was now disabled. It was never about the money. Who cared how much money Michael had? Michael put on a pair of latex clothes and cleaned off Angelica in a clinical fashion, before drying her off and leaving her on the bed. Naked.

'Thank you,' she said to him.

The power relations had shifted. Michael smiled. The fact she even said thanked Michael showed that he controlled the relationship. As Michael cleaned Angelica up, a small smile appeared on his face as he looked at the discordant grimace of Angelica. Angelica couldn't face or look at Michael, look at the husband who attempted to control her, her face filled with the pain and anguish of her new status as an object of her husband's pleasure. Angelica submitted to her husband reluctantly. Now she lacked control, Michael could do what he liked to her. It was a dream, his utter desire for domination and submission. Sex meant to control and penetration meant domination; the invasion and occupation of space of proximity. The annexation and control of his wife's body were gradually being fulfilled.

   'I think you will look good in your new clothes Angelica. It is time for new you. For you to become the wife that I have desired for years,' Michael smiled, as he tenderly put on the clothes of his silently grimacing wife. 'I always wanted to have control of this relationship. A wife must submit to her husband and you must submit to me. Amputation means amputation. Domination means domination and submission means submission.'

Angelica avoided eye contact with Michael for the rest of the day, looking away from him when he tried to engage with her with and stayed silent when he was about to speak to her. If wasn't going to show kindness towards her, Angelica would not engage.

Chapter 21

Memories are the fuel of mankind. Memories instigate happiness, pleasure and nostalgia, the fuel that drives passionate delusions of grandeur. Memories are also nightmares of past recollections, the agony of past decisions and traumas. For Angelica, the memory of amputation was that of torture. Some nights were the blissful sweet delicacies of sleep which were largely uninterrupted, the sleep of that of anaesthesia. Unaware of the past as propofol blocks memories and awareness. Other nights were hellish imaginations of trauma; vivid. Lying on her bed, she was completely paralysed, unable to move under the torment of the nightmarish visions that she endured. These horrendous imaginations she would experience happened to her at night and sometimes in the day. The sound of the hospitalized bleep of the ECG machine followed by the sounds of people talking, the sensation of choking, unable to breathe as if her breathing had stopped. There was the smell of burnt hair, so pungent to almost make Angelica puke up phlegm. Then there were the voices talking about things that Angelica did not understand.

What is Russell Portin paying us?

He is paying you all handsomely, perhaps a six-figure salary to each one of you.

Who is Russell Portin? Angelica screamed out in her agony. And then came the affliction of the wail of bone saws. The ordeal was excruciating agony as the saws severed the limbs of Angelica all for Angelica to wake up bawling in utter pain and fear, for her to look at her limbless body that she now owned as a mistake that had been created through this process.

Throughout these episodes that Angelica was afflicted by, Michael had become confused and bewildered by the experiences that she experienced on the various nights of the week.

'What is wrong Angelica?' he said to her in a startled voice.

'Oh, the agony!' she cried out in genuine pain before bursting into tears, 'I felt them cutting off my arms and legs... I felt the surgery... it was torture.'

This cry out in the middle of the night from the terrors she faced in her sleep made Michael uneasy enough to have slept on his couch on nights simply because he would not be woken up in shock from the screams. Eventually, he took himself as Russell Portin to visit Dr Nigel Johnson.

Dr Nigel Johnson had become reluctant to see Russell or Michael. He was not interested in meeting up with either Russell or Michael and this came about after the failure to create a business with them. It took weeks of persistent phone calls to his receptionist about Angelica's nightmares for him to take notice. Dr Nigel Johnson refused to meet him in Dallas and instead met him at the hospital he worked in. There were no comforts from the café and Dr Nigel Johnson stated he had a very short timeframe to see Russell. But this was no fun and games.

'I am seeing you because Angelica wakes up from nightmares about the amputations she had. She complains about the agony she was in and how she had recollections of the surgery...'

Dr Nigel Johnson was concerned about this. 'How long has she been having these flashbacks for? Can you tell me what she says about them?'

'She complains that she is powerless and talks about how she is immobile as she feels the surgery that she endures. She mentions Russell Portin, my name multiple times. Then she complains about hearing saws and agony as she feels her limbs being ripped off.'

'Shit. Right we need to act fast. I'll proscribe her some anti-depressants include Doxepin and Trazadone that she can take which should help her sleep. Just tell her to take these medications help with her sleep patterns and I will get them to you.'

'Can you proscribe medication to patients?'

'Well yes, I will just do it and add it to her notes that she has had depressive episode associated with amputation. I already mentioned and added to her notes that she has got depression. Easy enough to cover up.'

'Thank you.'

'No thank you. Our business venture failed but this could end us. Keep me updated with news on this Michael...'

'Don't use that name, I am Russell.'

'Right, Russell.'

When Michael got home, Kate Sunderland had been washing Angelica in the bath and now Angelica was watching yet more of her television program she always watched; Evangelical Protestant Pentecostal Television. This distraction from reality, that she could create a faith that existed through watching the television or the internet. The faith that she had in God was a faith entirely built via the media that she consumed, rather than a faith depending on a meaningful connection with transcendental forces. A faith that was fixed not upon Jesus or anything remotely like that but rather a faith fixed upon some enthralling preachers. Even after the sincerely held belief that God had told her through the television to have her arms and legs amputated, the preachers were enchanting, sending magnetic energy to their viewers. This magnetism had led many people in America to abandon sincere faith in God. After all, how could they claim to promote sexual purity and vote for a president who had many divorces or claim to ask for millions in donations whilst letting millions of Americans to suffer in poverty or without healthcare?

'I have never grown old of these worship songs, Kate. And to think God talks to us through the television or the internet as one minister puts it is so captivating,' Angelica said looking at Kate.

Michael said nothing, his mere presence was that of an autocrat. Captivating, controlling, manipulating and dominating, Michael could have easily been one of those preachers. Kate looked at him before sitting down away from him. Michael wrapped his arms around Angelica, who did not look at him, staring straight in front of herself.

'Hi, Angelica...'

'Don't talk to me. I want answers, Michael,' Angelica snapped.

'If I can't talk to you, there can be no answers,' Michael smiled.
Manipulation in part is to twist the words your opponent says and then
send them back at them.

'Why do you have to say that?' Angelica sighed.

'You were the one who said to me that you didn't want answers. If you
want answers, I have to talk...' he hissed in her ear.

'Fine! Talk as much as you want! Not that it matters!' Angelica
shouted.

'I have got you some anti-depressants for the nightmares you are
having. The doctor said that it is a common side effect of becoming an
amputee.'

Angelica breathed and hyperventilated, 'What I felt in my nightmares is
agony, Michael! You don't know what it is like to have a nightmare
where you are powerless, as surgeons remove your legs and arms the
excruciatingly agony of amputation!' she cried.

'Aww. Poor thing. You have some bad dreams. The doctor said it was
caused by depression and treatable by anti-depressants...'

'Why then are the constantly awful and repetitive, with the same thing
again and again, as if I was awake on the operating table when I had my
limbs amputated?' Angelica asked.

'Because you regret the surgery. That is why?'

'So, who is Russell Portin then?' Angelica interrogated.

Michael stood back off the sofa and looked out the window distance.
'He is a business partner. That is all. I have businesses with him...'

'You said you worked in the oil industry....'

'I never said that,' Michael rebutted, 'the trauma of surgery has
altered your memory. I have always worked in the finance industry. I do
derivatives trading, trading commodities, stock and currencies.'

'Who is Russell Portin then?' Angelica's voice became more
demanding.

'As I said, a business partner...'

'Why then do I distinctly have repetitive dreams of people saying about him in my surgery?'

'Subconscious thought patterns… I don't know… Having a quadruple amputation would be a traumatic event.'

'I remember Dr Nigel Johnson in surgery mentioning his name…'
Michael grabbed hold of Angelica, 'You are lying to me! That is a dream! It never happened…'

'Why then do I dream it?'

'Because…. because… anesthesia alters a patient's memory so they think they remember things from surgery but don't.'
The Dunning-Kruger effect; the belief that someone knows considerably more knowledge and expertise than they otherwise hold. Michael never had any knowledge or experience of anesthesia but now pretended to know more about anesthesia than an anesthesiologist. Michael may as well have been a politician.

'Is that true?' Angelica said.

'Yes. It is.'

'Oh well. It must be true. All these memories of the surgery are false. I am just making them all up… Do you think I am that stupid to believe you?' Angelica yelled.

'Do you know anything about anesthesia that you can enlighten me on? Please tell me. Oh, wait you don't. I have a degree in Finance and Economics so I think I know about anesthesia than yourself.'

Angelica doesn't respond to that and continued to watch the television. Kate was bemused by the squabbling, sitting on the chair awkwardly as Angelica and Michael battled it out. She had been ignored by both Angelica and Michael throughout the war of words.

'Kate, I am sorry for this argument. Angelica is confused about herself and her memories. She is making up lies and has complained about having false memories,' Michael admitted.

'It is okay Michael. I was worried when I first heard Angelica tell about these exceptionally detailed nightmares that she has been having. She can tell me explicit details, like smells of burnt hair and agony as saws cut through her tendons and bones.'

'Nothing but nightmares and false memories. After all, nobody experiences these events in surgery, so they have to be made up, imaginations based on her delusions and subconscious feelings. Isn't that right sweetheart?' Michael said patronizingly.

Angelica didn't dare to look into Michael's eye. Michael looked across to his stumped wife, who was more of a pawn than a queen. Michael now had the entire board to himself and could do whatever he wanted.

Chapter 22

'I am not wearing that,' Angelica whined.

Angelica was sat on the bed with luxurious black lingerie. The clothing was wrapped in clear plastic, polyethene. Shiny, sleek and kinky, it was the new patriarchal order that Michael was creating. Michael wanted life to be fun. Michael wanted his wife to be sexy. And the new clothing reflected the relationship realignment. Three latex catsuits, custom-made for quadruple amputee were the representation of Michael's desire for excitement. The catsuits were Republican-red, royal-teal and fascist-black. The colors of power, domination and control; conservatism and authoritarianism in latex. Out of surgery was born a new social contract. Michael was now the leviathan, with a manifesto of submission, discipline and control.

'You will,' Michael smiled, whispering in her ear.

'I won't. You can't make me. I won't do it,' Angelica cried her face welling up with tears.

'Decisions means decisions. Democracy means democracy. Freedom means freedom. Sex means sex. Look at all the things I do for you. I help you out of bed. I clean you. I make dinner for you. I clothe you. I do all of that for love. Now love is reciprocal, love means love. Submission means submission. Wives must submit,' Michael smiled seductively.

'The money was all blown on surgery that I have had and now you spend money on this?'

'We have plenty of it.'

'What do you even mean?' Angelica sobbed into the bedsheets.

'Money is not an issue for us. We have plenty of it. I am a financial trader.'

Angelica stopped sobbing and scowled at Michael. 'You told me this before. You told me this a few weeks ago. I do not understand why you would do this to me. Why have you even done this? What was the point?'

'You may be questioning why but let me say. It does not matter now. The past is the past. History means history...'

'Would you stop with those meaningless something means something. What you are saying is pointless. I don't understand why though you have kept the fact of which job you did away from me for so long,' Angelica retorted.

'I didn't want you to know. In case people asked about it. But now it does not matter. I make a lot of money trading.'

'I always remembered you working in the oil industry.'

'You see, there it is again. Your false memory. I never said that but it is good you believed I worked in the oil industry. Working undercover means fewer people keep an eye on you.'

'Who is keeping an eye on you?' Angelica growled.

'No one of interest.'

'It is obvious someone is keeping tabs on you. You mention it all the time.'

'Not all the time,' Michael replied.

'A lot of the time. You deny it because you fear someone. Tell me, who is it you are trying to run away from?' Angelica snarled.

'Nobody. I am running away from nobody. But that is not the problem. The problem is your refusal to wear the clothes that I bought you to wear. This I find to be a grave insult. But no matter, if you want, you can clean and feed yourself today.'

'Kate can help me...'

'She is not coming today. She is staying at her home today. I am the only one who can help you today.'

Angelica sighed and was agitated. 'I am not wearing that Michael. Where is my choice, my free will?'

'You made your choice to have your arms and legs amputated. No, I am having my choice over what you where...'

'You are controlling me, Michael! Your decisions, your desires, everything! Everything is controlled by yourself. You own me!' Angelica shouted.

Michael smiled, smoothing Angelica's hair. 'Aww. You poor thing. Too bad. You are going to wear these catsuits. I want you to. It's too bad that you don't want to wear it because I do. It is I who call the shots in this relationship. This relationship is now the one that I control. Wives, submit to your husbands. You shall submit to me,' Michael said voluptuously.

Angelica cried, 'Why are you doing this to me? Do you love me?' Angelica wailed.

'I love you so much,' Michael smiled.

'Then why are you doing this?' Angelica shouted.

'Because... I have feelings, desires and needs that have never been satisfied. I have fetishized latex ever since I was sexually aware. The church condemned such acts as depraved sinful behavior of the devil. I told nobody. Locking up these feelings inside because I would be condemned by others for acting in such a way.' Michael interrupted, turning towards the window and his eyes glazing with tears. This was the first time that he could express his sexual preferences without any condemnation from others. He controlled Angelica and so would not object to his desires.

'You could have told me....'

'You judged me. I told you and you snapped. You are the typical white Evangelical woman who dishes out judgement and condemnation like a demon in hell but offers no love or kindness. You Evangelicals denounce people without ever seeking to under other people. I wanted to have a wife who would participate in these acts. You would never have worn such catsuits before your amputation.'

Angelica was silent for a second. 'No, I wouldn't have...'

'So, the amputation was a way for me to enact my ultimate sexual desires. Putting my wife into a custom-made latex catsuit.'

'Do you think it is glorifying to God what you have just said?' Angelica snarled.

'And do you think it is glorifying to God turning away all your friends and family to have an operation they strongly disagree with? Do you think that the self-immolation of your body was justified?'

Angelica became frustrated, 'I was doing it to save my life! We were going to get the $3,500,000 pay-out! You wanted me to have it, you paid for it! How dare you criticize me for the surgery. You would not allow me to simply changed surgeons...'

'It was your decision. The decision rested with you and you alone. You could have had the final say, the final decision. But you didn't.'

Of course, Michael had been taking significant control of the situation at the time of Angelica having the surgery. Angelica tried to remember what had been said. The propofol had done its work and she couldn't remember so well. She thought that it was Michael that had controlled her decision. They would have had to paid out thousands of dollars to Dr Nigel Johnson as a means of opt-out fee. But Michael reasserted that it was Angelica's decision.

'You said we would have to pay $4,000 or so to cancel the surgery and that is why I chose to have the surgery.'

'You would have still been able to cancel the surgery. Anyway. Amputation has been done. You are now an amputee. You must accept the decisions you have made.'

'It wasn't my decision, Michael...'

'I assure you it was. Now you must accept the results of it. That having a quadruple amputation means well, being completely reliant on myself. To be honest, all I can say is that your amputation was part of my plan anyway.'

Angelica turned her head away from Michael before staring intently into his eyes, 'Why do you want to have these fetishes then? Why did you choose to have fetishes?'

'I didn't want them. The same way as a gay person doesn't choose to be gay or a lesbian choose to be a lesbian. I didn't choose to have fetishes or have a desire for latex. It is just who I am as a person.'

'But I do not want to be a part of these desires of yours.'

'This is not about choice here. Your choice has already been chosen by yourself. You are an amputee and therefore my decisions are also yours.

Where have all your friends and family gone? When has Elizabeth visited you?'

'You don't allow them to visit!'

'Stop trying to blame others for the negligence of your own responsibility. You could ask me to contact them. Don't you have your own cellphone? Couldn't you phone them up?'

'Why can't you do it?'

'Angelica. You do it if you want them to visit. Until then, I will allow them to visit if they contact us. But they haven't so that isn't going to happen.'

Angelica put the stumps of her arms onto her lap. She looked at her husband with some anger.

'Surely you could have reached out to them.'

'I don't need to.'

'Well, I want to.'

'Go on then. Contact them.'

Angelica was hesitant to suddenly reach out to people who she had disowned before the amputation. Admittedly, she was afraid that she would be mocked by Michael who would mock her trying to phone these people. Given that she would have to operate her cell-phone without hands, she would be lucky to be able to contact her friends and family. Moreover, they might not be interested in speaking with her again after all she had done to them. Still, she wanted to at least make the effort.

Her cell-phone was on her bedside table. It was a smartphone, one that could be used by voice-recognition software. She picked it up in her stumped arms and attempted to use the voice-activated assistant. Unfortunately, it had not been configured to recognize her voice. So, she attempted to call Elizabeth Londres but the smartphone would not work to her voice. She looked dismayed and sad when her eyes turned to her husband, Michael. Michael grinned. There was no use for contacting other people since she could not even use her smartphone.

'Oh, that is unfortunate. Your smartphone has not been configured for voice-recognition software,' Michael said flippantly.

'That is unfair! Oh, why does everything have to be unfortunate with me?' Angelica asked.

'You brought this on yourself. No use for self-pity. Accept your fate as and submit to me. Submit,' Michael smiled, smoothing Angelica's hair.

Michael had smothered Angelica. Angelica had tried to resist the control of Michael but she had now become his satellite, completely under his orbit. Wearing a catsuit was uncomfortable at first. Her entire body was locked into a piece of latex which became scorching hot thanks to the hot Texan days that she was in. When it was 71 Fahrenheit, it was torturous sitting in the sun and being cooked from the inside. She had been attached with a dog leash also, with a studded collar. Control, domination and submission, the regime change was now complete. Lying in the torturous sunlight was an ordeal. Her mouth became completely dried, her body sweat out. Then there were the drinks that Michael would give Angelica. Drinking was the only slight compassion Michael gave to Angelica, who he kept in the sunlight to be scolded. Then there was the torturous feeling of needing to urinate. Angelica held on, wriggling like a worm under a magnifying glass in the heat. To relieve herself would mean the dishonorable feeling of urine swishing around inside her catsuit. To Angelica, it did not matter though as she was nothing more than object any way at this point and so urinated inside her catsuit. There was slight relief on Angelica's part, as it felt somewhat liberating to be cooled down by her bodily fluids as she lied inert in the sun.

Michael would comb her hair, feed her and wash her in the evenings. This relationship was rather bizarre; Michael in caring and attending Angelica's needs would show affection and love but then put her back into the catsuit again and tying her by a dog leash to the table. This mixture of love and control was that of a master to a dog. And yet, Angelica, for all that she had been through, for all that Michael did to her, was fond of this relationship. Why she had become fond of a relationship that was completely demeaning to her was weird but then again amputating all of your limbs because you believed you had cancer was also absurd. The absurdity of love is one in which someone loves another person despite that person controlling them. Michael held dictatorial control over Angelica and could do to her whatever he liked. And for some reason though, Michael despite putting Angelica into a catsuit and tying her up, Michael showed affection to her at other times of the day. It was not like he wanted to show her who was most dominating in their relationship. He could show no kindness towards her anytime in the relationship.

This daily ritual of Angelica being put into catsuit was in the end altered to leave Angelica on the sofa, watching the television. She was still tied up with a dog leash on the studded collar but was not kept in the scorching heat of direct sunlight, which was less torturous. Various evenings, Angelica was picked up and taken by Michael into the bedroom, where would invade her personal space as a superpower controlling a sovereign nation. Angelica accepted these invasions, being penetrated was merely being a wife. Penetration means penetration. Penetration meant being a vassal, or a satellite of greater power. Freedom means freedom. Angelica had her limbs amputated to be free, she thought. At the time that was one of the major reasons. Now, she was being penetrated by her husband without any real freedom in it. She couldn't walk away from it. As a vassal of her husband, she would accept her position of submission. A vassal was always dominated and would remain submissive. The strong do what they will; the weak do what they must.

'You like submitting, don't you?' Michael asked voluptuously on top of Angelica's smooth shiny body.
Angelica looked at her husband in the eyes, who thrust himself onto her catsuit. It was a weird activity because it was rather difficult penetrating a zipped up catsuit. It was like signing an impossible political agreement,

messy and unguided. Angelica was sprayed with the sticky liquid that stuck to the smooth exterior of the catsuit. Vassalage and submission meant humiliation. And in the position of being nothing more than a helpless amputee in a catsuit, Angelica could only submit. Vassalage means vassalage after all. And bondage means bondage; amputation means amputation.

Chapter 23

Angelica was in her catsuit. She normally was. Michael was out of the house. Angelica was left alone in the house. If there was a fire, she would have been roasted alive. She sat there on the television watching her Christian television channels. As always was her relationship to Evangelical Protestant Pentecostal Television was her relationship to God. God always spoke through the television. Never through the Bible. That was how she decided to have a quadruple amputation based on what she believed to be God speaking to her through the television. So, her life involved watching these television programs to hope that she would gain anything new about God's plan. Today, there was nothing unusual about the program. There was the typical appeal to money, the phone in a prayer session and the prophecies of the future, of Iran attacking Israel sparking World War 3 and the return of Jesus to reign for 1,000 years. Unexpectantly, however, was not the break out of a war with Iran but a knock coming from the door. Awkwardly, Angelica couldn't open the door.

'Who is there?' Angelica bawled in a loud voice.
The knocking continued this time repeatedly before becoming a continuous knock.

'Who is there? Answer me!' Angelica shouted.

There were multiple bangs before the door flew open and what sounded like clicking of a gun followed. The sound of creaking floorboards reverberated throughout the house. Ghosts haunt houses but not houses that were 30 years old. Scratching footsteps scuttling throughout the house;
Angelica was petrified. She was in no position to run away, being in a red latex catsuit and being a quadruple amputee, she would have to accept whatever was coming to her. There were various clicks and bangs before the door to the room opened. Entering the room was an

African American man and white woman, middle-aged, wearing jeans and a dark blue coat with the words FBI written on it.

'FBI inspector David Miller and Angela Adonis here. We are looking for a Russell Portin, who we have been investigating for a while now due to a connection of crimes including money-laundering...'

Russell Portin? Michael Donaldson lives here. You must have got the wrong address,' Angelica replied.

'I am afraid not ma'am. You see, Michael Donaldson is connected to Russell Portin. How do you know Michael Donaldson?' David asked.

Angelica grimaced and sighed in exasperation, 'he is my husband. He is out at the moment. Why what has he done wrong?'

'We can't tell you everything right now. He is under observation himself,' David replied.

'Where is he right now?' Angela asked.

'He is out shopping.'

'He did this to you?' Angela queried, her voice with a hint of remorsefulness.

'Did what? It has got nothing to do you. What has Michael been doing?' Angelica replied; her voice filled with suspicion.

'We have suspected Michael has been doing money-laundering and has used multiple fake identities to avoid taxation in large scale tax evasion efforts. We are needing to gather some personal intelligence on him.'

'So, let me understand how large the scale of his money-laundering efforts is?' Angelica said.

'We are talking millions of dollars. I can't give you the exact amount because that would compromise the investigation.'

Angelica was aghast, her mouth wide open in absolute shock, 'millions of dollars? He has laundered millions of dollars?'

'Yes. We are trying to find evidence against him and well, you were in the house at the time. We could piece together more evidence against Michael and the wider conspiracy connecting himself. Dr Nigel Johnson is on our watch lists. We think there is a large conspiracy surrounding your husband.'

'Well, Michael is my husband. I can't rat on him. It would be wrong,' Angelica said, abruptly.

For all Michael had done to Angelica, for all of his domination, his total control over Angelica, Angelica still had loyalty to her husband. Why did Angelica still have loyalty to her authoritarian husband? Perhaps deep down, she enjoyed being dominated. There were some times a deep thrill in being controlled. Authoritarianism, that of being dominated and forced to submit to someone who has total control of your life had always been pleasurable. People enjoy being dominated and controlled, there was nothing wrong with that. Her husband gave her lots of attention now and only wanted to have sex every so often, perhaps once a week. And he was the only other human being she had talked to in months. Angelica wasn't going to simply let her husband go. Besides, he was the only person left in her life to protect her.

'What so you don't want to cooperate with us?' Angela asked, with disbelief.

'My husband is flawed. But I love him for who he is. I have nothing to say to you. Good day to you,' Angelica said.

'Your husband has potentially committed multiple large-scale crimes and has hurt you….'

'Listen, I love him and he loves me okay? There is nothing to say! Now leave me!' Angelica shouted.

'Do you have any friends or family?'

'Leave me!'

The FBI agents shrugged their shoulders and left her by herself. Angelica had now committed to her husband. He may have forced her to wear horrific clothes for his sexual fantasies, but he still loved her, in a possessive, dominating way. She felt protected by the fact that she was owned by her strong husband, even though he had left her by herself when he had gone shopping.

When he had got back, he appeared out of breath and seemingly was in a hurry. He became alarmed that he door had been broken.

'Hi cupcake,' he said, kissing Angelica on the forehead.

'Hi Michael,' she said exasperatedly.

'How have you been by yourself? The door's lock was broken when I came in. Any reason for it...'

'No,' Angelica quickly replied.

Michael glared at Angelica, 'Hmm. Very quick response. Everything okay here? Enjoyed watching your television? Gained any divine inspiration.'

'Yes, thanks. Perhaps we should have sex tonight.'

Michael did not know what to say. Why did Angelica suddenly blurt out with that statement? Angelica hadn't shown any interest in sex other since Michael had made her wear the two custom-made catsuits. The change was rather abrupt and with no real reason. What made her change in such a short space of time.

'Sure...' Michael said hesitantly. He didn't know what to say. It was not like he didn't want to have sex with her. He just didn't expect it.

'What do you want to drink? I have fruit juice if you want it or what or coffee?' Michael said.

'Fruit juice.'

Michael poured out the orange into a cup and watered it down as to give to Angelica with a straw in it. She gripped it with her two stumps and sucked out the juice. It was refreshing. Michael some days didn't give her much to drink. Now, the first thing he had done when he had got in made Angelica a drink. So much love that Michael was showing. It was as if all the days that Michael had been oppositional to Angelica, forcing her through the surgery was nothing now and Angelica suddenly became buoyed up with a love for her husband. Perhaps she wanted to take a vacation in Stockholm this year.

For dinner, Michael cooked Spaghetti Bolognese. A difficult choice to feed a quadruple amputee with. After dinner, Michael and Angelica snuggled up on the sofa and watched television together. For Angelica putting away her annoyance at Michael was more to do with the fact that he was the only person in her life. She had spoken to nobody for months now. It was merely Michael who she spoke to or had any relationship with. She hadn't gone to church or spoken with family members or with her old friends. Michael was the only person she had. That day she had the chance of exposing Michael. But she said nothing to the FBI, knowing that is she did that, she would no longer have Michael as he would be arrested.

There were new days with Michael. Michael took out Angelica for the first time in many weeks and perhaps months. Angelica lost track of time itself, stuck in her house, unable to do anything but watch the television for hours a day. The loneliness meant that she had connected with Michael. Who cared that he had done money laundering or had broken the law? Forget the past. Forgive and forget. The days came when Michael would take Angelica out, not in the business of the city but in the countryside where there was peace and quiet. There was just Michael, Angelica and the open sky in a field in rural Texas. Still, there was always the white van that appeared to follow behind. So really, even out in the country, it was Angelica, Michael and the random white vans that appeared from nowhere. Angelica was usually somewhat alarmed when the white van appeared. There was usually just Angelica and Michael eating a picnic in the middle of a field, Angelica enjoying the feeling an of wind going through her hair under the open sky. The emptiness of the field made her feel alive, that it was just herself, Michael and God in the whole of existence.

'Coffee?' Michael smiled at Angelica.
'Yes, thank you,' she replied.
Michael put a straw in the cup and Angelica drunk from it. Angelica smiled at Michael, her oppressor, her lover, her husband. There was nothing in her world now. Her friends had faded away, with no one talking to her at all. Her husband was her rock and was everything to Angelica.
'It is a lovely day today, isn't it?' Michael said to Angelica.
'Yes, but every day is so hot when I am wearing this catsuit.'

'You look so beautiful. You are the most beautiful woman in the whole world.'

'Why thank you,' Angelica said, her cheeks going bright red.

'You look so fabulous in your catsuit. I just wanted you to wear one. It's like my dreams have come true.'

Indeed, all of Michael's dreams had come true. Like a child in a toyshop, his sexual pleasures were hitherto unimaginably filled. There were no longer any times where Angelica would refuse to wear latex. Indeed, she wore latex every day now. Being bound up was naturally part of her life. Bondage means bondage and Michael was getting a great deal. Angelica, freed from the use of limbs, was now bound to her husband. How kinky. Angelica was so kinky being a sex object of her husband. Just looking at Angelica in her fascist-black catsuit turn Michael on. Before the amputation of Angelica's limbs, there was no fire in the relationship. And for the weeks after Angelica had been exceptionally hostile to Michael. But now, the ships had been burned down and so Angelica was left with one person in her life. And that person was Michael.

Chapter 24

Angelica smiled at Michael who was holding out her cell-phone. This was the first phone call from anyone after the surgery. It had been months of silence from Angelica's friends. Angelica had not gone to church for a long time and had not gone to the Bible study group either. Elizabeth had not contacted her, neither had any of her family. The bizarre situation is these people could have contacted Angelica. Perhaps none of them wanted to, but today there was one person who was interested in speaking with Angelica. It was Elizabeth, the one friend who she had completely ignored and despised, the one friend that had stayed close but she had rejected multiple times. Why did Elizabeth want to speak to Angelica?

'Hi, Elizabeth?' Angelica said in a voice of confusion. Michael had turned on the speakers of the cellphone. Angelica couldn't use the phone without voice recognition and she couldn't hold a phone as she lacked the arms to do it.

'Hi Angelica, are you alone?' Elizabeth asked. Her voice sounded apprehensive as if she was frightened of something.

'No, I am never alone, honey. I am always with Michael now. He protects me,' Angelica said with a beaming smile.

Domination and submission; the paradox of love. Despite her legs being amputated by a surgeon paid for by Michael, despite his domination and the millions that he made in trading, there was no hint of hatred from Angelica. Angelica's heart was now in Michael's lap simply because Michael was the only thing in Angelica's life. Her entire survival was in Michael's hands. There were no other people in her life. They had abandoned her after the decision to have her limbs amputated. Michael was the last person in Angelica's life.

'Oh, right,' Elizabeth sounded awkward, 'you wouldn't have a problem if I came around and saw you? I haven't spoken for months after your amputation. I had been meaning to contact you. I never did but today I decided to contact you.'

'That is most kind. Thank you, Elizabeth, you are so kind.'

'What time and day do you want to come around?' Michael interrupted. He needed to make sure that he was in control of the situation.

'Umm, well I am free tomorrow from three in the afternoon...'

'Yes, you can come around then. See you tomorrow,' Michael said, hanging up the phone.

Angelica glared at her husband, 'Why did you hang up on her?' Angelica whined.

'I was merely ending the phone-call.'

'You didn't give her an address...'

'She can text to ask me if she needs one. I don't see the point of keeping her on the phone if she didn't need to speak to us.'
Michael needed to control the channels of engagement, lest his wife wandered astray from him. She was aligned towards him and yet he feared that this alignment was only because he had effectively isolated her from the rest of the world. If her friends and family came back in contact with Angelica. Isolationism was essential for Michael's control of Angelica. So long as she had no way to contact to the outside world, he held power over her.

Angelica, who had gradually fallen increasingly under her husband's control now had a friend who she had ignored for months visit her. There was a strange amount of confusion surrounding Angelica, who did not understand why Elizabeth just randomly decided to visit her. It was not like Angelica had tried to regain touch with her friend. Still, it was best not to think too heavily into why Elizabeth had decided to visit. Otherwise, it would spoil the special event.

'It's time for you to have a shower,' Michael said.

Late in the evening, Angelica would have her showers. Michael would always help her have a shower. Having no arms meant that Angelica couldn't operate the shower by herself. Michael was always required, his presence total in every part of Angelica's life and body. Each square inch of skin on Angelica's body was reachable by the grasping gloved hands of Michael. Her body, merely a puppet to her husband's desires. Puppetry is a latex catsuit. Much of the skin was chaffed from being constantly put into a latex catsuit. Sweat and skin rubbed the latex constantly and Angelica's body smelt of dried sweat. Why Michael would be turned on by this constant pungent was not explainable, but the smell subsided when he washed down his puppet-wife. Besides, he would put her back into the catsuit after washing her.

'You will be clean after this,' Michael said, touching and feeling over Angelica's entire body. Angelica grimaced at the groping but after all that, she was merely a puppet. Puppets do what their masters do. Freedom does not exist with puppets.

After cleaning her, Michael put her back in the Republican-red latex catsuit, one of the catsuits that Angelica lived in. She was then carried to the bedroom. Puppets didn't have much when it came to consent. Angelica's Enjoyment was not the main consideration when Michael launched an incursion in Angelica's territory. Rule 1 of engagement; the strong do what they will and the weak do what they must. Angelica was certainly weak and could never stop her husband overpowering her. Her best chance of survival was to try to get on top, which was an exceptionally hard manoeuvre to accomplish. Otherwise, there was little Angelica could do to protect herself from the thrusting control of her husband. Weakness was Angelica's virtue and that would never go away.

The domination, submission and control lasted for minutes but in the end, as always, Michael ceased with his quest for control. He was a tired elk after mating. Men usually were. He went to bed after it, whilst Angelica lied inert, without being able to move. Sinking it was, sinking into her flashbacks. First was the sight of blue surgeons and then it was Dr Nigel Johnson speaking. Bleeps of the ECG echoed throughout the room. Dr Nigel Johnson held a scalpel and began to cut. Angelica though could not shout out or scream, being trapped, chained down in her nightmare. There was a tormenting agony as the characteristic burnt hair mixed with BBQ filled the room and the agony of a saw dividing tendons and muscles being ripped apart with scalpels. The flashback happened as always when Angelica was unable to move, stuck in a twilight between awoken state and asleep. Sleep was now a place of torture for Angelica, with dreams and the state between them being dominated by the memories of the past, the traumas of surgery and the nightmares of helpless agony.

Michael never listened to Angelica's cries in the morning about the nightmares she had. It was not very convenient. The flashbacks to the agony of her surgery were not something that Michael wanted to hear about. He was more interested in other things or rather was terrified of the implications of remembering the surgery. Angelica claimed that she had remembered Dr Nigel Johnson talking about someone called Russell Portin to do the surgery. And this was repeated again and again, the memory of Russell Portin paying Dr Nigel Johnson for the surgery. Of course, Michael had mentioned Russell Portin before but only in passing to Angelica and Angelica.   Today though, he would tell her about Russell Portin.

Angelica was sat in the sofa in the decaying living room. The television had been turned down. Stroking Angelica's hair, Michael smiled and breathed into the ear of Angelica.

'You ask me about Russell Portin,' Michael whispered.

'Who is he? Why did he pay for the surgery?' Angelica demanded, 'You can't lie about him to me, Michael! I know about him. He is in my dreams.'

'I am Russell Portin. It is I,' Michael said, his arms stretched out as if to want to hug someone, messianic in tone.

'How, what? Why? Why?' Angelica cried.

'I only wanted to protect you that's all. I needed to use a different name to protect my sweet precious cupcake. I couldn't let her die...'

'That is not true. You didn't have to change your name!'

'I have to do many things. I am a finance trader after all.'

'Is the FBI after you?' Angelica said.

'No, that isn't true.' Michael snarled.

'They came around not so long ago, stumbled in by mistake thinking that there was no one in the house when I was alone.'

Michael was immediately alarmed by Angelica's revelation. He couldn't hide from her much now. The conspiracy was now out in the open. The question was not whether Angelica knew, but how much she knew and to whether she knew enough information that she may be a liability to Michael. He became agitated and paced up and down the room.

'What did you say to the FBI, Angelica?'

'Not much,' Angelica whispered back.

'Tell me each word you said to them, I want a word by word replay...'

'I said that I didn't know what you had been doing and that I was shocked to hear that you were involved in a massive money-laundering investigation. They didn't give away much. When they asked whether I would help them, I declined.'

'What do you mean declined? They have bugged this house, haven't they?' Michael shouted.

'I don't know what the hell they have done. I couldn't have stopped them. I am a quadruple amputee for Pete's sake! How on earth do you think I was to fight them? Bite them with my teeth?'

Michael was very tense, his hands holding his head as if he had heard his friend was seriously ill. He shivered in fear. Perhaps the FBI had bugged the entire house or put a virus onto his laptops. Perhaps they were watching them now or listening to their conversations. There was no way to know the full extent of what was being surveyed. The Feds were onto Michael. The question was, how much time did he have?

'Has Elizabeth contacted me back, Michael?' Angelica said.

'Yes, why are you going to tell on me to her?' Michael growled.

'No what, no I love you,' she said, staring sadly into his eyes.

Abusive love. How dear was it to see the surrendered sad stare that Angelica had for Michael? Her eyes had lost all hope, now she was nothing more than latex doll to the wishes of Michael. Independence was lost to total control by Michael, who now essentially owned his wife. There was no freedom left for Angelica. Amputation means amputation. All sovereignty that Angelica had as an independent person was now taken by her husband. Michael could do whatever he pleased to her. But Michael was also the only person for months that even talked to Angelica. He was her rock and it was unthinkable no matter how vial he was to her, to get rid of him. Her love for him was total. He had taken her limbs it appeared. Now strapped to a surgical table, he had also taken her heart. She had resisted for months, her anger filled when he had merely let her fade away. The silence was her weapon of choice, to begin with, but by the end, Angelica was left with just pure, unconditional love for Michael. He could strap her down and rape her whilst surgically removing her organs and she would still love him. There was only Michael in the world. Michael and Angelica.

Now, though was the cuckoo of Elizabeth. This relationship, of Michael having total control and domination over his wife, was threatened by the re-emergence of Elizabeth. Out of all the people who reconnected with Angelica, it was Elizabeth. Angelica had been cruel towards Elizabeth but now she was in contact with Angelica. It appeared that the cruelty of Angelica had not gone too far with Elizabeth or there was something else at play with this relationship, behind closed doors. Whatever was going on, Michael had to be with Elizabeth and Angelica in any meeting that they had together. There would be no private meetings, not since Angelica admitted that the FBI was investigating Michael. Still, though there was a hope of Michael that Elizabeth wouldn't contact them back and would just leave them alone.

Such view, however, was wishful thinking as Elizabeth texted back asking for an address and time for her to visit. Michael's heart sank. He knew now that he had to prepare himself for Elizabeth. Elizabeth was up to something. Michael could sense it. Why would Elizabeth go to all this trouble to see Angelica, after all that Angelica had done to her and without having any interest in Angelica up until this point? Something wasn't right.

'Right when Elizabeth comes, I am staying with you in the room. I am not leaving you two alone together,' Michael said, in a frightened voice.

'What do you mean? I was allowed to meet up with Elizabeth without any problems before I had my legs and arms amputated. What is the problem now?' Angelica moaned.

'She cannot be trusted, Angelica. Elizabeth is up to no good, why else would she be coming to meet you after so long for no apparent reason? She must have a reason to meet you at...'

'She is my friend! What is wrong with you, trying to control my life...'

'I have done so much for you, Angelica. I love you. Love means love. I cannot allow anything to happen to our love. I just find you irresistible. I can't let you go....'

'You just don't want me to have a private life or anything that you can't control,' Angelica hissed.

'I thought you *loved* me...'

'Nothing is stopping Angelica coming around then?' Angelica said frustratedly.

'No. Just I want to be there to support you. You might need the toilet after all.'

'Yes. Because you have helped me to the toilet and bath me all the time.'

'I do everything for you,' Michael said, staring into Angelica's eyes as if he was staring into her soul.

Michael was right. He did absolutely everything for Angelica, on top being able to trade millions of dollars in trading accounts. Kate Sunderland never helped any more. It was just Angelica and Michael, alone, isolated entities in a world with no friends. Amputation means amputation. When you cut off your legs and arms for no apparent reason and lose your friends in the process, becoming a loner was inevitable. Angelica was a loner. Friends and family had all abandoned her. Her brother and sister of Scott and Nora had nothing to do with Angelicas and had completely cut off ties from her. The Bible study group she went to had not phoned her or showed any consideration for her wellbeing. Having a quadruple amputation against the advise of all your friends was not a way to build friendships. The result of the amputation meant that Angelica had one person left in the entire world. Michael. He was a fetishist who had perverse sexual desires of putting his amputee wife into a latex catsuit for days on end. Yet, this kind of desire was shown with a degree of affection. He would kiss Angelica and stroke her hair. There was no one else who remotely any interest in Angelica. Wilma said nothing to Angelica now, showing little interest in her crippled daughter.

Michael waited for the time that Elizabeth said she was coming. The doorbell went. Elizabeth had come. It was a surprise that after many months from the surgery, that Elizabeth even came to visit Angelica. Angelica was pleased to see her but there was a sense of discord between them. A cold-war tension was in the air as if superpowers were negotiating a treaty under the threat of nuclear war. Elizabeth sat facing the crippled amputee across the table in a chair that appeared to be old. For the months spent apart, Elizabeth was shocked to see that Angelica dressed in a custom-made cat-suit. Today, it was a fascist-black catsuit. It took Elizabeth completely by surprise.

'So, Elizabeth can I make you a drink?' Michael asked
'I would like a coke,' Elizabeth said authoritatively.

Michael left the room to make drink Elizabeth. There was an uneasy silence between Angelica and Elizabeth, neither people spoke to one another. The silence between them for the last few months had generated into silence now that they had met each other. Michael brought in the drinks, including a drink with a straw for Angelica. Michael smiled at Elizabeth, who just glared back at him.

'There you go Elizabeth, a coke for you,' Michael said.

'Thanks,' Elizabeth said bluntly, 'I need to be honest with you. Why is Angelica wearing a catsuit?'

Michael laughed, comically at the suggestion. Michael and Angelica really hadn't been seen in public together. Angelica spent vast amounts of time with either just Michael or alone by herself. There was no consideration about how other people would view Angelica wearing her catsuit. It didn't matter since she was always alone with Michael. Isolationist and a loner, wearing a catsuit was not going to be frowned upon if Angelica was spending the majority of her time by herself.

'You don't like that decision of clothes?'

'No, I think it is how can I put it, off. Angelica would never have worn this originally,' Elizabeth said.

'Have you considered that Angelica may have changed?'

'She may have changed. But she wouldn't have ever chosen these clothes. I mean why would she? Would she even have thought it was Christian?'

'Christian hey?' Michael smiled. 'Interesting idea hey. Christian.'

'I am a Christian still, Elizabeth,' Angelica said.

'Since when is it wrong to wear a catsuit in Christianity?' Michael cackled.

'It says about being freed from bondage... eh something like that,' Elizabeth replied, hesitant in answering a reply.

'Great use of theology. Perhaps you should write a PhD on why catsuits are a sin, Elizabeth. You truly have a fantastic knowledge of sexual sin,' Michael gloated.

Elizabeth gloated. She sipped some of her coke before putting the cup back onto the table. 'How do you afford the extravagance anyway?'

Well, I sold the last house for a start. That has given us a few hundred thousand dollars which I...'

'Run that past me, a few hundred thousand dollars?' Elizabeth spluttered.

'That is right,' Michael smiled. Michael didn't really talk about the money situation to anyone he knew. Not even Angelica. These financial costs were not talked about simply because the dark webs that Michael was linked to were deep and wide. Criminal was a word that could be used.

'So, you have made thousands of dollars but you won't purchase prosthetic limbs for Angelica?' Elizabeth said.

Michael walked towards the window, looking outside. The weather appeared to be overcast. A white van was parked outside as it always was. White vans. Appearing and then disappearing like ghosts, they had a rather strange appearance. Michael heard of the FBI were recently spying on him as it was reported to him by Angelica. He closed the blinds over the room, so the people inside the white van couldn't see into the house.

'I have made a decent amount of money recently. The house isn't that important, to be honest.'

'So, how much money have you made?'

'I can't give you an actual figure as that would be intruding on my personal life…'

'He has made millions,' Angelica shouted out. She looked at her husband with glazed eyes, not eyes of anger. They were eyes of sadness. Michael refused to meet them, looking intently at Elizabeth.

'You have made millions?' Elizabeth said.

'That isn't a number that I would say often,' Michael snaked like a politician.

'So, have you made millions, thousands or something?'

'Money isn't that important now. You have come around simply to attack my lifestyle and Angelica's lifestyle. I find this rather rude actually.'

'You know, you are right. I apologise for the abruptness…'

'No need. All is forgiven,' Michael replied.

'So, do you like the new house than Angelica?' Elizabeth asked.

'No, not really. I preferred the old house. This one is not the same,' Angelica sadly replied.

'The old house wasn't suitable for a disabled person. This is a more suitable house shall we say.'

'So, are you planning on getting prosthetic limbs?'

That was the awkward term. Prosthetic limbs. Angelica flirted with the idea of bionic limbs at one time. Technology, she hoped, could end her incapacitated state. She could utilize technology to end her disabilities and yet, there was nothing to suggest that she was ever going to get bionic limbs. They were the unicorns of a deluded patient, who had bought the treatment plan of her aggressively assertive surgeon Dr Nigel Johnson. The technology could solve mankind's problems like border checks that caused food shortages, or technology that could solve climate change. So, Angelica could receive bionic limbs. Or so Angelica thought. In reality, bionic limbs were decades away. She had her legs and arms amputated and there was no technology to replace the limbs lost. The lost limbs were gone forever.

'We haven't talked about it,' Michael replied with a pleased expression. Lying of course, but Angelica did not call him out for it.

'Why? That is an exceptionally important thing. Amputees lose their entire independence and their freedom and without prosthetic limbs, they will never gain back their independence.'

Independence, freedom and sovereignty were concepts that no longer mattered to Angelica. She had her legs and arms amputated to take back control over cancer. There was no talk now of cancer. No consideration at all of whether there was cancer in the first place. Cancer, which had become a sort of booger man that hung-over Angelica never really existed at all. Cancerous cells were taking over her body like Mexicans taking over her body, as Dr Nigel Johnson said. Being free from cancer meant, well, being free from cancer. Cancer means cancer. Mexicans mean Mexicans. Amputation means amputation. Taking back control meant losing all control. Amputations have that kind of effect.

'Freedom means freedom,' Michael replied.

'What are you saying?' Elizabeth asked, confused with such a meaningless statement.

'I am saying what I am saying. Freedom means freedom.'

'Okay? That is rather weird,' Elizabeth frowned.

'Independence can never be appreciated without understanding the necessities of mankind, that man is by no means an island and that we work together for our existence. I mean we are individuals of course and we must stand on our own two feet...'

Michael's half-hearted attempt at political theory was nauseating. Elizabeth sighed. She didn't come around for political debate with a contradictory Trumpist libertarian.

'Alright enough with the political discourse. That is not why I am here...'

'Why are you here then?' Michael grinned.

'To see Angelica.'

'Well good, you have seen her. Time for you to go...'

'Wait. That is not it is it? I want to spend longer than that. How is life with you, Michael? I haven't been able to consider what you are considering at the moment. It must be hard looking after Angelica all by herself. I am sorry to sound so negative.'

'No, it is fine. Yes, life is okay. I find it hard, life with Angelica. To be honest, though, being a financial trade makes life easier. I fit my life around Angelica.'

'I always thought you were in the oil business.'

'Your beliefs are mistaken. I never was in the oil business.'

The quiet financial trading that Michael had been trying to do on the side. It was possible to do, since you could put in trades and do research throughout the day and didn't require the total full-time job. He could make the money required for him to live off and support Angelica.

'So, your claims about the oil industry and working in the oil industry was incorrect?'

'I never said I worked in the oil industry.'

'You did to me, multiple times.'

'Well, I think that was a false memory.'

'Are you questioning my memory, Michael? I think I know what memories are right or wrong.'

'Your memory was false. We have them all the time.'

'I see. So, your financial trading, tell me about it. It seems that you are good at trading.'

'Quite. I earn a lot of money.'

'So why aren't you in a better house. I mean let's face it, you could afford a better house, couldn't you?'

Michael smirked. There was nothing to suggest that he was going to say the truth. He could have said anything he liked and it would be correct. Or that he could change the truth and change the memories of the past. Such power was not to be underestimated.

'We don't need a better house, Elizabeth. We needed a house that could function for Angelica's disabilities,' Michael replied. It was easy to fabricate false memories.

'That is new. Who bought your old house?'

Angelica glared into the hesitant eyes of Michael. Michael didn't appear stressed, despite the threat of these questions looming over him. He appeared completely unfazed by this form of integration from Elizabeth. 'It was a man called Russell Portin.'

'What relation is he to you?' Elizabeth interrogated, with a forceful approach.

'Meeow! Sounds like a tiger is on a prowl, hey Angelica?' Michael laughed. Angelica appeared concerned. Russell Portin was Michael with a Panama passport. Michael sold his house into a Panama citizenship account, even though he wasn't a Panama citizen and Panama didn't recognize dual citizenships. Michael was clever that way.

'I am being serious. How is he connected with you?'

'An acquaintance of mine, that is all,' Michael said light-heartedly.

'You aren't answering the question.'

Michael twitched and adopted a defensive position, 'Personal details like that I will not give away. Russell and I are good colleagues and regularly contact one another...'

'How often is regular?'

'Once a day actually.'

'Is he on your phone contacts?'

'That information I am not discussing. Sorry. That won't happen.'

'Shall we talk about something else?'

Angelica and Michael looked at each other in a state of bemusement. Elizabeth had never been quite like this before. There was no reason why she would be so aggressive in her pursuit of questions. Perhaps it was a change of character. Or perhaps worse, was the potential for her to be some kind of mole on Michael's behavior. 'Quite. I am not talking about all my personal life.'

'So, what has it been like for you guys then since the surgery? It seems that it has been very quiet?' Elizabeth said.

'It has been very quiet. Nobody has talked much to me since the surgery. I have only had Michael and Kate on a few occasions. Not that it has been a problem but I have found that everyone has seemed to abandon me after the surgery,' Angelica said with a deep sense of regret.

'I don't think you helped yourself to be honest. You were too aggressive toward people who were trying to help yourself.'

'How is your job going, Elizabeth?' Angelica replied.

'It is okay thanks. Rather busy and things. I am more interested in what Michael does. Being a trader sounds great.'

Michael became more confident and relax, 'I have made a lot of money. I have put derivatives and currency trades on all sorts of things. Like I shorted the pound when they voted to leave the EU...'

'Really? Tell me more.'

'Insider information. Exit polls allowed me to bet against the pound. I made a small fortune. I made a small fortune on certain stock options that did well after Trump was elected.'

Elizabeth grinned. 'Your trading sounds interesting. I wish I was a trader over being a nurse,' Elizabeth said, voluptuously.

'If you want to follow the money, trading is the way to go. Betting on the fundamentals can make you a lot of money.'

'Fundamentals?'

'Yeah. It means making decisions on the big picture rather than small picture. My strategy is using politics as a tool to get my desired outcome. Whether that be the EU referendum in the UK or whether that be the 2016 presidential election, I have even put money into various campaigns to influence the outcome. Like the push for a Britain leaving the EU with No Deal, a lot of people including myself are shorting British stock and currency on the belief that the UK's economy will crash. I made a lot of money on hedging on UK stocks and currencies.'

Elizabeth looked stunned at what Michael had been saying to her. The fact that Michael was able to give her that information made Elizabeth more abrupt in what she was saying. In the end, it was time for Elizabeth to go. Elizabeth left and shut the door behind her before stepping into the white van that had been placed outside the house and driving off. Michael grunted and looked at Angelica.

'We better get our things packed. We are moving out...'

'What? What on earth are you on about Michael?'

Michael sighed, 'Don't you see? Elizabeth came around here as a trap. I bet the Fed wired her to snitch us or me in particular. If we stay here, they will come and arrest me. We need to get out of here.'

'Where will we go and hide?'

'Well, I have somewhere in the Mountain West. Out there, no one will catch you. They won't be able to find someone like us. We just hide out in a log cabin I own.'

'You own a log cabin?'

'There isn't much time to explain all the little secrets about myself. Put it to you this way. I know this was going to happen sooner or later. It was either now, or some other time that we would have had to do it.'

'Wait... No. This is ridiculous. Going to a log cabin in the middle of nowhere. How on earth can I trust you?' Angelica shouted.

'Do you want me to get arrested?'

'I have no arms or legs, Michael. What if a bear breaks in and attacks me? I am utterly defenseless out there.'

'That is why I will stay with you all the time. I have my rifles with me. There won't be any trouble.'

'We will stick out like a sore thumb up there. If I wear a catsuit all the time, it will look out of the ordinary...'

'Which is why I won't make you wear it outside of the cabin if we are going into any of the towns. It'll be different when it is just you and me.'

Chapter 25

There were multiple white vans parked outside on the road. In the dead of night, the white vans emptied, filled with people dressed in dark blue, with the yellow words of FBI written on their backs. The single-storied house that they were raiding, home of Michael Donaldson, should have been easy. Catching him was now merely a formality. Fed had now caught up to Michael Donaldson. Suspected to have laundered millions of dollars through a Panama bank account that he had opened with a fake passport. ID fraud, money laundering, tax evasion, financial fraud were all crimes that he was associated with. He had funnelled money into the hands of political campaigns and there was evidence they had of insider trading that he had used in various elections. Having admitted what he was doing and after the investigations on tracking the money associated with his accounts, they were ready to make a move. Guns were armed and ready. With a battering ram, they broke into the house and shouted entering every room.

'FBI! Don't move you are under arrest....'

Nothing. The house was darkened in the shroud of night. The house had been abandoned. On the table in the living room, was a note. Michael was 5 steps ahead.

Hi there, Feds. I know you were coming. I have been waiting for you to come. For over 15 years I have been waiting for this. It is such a shame though that I am always 10 steps ahead of you. My outgoings, my spending on Panama consultants and my "friend" Russell Portin was all just a way to funnel more money, out of reach for your pesky hands. And the icing on the cake was making my wife Angelica an amputee. Boy, sending her to have her arms and legs amputated was how can I put it, a rather gratifying experience. Using her surgery as a form of a tax-deductible is rather sexy, to be honest. Angelica is with me. You tried to interrogate her and she told me what you were up to. I wasn't surprized. The white vans were too obvious. I knew what you up to. And did I think

*that Elizabeth was there to just see Angelica? No. I knew that she was
your mole. That was why Angelica was always alone. I had no reason for
her to see others. She is mine alone.*

*I don't know what you are going to do now. You could close the borders.
That worked to stop Mexicans coming over the border. I am heading
somewhere else. You aren't going to stop me. Once I have gone off the
radar, you'll have no hope tracking me down. I admire your attempts to
catch me. But there again, you failed. I won. Get over it.*
Best Wishes
Michael

'Damn, he has got away,' David grunted.
'Do we have any leads to where he has been heading?'
'No. I have no leads.'
'What about money?'
'Keep a check on any outflows of cash or credit he is using. The Panama
authorities have been contacted though they are unwilling to disclose
anything on their citizen's information.'
 'We'll track his bank accounts. There should be money flowing out
sometime. Let Panama know of his fake ID.'

Living on the run was the life of convicts, criminals, pirates, rebels and
fraudsters. Doing so with an amputee wife was going to be a challenge.
Still, Michael had planned for this for years. What to do if you were
being chased by the FBI and the police? Hide in the mountain west,
Montana. Near a hamlet sized town called Troy, Michael owned a small
log-cabin house. It wasn't listed under any of his other two identities.
So, knowing that, he could effectively bury his past whilst living in the
wilderness. Besides, hunting the local wildlife, using firewood locally
meant he cut down his spending so less money circling. The lack of
information on his whereabouts meant it was possible to hide in plain
sight. Hopefully, that would work. Still, there was the driving. For miles
and miles, through the open road and open skies, Michael and Angelica

headed North. Like pioneers on the route to a new life up in the Mountain North, Michael and Angelica would begin life in complete isolation from the rest of the world.

Isolationism was a problem. There was a semi-isolationism in Texas. But there were people. Michael did communicate with people and went shopping, trading in currencies, stocks and commodities. Now, Michael was going to isolate himself. After the investigations, it had finally come to this. Isolation in Montana. An Anglo-Saxon future. Angelica was somewhat restless. They had been driving for hours. Michael refused to stop for miles of driving. Of course, Angelica could do no diving herself. After taking back control over cancer, she had lost her independence. Taking back control meant losing all control. Gaining independence meant having no independence. And amputation means amputation.

'How much longer have we got?' Angelica groaned. The sunlight was beginning to fade. The sunlight went from golden to now a pink, twilight pink and crimson filling the sky.

'We need to do another 150 miles. We need to stay down low at a motel,' Michael said, urgently.

'Well, I am tired...'

'Too bad! We have got further to go. A good job I keep my gun on me. When you are carrying $70,000, a gun is your lifeline.'

Michael had $70,000 in cash that he had withdrawn from numerous ATMs. The fact he had $70,000 just lying around in his bank account but couldn't pay for Angelica to have a better surgeon or pay for the Article 50 breakaway clause was not something that Angelica was thinking about right now. The past lies and misrepresentations by Michael had simply gone over Angelica's head. She loved him and that was that. Still, she was irate that they were not pulling in for the night. For Michael though, it was simple. The further he went down the road, the road to oblivion and insanity. There was no pulling away from it now. Marooning himself in the Rockies was the most appropriate option. The

Fed would never find him in the Rockies, he had planned and calculated. Self-imposed exile was the only option now.

After driving down the road of seclusion, the sky finally fell from twilight to black, as the shrouded curtain rolled over the day and turned the land to darkness. They had stopped for the night and pulled into a delipidated motel by the side of the road. After getting the key, Michael and Angelica slept on the ground floor. The room appeared to be falling apart, with the bed that had been broken and a light that flickered dimly. Still, it was a place that accepted cash in hand, easy to avoid the Fed if you didn't leave a trail of money transfers. At night Angelica and Michael sat looking up at the rotten ceiling. A firm pungent smell of urine, cigarettes and excreted waste hung in the air like a ghost. There was a strange despondency between the amputee and the husband. They were both awake, both knew each other to be awake but didn't talk to each other. Until Angelica made the first move.

'I wish that I didn't have my limbs amputated,' she said quietly. This she had said before that she had regretted the surgery. This time, she was direct about it.

'Well, it was to save your life from cancer. You needed to take back control over cancer. You needed to be freed of cancer. Cancer was eating you up like a Mexicans over the border wall. That is why you had your legs and arms amputated.'

'But I have lost all control over my life. I am dependent on yourself. I have no freedom left.'

'You are free. Free from cancer. Free from cancer that was going to kill you.'

'But I have lost everything in the process.'

'Cancer was taking you over. That is why you needed all your limbs amputated. Trump is building the wall to stop Mexicans from taking over America. Likewise, you amputated your limbs to stop cancer taking over your body.'

Cancers took over the bones of people and would take over an entire body. This child's level understanding of cancer was what allowed Angelica to even agree with amputating her limbs, to begin with. Anyone could be persuaded if they lacked an understanding of reality. When a person lacks the knowledge to be able to make informed decisions, without knowing the consequences of the action that they plan to commit, they are doomed into a state of delusion. Delusion is a powerful state of mind. It had distorted Angelica's mind completely, allowing her to completely commit to having all her limbs amputated. She did this in part because she believed that she would have received a pay-out of $3,500,000 that never came to anything more than just a complete lie. Amputation was also decided upon as an action because it was a way of getting completely rid of cancer and taking back control of Angelica's body. By taking back control over cancer, Angelica was able to be free of it. Taking back control was a radical decision, meaning that she was now unable to live a life external to Michael's own life. This was okay of course. Michael was able to take care of her completely. Reliance on Michael did not mean that she ha lost her liberty and freedom.

'Why am I like this?' Angelica whined, rhetorically.
 'Because that is how it is. Freedom costs. For you, freedom cost your arms and your legs. You are free of your cancer. Freedom always costs.' Freedom does always cost. For Angelica, it cost her an arm and a leg, quite literally. 'Freedom is the most important thing that a human can have. Freedom is costly. Do you not know the sacrifices our soldiers went through so that we can be free? Likewise, freedom for you means so much now that you have lost your arms and legs. How can you enjoy life if you aren't free?'
'But I have no arms and legs. How can I be free?'
'Do you not see it? That is freedom. You are free, free from the life of cancer.'
Freedom, of course, means different things to different people. Some people think freedom includes access to healthcare, education and

welfare because if you lack these things, you cannot enjoy the benefits of freedom. Others simply think that freedom is simply the lack of interference from others. Freedom for Angelica meant losing her limbs. That after all meant she was free from cancer. Freedom from cancer would mean freedom. It did not mean the freedom to live a life without Michael. But it did mean that she could enjoy some life at all.

'But a life of cancer isn't real life at all. It is death. I would have died if I didn't have the surgery.'

'Exactly.'

'But I am not free though am I?'

'Freedom doesn't require you to benefit from freedom. Freedom is freedom in itself. You don't need anything else to benefit from freedom.'

Freedom means freedom, according to Michael. Freedom did not just mean freedom to Angelica, though she ha not really a fully defined theory regarding this concept. Freedom meant more than just being free for Angelica. For how could someone be merely free if they were unable to do anything? But for Michael, freedom was merely the freedom from restraint. No one was restraining Angelica. She was free in that regard. But she was unable to do anything. Freedom meant being free from restraint. And even that wasn't Angelica since she permanently wore a catsuit. Freedom is freedom if you permanently wear a catsuit?

The next day was a rush across the open plains, north heading into the tail end of the Rockies. The open sky became filled with the craggy outcrop of rocks, mountains stretching for miles. There was not a cloud in the sky, open sun on the scorched earth and rock below. The road winded and meandered into the landscape, snaking itself around the rough ground that began of the Rocky Mountains. To Michael and Angelica, they were small specks on the great horizon, swallowed by the vastness of the infinite mountains. The road appeared to be desolate, with the rare vehicle passing them, perhaps the odd car, SUV or truck but these were once every ten minutes or so. Other than that, it was just Angelica and Michael. This had always been the case after Angelica's amputation. Angelica never was with anyone else. Elizabeth's visit did not change the status quo.

 The road went for miles. Eagles circled in the sky, soaring above the SUV like a mandate from heaven. There were far fewer vehicles than there otherwise had been. Michael was preferring the quieter roads in the Rocky Mountains. There would be no state troopers. He wasn't being watched by the FBI. Quiet roads were the way of going off-grid. Michael was on a journey away from the past towards a new destination of freedom in the wilderness.
 'In our new life, we will be free. There will be no constraints, no bounds, free wilderness,' Michael said.
'You may be free to enjoy this new life, but I won't be able to. Not with being an amputee,' Angelica sadly replied.
'Nonsense. You are with me. We are free together.'

Well, sort of. Angelica's freedom was completely tied to her husband. A satellite state is free in-so-far as their master free. Freedom is relative. Freedom for a dominatrix is the freedom to practise their sexual deviancy that the freedom of a church-going Evangelicals would find abhorrent and disgusting. Freedom for a commodity trader is to make millions of dollars whilst other people barely survive on a minimum wage job. Freedom for Michael to have the pleasure of Angelica's body to be encased in a latex catsuit meant Angelica's slavery. Angelica was free in so far as she had some kind of freedom of speech. Other than that, she had little to no freedom. Over the mountains and through the forests of the Rockies, there was no freedom from Angelica to abandon Michael. She could object. But that was the only freedom she had. The First Amendment, whatever that was worth.
'So how far do we have to go today?' Angelica asked.
'My plan is always around 400 miles or so. 8 hours driving. We need to go as far as we can in a single day,' Michael replied.

'Is that a good idea? We may need to stop for breaks and the road is quite treacherous.'

Mountain roads were always treacherous. Winding in the craggy ravens of the Rockies was never going to be an easy road trip to freedom from interference. Particularly when Michael was driving 400 miles a day. Still, he managed it with the breaks by the roadside lanes and then set out in quick order. The police never managed to track him down. Evading through the wilderness of the mountains, he managed to get from Texas to Montana in three days with no detection. Avoiding the interstates and major highways was important. After all, the interstates were crawling with state troopers. Over the many hours of travelling, over the days of travelling through the mountains, through the forests and past rivers, they had finally made it. Without being detected.

All, alone, independent and isolated in a rural cabin in the middle of Montana, over 7 miles from the nearest town, was Angelica in her fascist-black catsuit. Of course, Michael was never going to get rid of these items of clothing. They were too, enjoyable. Too sexy. To see his wife constantly wear a catsuit when she was an amputee was for Michael all the reason for her to have the amputation at all. Total domination. Total submission, there were no treaties to bind Angelica to equality, to freedom of speech or anything that meant some kind of liberty. Article 50 meant amputation. Being a quadruple amputation in Montana, miles from any town or form of civilization was, well, a form of isolationism. Marooned in a dark pine forest, Angelica sat facing a crackling fire waiting for her husband to return. Luckily, she wasn't alone. As always God was with her, in the only place she knew God to be. God with us, on the television. Nothing changes, the same Angelica who would watch the endless amounts of EEPPTV and she could watch this uninterrupted as Michael would spend hours away from her. Michael, with his libertarian instincts, was out in the wildness as a character from an Ayn Rand novel, being a pure individual, with no regards for anyone else. Not even his severely disabled wife, who he abandoned all by herself in the cabin. If he was attacked by a bear or if the cabin was set alight by the fire, then Angelica would be dead. She was helpless. Not that she wasn't helpless in Dallas. Michael could do whatever he liked. But now, she powerless and isolated. Her friends and family now merely memories of the past, nothing more than the ethereal mist that floated inside her imagination. The relationships that she had trashed, the family members scolded were nothing to her now.

Isolationism. To be alone, independent and sovereign. This is what isolationists want to believe. But Angelica was alone but she was certainly not independent. Being completely dependent on her husband Michael, Angelica was now his toy. Even in the time she was alone, she would be unable to get up and break free, run away or anything. Her fate was this fate for the rest of her life. Michael was away, hunting for elk. But he would return. Meat for dinner, as it always was followed by enforced sexual routine. Angelica could not change the state of affairs. She could object, as her last freedom was the freedom of speech. But then again Michael would not listen to her. Isolationism meant she was alone, with no one to turn to.

Michael returned from his hunting. By the strength of himself, he had carried an elk, which he had dragged from his SUV from when he had gone hunting. The massive animal was dropped onto the floor. Angelica looked at the animal and then looked at Michael with a sinking feeling. 'We have all that elk?' Angelica whined.
'It will last us for well over a week. This is a fantastic piece of meat,' Michael smiled.
'So, we are relying on eating just an elk then?'
'We'll buy somethings at the nearby grocery store.'

When Michael meant nearby grocery store, he meant a store which was over 12 miles away. It meant around 25 minutes in the SUV. Which was sort of close? Close to an hour round trip, given how windy the roads were. Hardly a 10-minute trip to the local grocery store. Still, was better than living in the part of Minnesota surrounded by Canada. The road to the grocery store was desolate. The lands surrounding the town of Troy in Montana was heavily forested, giant mountains in the distance were impending monsters on the town. Various houses were scattered around the area, creating the vague remanence of a town, even though the houses were not linked together in any form of streets. Troy was nothing more than a loose collection of houses that loosely resembled a town. There were a few churches like in most towns in America, though the Mountain West was not nearly as Evangelically aligned as the Southern United States of America. But other than a few shops and a small library, Troy was a town without many services. It was a tiny, with little over 800 people. So, the small grocery was one of the only shops in the area. Michael parked up the SUV by the side of the shop and walked into it, pushing the disabled Angelica into the shop with him. The shop was small, the aisles were not particularly suitable for a wheelchair to be pushed through them. Still, Michael continued. Various local people looked at the couple but did not stare, minding their business to what seemed an odd couple, new to the area. After collecting various items on the grocery shop, they went up to the checkout. A wanted poster was attached to the counter. Michael was spooked out.

Wanted: Michael Donaldson. Also known as Russell Portin. With a quadruple amputee wife, last seen in Texas 6 months ago. Criminal suspected for money laundering, tax evasion, fraud, financial embezzlement. Details on sightings can be reported to the local sheriff's office or FBI offices.

A picture of him with him pushing Angelica was attached to the poster. He glanced at it, as the shop assistance packed his bags of shopping and after he had paid, Michael and Angelica exited the shop. In the SUV, Michael stared into space as he let the wanted poster settle in. He had moved to the other part of the country, abandoning his life in Texas all for him to be able to hide from the authorities. Hiding had failed. It was

a matter of time before the FBI caught up to him. Driving home in the forested hostile region, there was silence in the SUV. Angelica was fearful of the tension that was found in Michael's stance. They had gone multiple times to that particular grocery store and there had not been any wanted poster. It was only now there was one. Perhaps it was only recently that they had been found out.   Still, it was worrying times.
'I do enjoy the roasted elk you cook,' Angelica laughed anxiously, trying to defuse the ice.
'Oh… Haha. Great. That is good,' Michael replied, nervously. He wasn't interested in cooking elk or anything.

This kind of low-level chatter was in part due to the reality that Angelica couldn't communicate with anyone. Being a sort of hostage of Michael, she had only spoken to him. There was no contact with anyone other than him. So, there was nothing really to engage with. Just menial subjects of communication. Michael though wasn't particularly interested in conversation as he feared for whether there was a police car waiting for him in the drive. There was no time to relax since the Fed or police could come for him at any time.

When he was home, Michael decided to sit by the window, looking out of the window. Angelica lied on the sofa, after being put back into her catsuit, she curled up into a sort of fetal position. Interaction between Michael and Angelica had all but died that afternoon. Michael now realized that he was, like Angelica his wife, alone. The life that he had created, the life of criminal financial activities had now caught up to him. The amputation of his wife's limbs, a part of financial wizardry by himself to lower his taxation was yet more evidence to be used against him. There was no more enjoyment of the great outdoors and freedom in Montana. He could go out hunting elk and the elk that he had shot would feed Angelica and Michael for weeks. However, Michael who thought that he could exist on the fringes of civilization and have the great open doors for him to hunt whilst laying low from the authorities, his hopes were shattered. The months in hiding from the Fed had come to nothing. As the darkness came, the curtain of the night shrouded the light of day, Michael sat by the fire next to his crippled wife who he had put in a catsuit. What was the point of amputation anyway? Why did amputation mean amputation? After all, it did not need to happen. Michael knew that amputation was not necessary. Angelica, the disabled wife that was dependent on him did not need to have all her limbs amputated. Amputation does not need to be amputation. Bone cancers sometimes require amputation of a limb. But quadruple amputation was never necessary. In such a mad world though, Angelica's amputation was nothing more exceptional than a country devouring itself over political processes. Still, at least it wasn't Brexit.